". . . nine . . . eight . . . seven!"

"Hey, babe, you found me!" Molly saw Scott's eyes crinkle the way that always made her heart skip a little bit, and smiled back at him. He leaned down to her ear and raised his voice.

"I have something I want to talk to you about. I've been looking for you."

". . . six . . . five . . . four!"

Molly caught a glimpse of all the fawning women Scott had been dancing with earlier and cocked her head with a smirk. "Looking hard or hardly looking?"

"Huh?" Scott squinted.

". . . three! Two! One! Happy New Year!" Molly's friends threw handfuls of confetti in the air, making Molly cringe at the sight of the mess, and started blowing their noisemakers. Couples kissed and friends hugged each other. Jenny and her college roommate began singing a very drunken version of "Auld Lang Syne" while the televised crowds in Times Square danced in the streets.

Scott moved closer to her, and she felt his arm snake around her waist, once again drawing her in.

Molly wrapped her hand around Scott's neck to move his head toward hers. His thin lips pressed against hers with a warmth that always spread through her like the heat she'd feel from a fresh cup of tea, though a spiked one, hot toddy–style. Molly raised her eyelids to look at her boyfriend through the haze the candle smoke had created and saw that his martini-olive eyes, murky now through the cloud of alcohol, were focused only on her own. It was going to be okay.

"Molly," Scott said.

Before she could move, Scott dropped down one knee. One of his hands grasped both of hers, and up to her chest the other held a small, black velvet box. The box was open, and inside something glittered in the candlelight, flashing against the black silk. People around them started to catch on and back away, creating a small clearing around the pair. Molly looked at Scott's earnest face, the beads of sweat rolling down his forehead, then down at the brilliant diamond ring on display. *Wowza,* she thought. *That thing is big.*

"Will you marry me?"

All the Difference

LEAH FERGUSON

BERKLEY BOOKS, NEW YORK

BERKLEY

An imprint of Penguin Random House LLC
375 Hudson Street, New York, New York 10014

This book is an original publication of Penguin Random House LLC.

Library of Congress Cataloging-in-Publication Data

Ferguson, Leah.
All the difference / Leah Ferguson. — Berkley trade paperback edition.
p. cm.
ISBN 978-0-425-27938-0
1. Young women—Fiction.   2. Pregnant women—Fiction.
3. Decision making—Fiction.   I. Title.
PS3606.E72556A79 2015
813'.6—dc23
2014045341

PUBLISHING HISTORY
Berkley trade paperback edition / September 2015

PRINTED IN THE UNITED STATES OF AMERICA

10 9 8 7 6 5 4 3 2 1

Cover art by Nina Tara.
Cover design by Lesley Worrell.
Text design by Kristin del Rosario.

Penguin
Random
House

For David,
with thanks for the laptop(s)

Yet knowing how way leads on to way,
I doubted if I should ever come back.

—ROBERT FROST

CHAPTER ONE

New Year's Eve

"You've got to be kidding me."

Molly Sullivan stared at the thin white stick she held in her fingertips. She couldn't keep her hand from shaking. The wand vibrated back and forth like a baton conducting the most cacophonous piece of music ever performed.

She sank down onto the closed lid of the toilet seat.

"You have *got* to be kidding me." The words bounced off the beige walls of Molly's tiny upstairs bathroom. She concentrated on the feel of the cool tile beneath the bare skin of her feet, forcing herself to slow her breathing down, and willed her body to stop trembling. It didn't obey.

The test she'd used was one of those no-fail electronic ones. There was no second line that might not really be there, no vague plus sign that could raise a doubt of its accuracy. What Molly gripped in her hand, now moist with sweat, was a test—her third of the morning—with a window designed to say "pregnant" or "not pregnant." She looked at it again, and closed her eyes.

It definitely said "pregnant."

But it couldn't be true. There was no way. No.

Molly opened her eyes again and swallowed hard. Denial is an uncomfortable emotion for somebody afraid to make mistakes.

"Coffee. Coffee can fix this," she mumbled, and braced herself to stand up. Then she remembered that there was supposed to be a rule about pregnant women and caffeine, and her legs buckled underneath her again.

She didn't know how she was going to do this. It wasn't in her plan.

An awful metallic taste rose in the back of her throat, and Molly forced herself upright to reach for her toothbrush. She leaned against the shining granite countertop, grateful for its firm support, and swiped the brush around her mouth without looking in the mirror. She knew what she'd see, and that it wasn't going to be pretty: hair flattened to one side of her head from sleeping in the exact same position for nine straight hours. Eyelids puffy over purple-shaded skin. Forehead and cheeks blotchy with broken veins from too many sudden bouts of morning sickness. Molly didn't know why she'd been so surprised by the positive test. She'd been experiencing almost every symptom Google had warned her about.

Molly jabbed her toothbrush back into its holder and stumbled in the direction of the kitchen. She hadn't felt like this since the night she went to that karaoke bar with her friend Jenny and drank so many of the margaritas on special she ended up performing the Eurythmics' "Sweet Dreams" in a singing voice a little too close to hollering. Both the melody and the backing vocals, she winced to recall. In their entirety.

All of a sudden she felt nauseous again.

Molly reached for the coffee filters she kept in the pantry before she caught herself, groaning, and reached for the herbal tea bags instead. *This,* she thought, *cannot be happening.* She was thirty years old, knocked up with a baby she'd planned to want but just not quite *yet,* and the only way she'd know how to deal with it would be to dust the furniture so well she'd wear lemon-scented tracks into its wood stain. Molly had to make sure the little realities in her life were organized—scrubbed clean, shining, and sorted to perfection—before she felt confident enough to face the messier, more abstract ones. *Because that's helpful,* she thought, and opened the cabinet that held her cleaning supplies. She couldn't tell if the nausea rolling around her stomach was from being pregnant or just from knowing she was pregnant. Either way, she knew her house was going to end up spotless.

By that evening, Molly was on her hands and knees on the hardwood of her living room floor, scrubbing marks off the white baseboards with an eraser sponge. She was still wearing the old Amy Winehouse T-shirt she'd slept in, along with yoga pants she'd pulled from the folded stack of identical pairs she kept tucked in a dresser drawer. Her long brunette ponytail swung as she scoured the wall with a fury she didn't know she possessed.

Molly knew what she was doing was ridiculous, and she finally sat back on her knees, frustrated. She threw the dingy sponge to the floor, looked at it for a moment, then picked it back up and turned her attention to the darkening day outside her front window. Liz Phair was belting "Johnny Feelgood" from the stereo speakers, singing like she was mocking Molly, laughing at her. "I hate him all the time," Liz sang, "but I still get up when he knocks me down . . ." Molly curled her upper lip and shook her head in resignation.

She stood up, brushed herself off, and shuffled into the kitchen to set a plate of leftover carbonara into the microwave to reheat. She shuddered and wrapped her arms around her waist, hugging her elbows, and looked at a photo that hung on the side of her stainless steel refrigerator. Molly looked so happy in the picture, her arm slung around the waist of the man next to her. She should've called him by now. He'd have wanted to be here, too.

She thought about the night it all started, a few years earlier. After work one Friday evening she'd wandered into the Barnes & Noble that loomed over a park on Walnut Street in the same neighborhood as her office building. A bunch of coworkers had left at the strike of five o'clock to head over to McGillin's Olde Ale House for the usual happy hour festivities, but Molly was feeling a cold coming on, so had decided to stock up on some reading material for a weekend of self-imposed quarantine instead. Wandering around a bookstore on a Friday evening was a treat for her, anyway. She'd buy a latte from the Starbucks and thread in and out of the aisles of the fiction section, checking out the cover art for the new releases, looking to see if that hardcover she'd had her eye on was out in paperback yet.

She had paused by the children's area to smile at two toddlers chattering back and forth as they played with some cars on a train table. She was standing in the middle of the aisle between the literature section and the children's room, coveting a little girl's Converse All Stars, when he came ambling toward her for the first time. He had a grin spread wide on his face and a book held in a loose grip by his side.

"They're cute, aren't they?" he said, nodding toward the children. "I've always said I'd want kids of my own, but only if I could get a guarantee that they'd never cry and never poop." He chuckled, gauging Molly's reaction, and reached up to brush his dark hair off of his forehead.

Molly glanced up and met this stranger's green eyes. She was only weeks out of a relationship that had ended before she was ready to let it go, so she was wary of new men. But Molly noticed that this man's clear eyes were the color of olives, and that they were focused on her. She felt the quiet thrill of his attention, and mistook it for the feeling that she once again was in control.

"Hey, if you can find a kid like that, you'd have women lined up to help you raise him. Probably some men, too." She grinned.

"I would, wouldn't I? Babies are like dogs. It's a proven fact that just holding one makes a man ten times more appealing to women. You agree with me, right?" Molly could swear his eyes sparkled as he looked at her. *Ooh, he's flirting with me,* she thought. *Keep it coming, dude.*

"Ah, well," the man in front of her continued. "Guess I'll just have to take my chances and see what life brings me. Though I should probably focus on finding the right woman first, and worry about the kids later, shouldn't I?" He looked at her in a way that made it seem he was implying more than his words let on.

Molly took a moment before she responded, as she was distracted by the line of muscled shoulders under his coat. He raised his eyebrows with amusement, watching her look him over, and it had the effect of crinkling the skin around his eyes in a way she found endearing. He was tall. Really tall, actually, with those shoulders and a broad face with a square jaw she thought only existed in Calvin Klein print ads. His brown hair was the kind of wavy she had always wanted for herself, and he wore it tousled and swept back from his face, like he couldn't stop running his hands through it. He dressed like most of the professional men she avoided in the bars, who talked too much about the mothers they lived with in South Philly and whether the Sixers would finally get a shoulder up on the Celtics: dark jeans, black T-shirt, sleek black leather jacket that fell to his hips. But on this guy the Philly uniform seemed different, intriguing. He looked like he could either be an advertising exec or a bartender.

Hey, baby, you can mix my drink anytime, she thought. She laughed to herself before realizing too late that she'd snorted out loud. Molly coughed, hoping he hadn't noticed. He tilted his head with a bemused expression and nodded at her hands.

"What, no books? You just like to come to the bookstore on a Friday night for the five-dollar coffee?"

"Of course not! The five-dollar coffee is just the beginning," Molly teased. "Don't let the empty hands throw you off. I have the rare ability to turn book-shopping into an epic event. It's not like a person should just walk into a bookstore and settle for the closest thing she sees."

He had leaned against a display, his expression amused, waiting for her to continue. Encouraged, Molly gestured at the stacks around them. "It's all a matter of instinct and fate: What'll it be tonight? Young adult? Historical fiction? The latest vampire series? It's too exciting a process to rush, frankly. These things take time." She took a sip of her coffee and looked at the handsome stranger standing in front of her. She liked having this feeling again, the charge of someone's interest, the adrenaline jumping through her veins. He straightened and laughed, sliding the book in his hand behind his back in an exaggerated arc.

"Then I probably shouldn't tell you that I ran into the store to pick up the latest Nicholas Sparks novel for my mom's birthday, should I?"

"Nope, you totally shouldn't. At least the book's not for you, though."

Molly turned her head to look at this new man from the corner of her eye. "It's not secretly for you, right? I'd have lost all respect for you then."

He leaned forward, closing the distance between them until she was certain he could smell the latte on her breath. But he didn't seem to mind, and took a step closer.

"So you're saying I've earned some of your respect? I was starting to think that I was going to be like one of your books— I'd be lost among the shelves until you decided if fate would make you lean my way."

"And why would I want to lean your way?" Molly tilted her head as she smiled up at him. Her heart was thumping in her chest.

"Well, to see how irresistibly charming I am, of course. And how else would I be able to persuade you to join me for a drink?"

Standing in her kitchen, Molly ran her hands over the muscles of her flat belly. The microwave hummed. The man's name had been Scott Berkus, and he'd been in her life off and on for the last three years. Soon enough he'd be at the door. She would wait to tell him then.

"No, no, no," Molly muttered. A wave of dizziness washed over her, and she slid down the face of the cabinet into a cross-legged heap on the kitchen floor.

There was another person in her belly. There was a creature, with cells that multiplied and a body that was growing, attached to her insides. It had been living off of her for weeks. Molly retched. This was happening.

This was happening.

The microwave beeped. The smell of homemade pasta wafted through the kitchen and forced its way into her awareness, replacing the sinking sensation of realization with a new feeling, this one roiling around in her stomach, sloshing against its walls, climbing up her throat like the legs of an angry spider. Molly lurched over to the trash can, opening it just in time.

It was New Year's Eve. In three hours she was supposed to be on the doorstep of her best friend's house, on the arm of her boyfriend, entering the same party she'd been attending every year for most of her adult life. It was routine by now, the music she'd hear and the drinks she'd pour, the jokes they'd make, but tonight was going to be different. This time everything was about to change. Molly wiped her mouth with a fresh napkin and set the untouched plate of warm food back into the refrigerator. She had to get ready.

A short while later, the doorbell was buzzing like a wasp caught in her door frame. Molly patted some gloss onto her lips and ran down the stairs, the polished hardwood slippery against her bare feet. At the bottom, she paused for a moment to let her nerves settle themselves, then opened the door to greet her boyfriend.

"Hiya, sweetheart." Molly reached up to plant a kiss on Scott's lips and glanced at the wrought-iron clock that hung over the fireplace mantel. "Nice of you to appear."

"Oh, hey, I'm not that late, am I?" Scott's gaze traveled the length of Molly's body and he wiggled his eyebrows in a hopeful leer. "Though if I'd known you were going to look this good, I wouldn't have stuck around my parents' house for so long." Scott placed his hands low on Molly's hips, guiding her back into the living room, and leaned down to nuzzle his nose against her neck. She had to tell him, she knew.

"How did I get so lucky to land you?" He mumbled the words against her skin. "You even *smell* good." Molly felt the muscles in her neck constrict, and slipped out of his arms.

"It's the same perfume as always," she said, keeping her voice bright. "You know me."

"That's what I love." Scott tucked his finger under Molly's chin and held her gaze for a moment. "I always know what I'm getting with you."

No, she thought, she didn't have to tell him yet. Not yet.

Scott rummaged for something in the pocket of his sport coat. "Oh, and hey, my mom wanted me to bring this to you. Said she forgot to give it to you at Christmas." Scott pulled out a small gift and presented it to Molly on an open palm. She recognized the trademark robin's-egg blue of the box, though she'd never seen it outside of a magazine ad before.

"But why would she do that?" Molly, her forehead furrowed, glanced up at Scott before untying the white bow. "She already gave me so much."

Scott shrugged his shoulders and slouched against the wall. "You know my mom. She tends to overdo it a bit. Compensation for my forgotten childhood and all." He used a finger to dangle the silver heart locket in front of Molly. "Besides, you know she adores you. I think she sees you as her prodigy, Miss Executive."

Molly opened the locket to find pictures of her and Scott already cut and placed inside. She swallowed hard. The glossy necklace was more ostentatious than her usual style, but she knew she'd wear it. Monica would expect to see it on her the next time they got together. Molly laid the necklace back in its iconic container. The bauble must have cost more than Molly's monthly rent. She wondered how many gifts were going to be lavished on her once Monica found out she was getting a grandchild.

Scott brushed past Molly into the room and turned to face her. "Yo, how do I look?" Scott threw his shoulders back and placed his hands on his hips in a male-model pose to give her a good view. "Pretty hot, right? You going to be proud to have me as your date?" He watched Molly look him over, his smile faltering as he waited for her approval.

"Tonight is a big night, after all, Molly." He paused. "For you, I mean, what with all the champagne and fireworks and that stuff you women seem to like so much. I'm just hoping to make some fireworks of our own later," he said, lowering his voice, "if you know what I mean."

"Oh, God." Molly groaned and clutched her stomach with a hand before she could stop herself.

"What?" Scott's dark eyes were wide behind his thick lashes. "What's wrong? You need some water?" He pronounced it "wooter," as only a born-and-bred Philadelphian would do. He looked uncomfortable.

"No, I'm fine. Just forgot to eat dinner, that's all."

Scott laughed. "You? Forgot to eat?"

"Weird, I know," Molly said. "I was cleaning." She and Scott looked at each other for a moment before Molly cleared her throat. The words she needed to say seemed to be lodged in her windpipe.

"Let me just grab my lip gloss and my pocketbook, and I'm set to go," Molly said. She started for the stairs. "Can you turn off my iPod? I don't want the battery to run down while we're out."

"Gladly," Scott shouted from the kitchen. "What were you listening to this time, anyway? Your folksy stuff or your emo music?"

"Not sure you could quite call Liz Phair either," Molly called back. "In fact, she'd probably keel over in front of her NOW poster just to hear you say that." She was tidying the hair products in her bathroom cabinet and couldn't hear Scott's response. "The woman's an indie icon," she continued. "Have you never heard *Exile in Guyville*? She did a song-by-song response to the Stones' *Exile on Main Street*. You should really give it a listen sometime."

"I'm good," she heard him mumble in the silence that followed as the speakers over the fireplace downstairs went quiet. Scott called up again, his voice louder this time as he stood near the front entrance. "Unless you've got some Poison on that iPod, I'll be in the car. And don't be late!"

Molly stared in disbelief in the direction of the stairs. No one ever needed to remind her to be on time.

"Me, late?" she yelled.

"Mol, I'm kidding! But I don't want Jenny getting all salty with me again. Besides," Scott's voice turned singsongy, "tonight's a big niii-iiight. It's New Year's Eve, baby! Let's get this show on the road already!"

Molly heard the hard click of the front door when it shut behind a whistling Scott as she slipped into a pair of metallic red stilettos. She'd chosen to wear them because she knew they played off of the deep charcoal silk tank she'd paired with a black leather skirt, but now it seemed like a ridiculous ensemble for an expectant mother to wear. Molly glanced in the mirror just in time to see herself turn pale. She forced herself to keep looking. She'd gotten her collarbone-length brunette hair treated with the subtlest of red highlights at a salon off of Rittenhouse Square that week, ignoring the absurd fact that she was paying three hundred and twenty-five dollars just to emphasize the deep green of her eyes. Silver chandelier earrings peeking through the curtain of hair and a cascading chain necklace added sparkle that reflected off her skin. She brushed a wisp of her long bangs off of her forehead. No one else had to know, she thought. At least, not yet. Not before she'd had a chance to understand what she had to share.

Molly prided herself on her stability—the way she was able to maintain her job, and friendships, and family connections with an ease that rarely left her floundering. Her relationship with Scott was the only facet of Molly's life that she couldn't keep consistent, and the positive pregnancy tests in her trash can weren't going to make it any easier. They'd have a few good months as a couple, then separate for a while before falling back in together with the same intensity as before. It was the same pattern each time. It reminded Molly of Velcro—they kept getting tangled together despite themselves, snagging all sorts of detritus along the way. Every time she tried to remove herself from Scott, every time there was a problem that didn't seem like it could be fixed, another hook appeared, bringing her back, until Molly finally decided to just let herself stay attached. After all, her persistence was the trait that had gotten her so far ahead in her PR career. She assumed it had to eventually work in her personal life as well.

The sound of a Porsche's horn echoed from the street outside, and Molly hurried down the stairs. She snatched her coat from one of the hangers that were evenly spaced along the bar in her front closet and pulled it on. The car horn beeped again. Flipping the switch on the tabletop lamp beside her, Molly glanced around her first floor once to ensure every object was in its proper place. She stepped out into the dark to meet Scott, shutting the door on the warm light behind her.

Scott found a parking spot in Old City in record time, despite the early party crowds clogging the narrow streets on their way down to Penn's Landing. The crisp air draped itself over the squat rooflines of the old row houses, a thin blanket of cold weaving itself among the ivy and leafless plants tucked into the flower boxes that adorned the windows of each tiny home. Molly stepped with care along the brick sidewalks, clutching Scott's arm for support as they made their way across the cobblestones to the front of Jenny and Dan's apartment. In a stretch of Philadelphia night sky that broke through the web of treetops and dormer windows above them, she could see a misty halo hanging around the moon, foreshadowing a rainy day to follow. Molly squinted in disappointment, dismayed by the prospect of being trapped inside on the first day of the New Year, until she spotted a few stars that had managed to peek through the clouds. With a sigh of approval, Molly let go of Scott's arm to step to the top of the stoop.

"Molly!" Jenny Waters-Kim threw open the door. Her voice was loud, brassy, and always seemed to carry a hint of a laugh rumbling below her singsong alto tones. "You're here!"

Molly's best friend threw her arms around her neck. "Oh my gosh, I was afraid you were going to bail on me. Every single year, I'm like, uh-oh, she's not gonna come! I know she's gonna get all crazy-sweatpants-cleaning-lady and want to stay home, but by golly, you never fail me!" Jenny gave her another squeeze. "And *that's* why I call you my bff, you bff!"

She leaned to the side of her embrace to look Molly in the face. "Oh, sorry. Am I choking you?" Jenny extracted her arms from around her friend's neck. She was wearing a shimmering black tunic over black leggings and had piled her arms with rows of silver bangles that jingled and caught the light every time she moved her hands. They clanged together again as she turned to Molly's boyfriend.

"Hey, Scott."

"Hey, Jenny," he replied, the corner of his mouth drawing up into a slow smirk that was as sexy as it was sarcastic. "I'm liking this vibe you've got going tonight," he said. He moved his eyes down the length of her outfit, nodding in approval. "The look is like carnival gypsy meets hipster princess. You should put on a show."

Jenny gave Molly a sidelong glance before rolling her eyes at Scott. "Yeah, Scott, I'll do that. Like Audrey Hepburn in that dance from *Funny Face*, only with vodka. I've got it all planned out."

The suave facade dropped away from Scott's face as he tried to understand the reference. He had a knowledge of films that rivaled any information Wikipedia had to offer, but not of the kinds of movies that involved beatniks and berets. Jenny laughed and reached for Molly's sleeve. "I can take your coats if you want. Dan's mixing drinks in the kitchen."

Daniel Kim had been Jenny's high school sweetheart. As they told it, they'd been seated beside each other on the first day of Ms. Thompson's geometry class at Archbishop Ryan High School and hadn't been apart since. They'd both gone on to play soccer for St. Joe's and had spent much of their time in college in a friendly competition to see who could get the better grades. They'd both ended up graduating summa cum laude, with Jenny's GPA just one tenth of a percentage point better than Dan's. They'd stopped competing after that.

"Hey, do I see Jägermeister?" Scott exclaimed, and returned Dan's wave. "I haven't had that stuff since college. That's the shit right there!" He planted a quick kiss on the top of Molly's head, one foot already leading the way through the small crowd to the kitchen. Molly acknowledged Jenny's incredulous look with a playful shrug.

"What are you gonna do?" She laughed.

She spotted a small bowl of chocolates on the table by the door and moved closer to them, her unsettled stomach rumbling. She could hear Corrinne Bailey Rae playing from the stereo in the corner and breathed in the aroma of a vanilla-and-balsam-scented candle. Her friends had painted the apartment in soft, neutral taupes and greens, with lots of bamboo and the occasional canvas of framed Korean art Dan's grandmother had given them. Their light-colored furniture was sleek but comfortable, accented with large floor pillows perfect for lying around with a glass of wine and good conversation. Jenny joked that they were single-handedly supporting IKEA's mid-Atlantic profit margin, but Molly felt so welcome there she sometimes didn't want to leave.

"Sooo." Jenny was still standing close beside Molly, craning her neck to look in the direction of the kitchen. Her blond hair tumbled down her back in a waterfall of curls. Jenny was a petite woman with the tiny features of a porcelain doll, complete with big blue eyes and dark lashes as thick as paintbrush bristles. The only feature that didn't fit her doll face was the smattering of freckles across her nose and cheekbones. Jenny had given up trying to conceal them long ago, for which Molly had been glad, because the endearing speckles were the best hint of the personality that lay beneath them.

"Do you think tonight's the night?" Jenny continued. She pointed her chin in the direction of the people huddled in the adjacent kitchen. A low wall separated the two rooms, and they could see the men joking with each other. As they watched, Scott threw his head back in laughter, and then, as if he could sense Molly's eyes, he turned to smile at her, raising a flirtatious eyebrow. For a brief second, Molly felt like she was the only person in the room. Scott turned back to Dan, and the sensation disappeared.

"Oh, Jenny," Molly said. She shook her head and lowered her voice. "I don't know. He hasn't been acting any differently. You'd think if he were planning something he'd seem anxious, or on edge, or . . ."

She gestured in the direction of the kitchen, where Scott was raising a full shot glass with one of her friends from work.

"God, I remember back when it was you two. Dan was driving me nuts." Molly paused. "Scott seems completely chill."

Jenny smirked. "Molly, it's Scott. I don't think that man's been nervous a day in his life."

"Yeah, he has," Molly was quick to say. She looked at her boyfriend. "He just hides it well."

Jenny threw her a sharp glance. "I didn't mean that the way it sounded," she said. "I meant, you know, how Scott's just so laid-back about some stuff, that's all. I never imagined you'd end up with someone quite so type B."

Jenny was quiet for a moment, then continued. "But we had some awesome times, the four of us, when you guys started going out. Scott's fun. And I think Dan's taken him on as some sort of goofy big brother." She shrugged. "I guess I just want him to be more of that man who's going to ride in on a white horse with a rose between his teeth for you."

Molly snorted. "Are you serious? Liam didn't even do that back when he and I were dating. And he was about as close to a knight as I was going to get." She laughed as she thought of her ex. "Even when he was galloping away."

Liam and Molly had been a few months into their relationship when his college girlfriend moved back to town. The pair had known each other since childhood—they'd skinned their knees on the same playgrounds, competed on the same swim team in high school, volunteered to build houses together in Haiti during their college breaks—and when Stephanie had asked him for another chance, wanting to see if their history meant they could have a future, Liam felt obligated to see it through. By honoring his old girlfriend, he had to hurt his new one, and yet Molly had never begrudged him his decision.

Molly mumbled now through a mouthful of dark chocolate. "I like lilies, not roses, anyway, you know that. Scott is not a fairy tale. He's just real, problems and all." She swallowed the candy. "Though a horse would be kind of cool . . ."

The women stood in silence for a moment, each picturing the scene. Jenny shook her head.

"Drink?"

"Uh." Molly hesitated. She concentrated on unwrapping the last chocolate while she thought. Jenny glanced at the candy dish, now almost empty, and frowned at Molly in a silent question. Molly was just about to answer her, to finally tell someone and make it real, when she spotted Scott in the kitchen, joking with a woman she didn't know, and stopped.

"A drink sounds good." Molly looked up and smiled. "But I'll get it. Let me go to the bathroom first. This skirt's so tight I've got to make room for anything else going in my body."

An hour later, Molly was holding a short glass of scotch that she'd watered down excessively in a successful, if unappetizing, attempt to pass the drink off as her usual choice. She took a sip from it and tried to hide her grimace. She thought of the pregnancy test, now wrapped in tissues and stuffed into the very bottom of her bathroom wastebasket, and put down the glass. How ironic, she thought, that at the one moment in her life when a woman could really use a stiff drink, she wasn't supposed to have one. Her head felt heavy, her eyes fuzzy and dry from fatigue. She wished she could just go back to bed and start over. The day, the year, all of it.

She leaned against the wall of the dining room to watch the crowd in front of her. Jenny and Molly had a wide circle of friends they'd made through their work at Shulzster & Grace, a big public relations firm in Philly, and by eleven thirty most of them were singing along to Janelle Monáe's "Tightrope" and drinking one of Dan's champagne cocktails.

Scott was happy, the life of the party, dancing in the center of a group in front of the fireplace. His hair was flopping in glossy clumps around his cheekbones, and another button on his shirt was opened to show off his smooth chest, now shining with sweat. The women around him laughed, each preening until he grabbed her hand for a spin around the floor. He moved well to the music, by all appearances oblivious to the attention on him, but careful to dance with each person in turn. Molly watched Scott empty his champagne glass and reach for another full one on the mantel. It looked like she was going to be starting off this new year the same way she did the last: trudging to Wawa for some Gatorade and a hoagie. Molly yawned. This time, though, it'd be a little harder to get off the couch herself.

Molly eased her way closer to her boyfriend, catching Scott's eye to laugh at his terrible attempt at the robot. She felt the familiar pull as his gaze singled her out, drew her in. She thought she could smell his cologne mingled with the scent of candle smoke and sweat, and watched him looking at her, separating her from the rest of the people in the room. Without thinking, Molly placed her hand over her stomach, protecting a secret she'd only just found out she was keeping. She watched Scott, in the center of the room, at the center of attention, from her spot on the edge of the crowd.

Molly's thoughts strayed to a recent fight they'd had. It had been the end of November. Scott had cajoled her into going to his parents' house for Thanksgiving, even though her favorite aunt was flying in from Minnesota. She hadn't seen Aunt Cookie in two years, and she only planned on being in town for a few days before heading home to Minneapolis, but Scott insisted that if he and Molly, as a couple, were supposed to be getting more serious in their relationship, it was about time they spent the holidays together. And since they planned to stay with her parents for Christmas, he'd thought it was only fair they spend

Thanksgiving with his. Which *was* fair—Molly just missed her
aunt Cookie.

Thanksgiving found Molly sitting in a cavernous dining
room in Montgomery County, making small talk about sweet
potatoes.

She remembered how miserable she'd been, how uncomfortable and long the hours were. No one who lets herself be bullied
is going to be happy with what happens next. Molly was used to
huge, chaotic, loud holidays with her big family. That afternoon,
it was just Molly, Scott, and his mother seated around a quiet
table draped with russet-colored linen, sipping their chardonnay
from hand-cut crystal. They asked each other to please pass the
fresh cranberry sauce while Scott's father threw tantrums in front
of the Cowboys game in the next room. No quiet dog under the
table waited for a dropped crumb. There was no teasing or jos-
tling for the last piece of pie. It was just the three of them, a small
turkey from the caterer resting on heirloom china, and Sade playing in the background. The Sade is what put Molly over the edge.

So she sneaked off to the bathroom to read texts from her
brothers, even though each quip, every update about Uncle
Frank's whiskey intake, and one voice mail from her goddaughter Samantha sank Molly more and more into a homesick funk.
Scott, of course, had noticed, and they'd gotten into a huge argument about it on the car ride back to the city. Scott said she was
being selfish. Molly thought he'd cornered her. When Scott
parked his car in front of her house, he was still shouting while
Molly got out on the sidewalk in tears. He'd sped his fancy little
car away before she could even slam the door.

They'd spent two weeks apart, although Scott had left daily
voice mails. At first the messages were kidding, trying to blow the

whole affair off as a silly misunderstanding. And then her silence must have gotten to him, because he quieted down. He began to apologize for yelling. With a gentle voice, he said he regretted taking her away from her family on such an important day. She started to think that maybe she was just overreacting, that she'd been responding to an ultimatum that wasn't really there.

So one day she picked up the phone. He came over, and they curled up on the sofa together to talk. He was humble and cha-grined, and she'd felt understood. He smelled like soap and fresh cologne, and had brought her a large bouquet of red dahl-ias and a thin bracelet of white gold. She was comforted by how gentle he was with her. When he placed his arm around her shoulder, she let him. When he leaned in to brush his lips against hers, she didn't resist.

That was six weeks ago. Molly felt the contents of her stomach roll over inside her. She remembered how they'd ended up lying together that evening, under a blanket beside the lit fireplace, their clothes scattered around them, heads on throw pillows that had fallen off the sofa. She recalled feeling satisfied but strangely guilty, like she was a kid who'd stolen a cookie out of the jar right before dinner. She hated him. She loved him. And neither one of them had bothered to get a condom from the bedroom.

A sudden clatter of applause and cheering brought Molly back to the present. Jenny had turned on the television, and the host was counting down the seconds until midnight. Molly blinked her eyes hard and stood up straight. She worked her way through the throng of people in front of the big fireplace over to Scott, who was draining the last drops from a glass of champagne.

It was time, Molly thought. She would tell Scott, and they would take the new year to let the news settle, figure out what to do next. She wouldn't rush life this time, wouldn't plan, would allow all the jagged edges of her fears to soften up on their own. It would be okay, Molly thought. So she didn't know what would happen next. She was having a baby. It would be okay.

Molly saw Scott catch her eye. He flashed a wide grin and set his empty flute on the cluttered mantel. He patted his pants pockets, like he was afraid he'd misplaced his wallet, before reaching his hands out to Molly to draw her closer. She saw that his chest was still slick with sweat, and he swayed just a bit in his British-made shoes.

". . . nine . . . eight . . . seven!" Dan and Jenny were bouncing up and down a little, noisemakers at the ready.

"Hey, babe, you found me!" Molly saw Scott's eyes crinkle in the way that always made her heart skip a little bit, and smiled back at him. He leaned down to her ear and raised his voice.

"I have something I want to talk to you about. I've been looking for you."

". . . six . . . five . . . four!"

Molly caught a glimpse of the fawning women Scott had been dancing with earlier and cocked her head with a thin smile. "Looking hard or hardly looking?"

"Huh?" Scott squinted.

". . . three! Two! One! Happy New Year!" Molly's friends threw handfuls of confetti in the air, making her cringe at the sight of the mess, and started blowing their noisemakers. Couples kissed and friends hugged each other. Jenny and her college roommate began singing a very drunken version of "Auld Lang Syne" while the televised crowds in Times Square danced in the streets.

Scott moved closer to her, and she felt his arm snake around her waist, once again drawing her in.

"Oh, never mind," Molly said. She wrapped her hand around Scott's neck to move his head toward hers. "Come here."

She took a deep breath.

"I actually have something I need to tell you, too."

Scott's lips brushed Molly's, and a familiar warmth spread through her like the heat she'd feel from a fresh cup of tea, though a spiked one, hot toddy–style. He pressed her body to his, hands on her hips, pulling her tightly against him. His fingers moved up the sides of her body and along her bare arms, trailing until they came to rest on her hands. He clasped them in both of his and moved them down to rest against his heart. Molly raised her eyes to look at her boyfriend through the haze the candle smoke had created and saw that his green eyes, murky now through the cloud of alcohol, were focused only on her own. It was going to be okay.

"Molly," Scott said.

She took in his face, startled by the expression she saw there, and opened her mouth to respond. Scott shook his head at her, and placed a light finger against her mouth. The sweat from his skin felt cold against her lips.

Before she could move, Scott dropped down on one knee. His lips were moving, but Molly couldn't hear what he was saying. One of his hands grasped both of hers, and the other held a small, black velvet box. The box was open, and inside something glittered in the candlelight, flashing against the black silk. People around them started to catch on and back away, creating a small clearing around the pair. Molly looked at Scott's earnest face, at the beads of sweat rolling down his forehead, then down at the brilliant diamond ring on display. *Wowza*, she thought. *That thing is big.*

She opened her mouth again, started to say something, then closed it. Molly looked up from Scott's face and met Jenny's eyes. Her friend was standing beside Dan with her arms crossed against her chest, watching her with an expression Molly couldn't read. Molly's own face felt slack, blank. She could hear the tinny sounds of the revelers in Times Square cheering through the television.

She'd thought it was going to be okay.

Molly looked back down at Scott, who had shifted his weight off of his knee and onto his other foot. He repeated the words.

"Will you marry me?"

Scott dropped the ring a little and raised his eyebrows, waiting for an answer.

CHAPTER TWO

January

If She'd Said No

She heard the rumbling sound like it was an echo from another life, rolling in on soft waves at first, then growing louder as she became more aware of it. Her eyes were closed, she realized, and she kept them shut, staring at the absolute blackness in front of her. It was so calm here, so peaceful, and she didn't want to leave this spot. The rumble grew, though, thrashing around between her ears now with a determined force. Molly's eyes flew open.

She'd been snoring.

Molly blinked a few times, then turned her head to the right to see the other women in the class coming out of corpse pose. Without moving, she watched the yoga instructor across the room give her a serene smile before she touched her palms together in front of her bird-frail chest. The lithe woman bowed to the group facing her.

"*Namaste,*" the teacher said. Her soft voice floated across the room and over the faint rumbles still resonating in Molly's head.

The other students were sitting up now, legs crossed with measured grace in front of them, mirroring the instructor's movements.

"*Namaste,*" they replied. As if they'd uttered a secret code, the relaxed atmosphere of the room disintegrated. The students began rolling up their mats, chatting to each other in subdued voices. Molly continued to lie in place on her back, her legs splayed in *savasana*, her palms thrown open to the ceiling in a gesture of hopeless resignation. She stared upward, lying in the back of the room while the rest of the class filed out, throwing her curious glances on the way.

She was so tired. The muscles in her body were heavy against her bones, and she felt like she couldn't move them if she tried. But she didn't want to try. She didn't want to leave this darkened room and walk back into the cold daylight of a noisy street. She didn't want to go home to her empty house. It was too quiet there. Way too quiet.

The yoga instructor unplugged her phone from the speaker system and the music came to an abrupt stop. Molly sensed her hop down from the stage in the front of the room and heard her whisper something like *good-bye* as she padded away. The door clicked shut, and she was alone.

Molly rolled over to her side and closed her eyes again.

A week later, Center City was noisier than Molly expected it to be on a Saturday afternoon. The sidewalks were filled with people scurrying along, weighed down with the holiday packages they were returning and the groceries they needed to replenish now that their refrigerators were empty of leftover turkey and half-eaten pie. Couples strode hand-in-hand against the breeze while parents steered their children through the crosswalks. Occasional office workers, work bags thrown over their shoulders, trudged out of offices on their way underground to catch SEPTA trains to the suburbs. Molly was rooted to the sidewalk, working her way through a bag of M&M's while the rest of Philadelphia moved around her. She was staring at the window display of the store in front of her with a sort of curious fascination when its door swung open. The mechanical bell sang a weak alarm.

"Why, Molly Sullivan, is that you?"

Molly heard the voice, the bright tones of it tripping across the frigid air of Chestnut Street like a stone skipping across a shallow lake. Molly didn't turn her head. She chewed the last bit of chocolate until it was nearly liquid and shoved the empty bag deep into a pocket of her peacoat, all the while keeping her gaze straight ahead of her, buying time.

The voice belonged to Scott's mother.

Molly was standing in front of a maternity store.

"*Shit.*" Resigned, she whispered the word, then turned to face her would-be mother-in-law.

"Monica!" Molly's voice was loud and high, and she stopped to take a breath, the smile on her face so artificially wide she could feel her eyes squinting closed. "Yes, yes, it's me!"

Molly reached forward to grasp Monica's elbows with her hands when she approached. Scott's mother kissed both of her cheeks, and Molly recognized the scents of hair spray and Chanel No. 5 that the statuesque woman wore like a suit of armor.

"Well, just look at you," Monica said, and stood back to hold Molly at arm's length. "My goodness, darling, you just get more beautiful every time I see you. I swear, you're positively *glowing*. Tell me, what's your secret?"

The skin on the back of Molly's neck flushed hot.

"Oh," Molly said. "Um, thanks? It's probably just this new yoga class I've been trying out."

"Well, I must be doing something wrong, then," Monica laughed, "because I've been doing yoga for *years*, and I don't look as healthy as you do right now. My Lord, girl, even your *hair* is radiant!" She shook her head in delight. "I *must* get the name of your studio. Whoever's responsible for doing that to you must be able to work wonders with a middle-aged lady like me, right?"

Molly pressed her lips together to stop a hysterical giggle from rising out of her throat. She felt like she'd walked onto the stage of a very bad play.

"Well, Molly, I can't tell you how *happy* I am to see you." Scott's mother stood straighter, throwing her shoulders back so that her Burberry coat fell from them in a straight, well-tailored line. Molly found herself mirroring her actions, and sucked in her bloated stomach as best she could. She was regretting the last of those M&M's.

"I was afraid I'd never see you again," Monica continued. "What brings you here today? Has that best friend of yours finally decided to settle down and have children?"

Molly glanced toward the clothes in the window beside them. She'd been looking at an expensive sweater dress, imagining what it would be like to see the swell of her own belly outlined by the narrow coffee-colored cable-knit.

"No, no, Jenny's not pregnant yet, though I've been wondering that myself. I'm just preparing for the day it happens, I suppose." Molly tried to laugh, but the sound got lost in the cold air. She shifted her weight. She wanted to lie down.

Monica took a gloved hand to her hair, patting the straight blond bob. She looked at the dress Molly had been admiring, then let her gaze fall over the other winter-weather outfits on display. The faceless mannequins stood poised in the window like they owned it, their round, symmetrical stomachs perched on too-tall, too-thin frames like balloons taped to street signs. She turned back to Molly.

"I couldn't wait for the day it was you." Monica tilted her head, as if waiting for the words to meet Molly's consciousness. "I was just thinking that, the whole time I was in there, getting a little something for my niece's girl. I wished it was you."

Molly's glance fell on a diamond bracelet clasped over the kid leather gloves covering Monica's wrists. The flashing jewels winked at her in the harsh sunlight.

"It's not too late, you know," she continued, and when Molly looked back at her, she was shocked to see a plea in Monica's eyes. Molly had never known Monica to beg for anything. This was the woman who'd maneuvered her way to the top of the best architectural firm in the city before she'd turned forty. Monica usually got what she wanted. "I'm sure you and Scott just had a silly misunderstanding. You could patch it up, couldn't you?"

Molly shook her head. She had her reasons for walking away from Scott, even if she wasn't ready to articulate them to the intimidating woman standing in front of her.

She glanced at the window display again. She really liked that dress.

"Monica . . ."

"No, don't tell me." Monica held up her hand. "I can't imagine that you two could really be over for good. Just think about it, okay? About coming back to my son?" She reached forward and took hold of Molly's bare fingers in her own.

"I miss you." She looked at Molly with a sad smile. "It was nice having a daughter around."

Molly nodded. She felt like a tourist who'd gotten lost and couldn't understand the accent of the person giving her directions. She'd stepped into a country that seemed an awful lot like the place she'd come from, but was still foreign enough to make her homesick. It was an unsettling feeling, being surrounded by everything familiar, but not belonging to any of it. Her eyelid started to twitch.

"Well." Monica dropped Molly's hand and sighed. "In the meantime, how about I take you out for a cappuccino? What about that lovely café we used to always go to after our shopping trips? Just for old times' sake? I drove the Jag in today, the blasted old thing, but it's parked right around the corner. What do you say?"

Molly looked down at her shoes. A young man with a scruffy beard passed by very close to them. Monica shifted her purse to the other shoulder, her gaze still on Molly, waiting.

"I—I can't, Monica. I'm sorry." Molly's mouth had gone dry, and the words caught in her throat. She longed for a cappuccino, with extra foam and a design swirled into the top by a trained barista. But coffee would have led to dinner, with wine by the bottle and desserts with French names, and the platinum credit card always, always, being passed to the server without ever a glance at the check's total.

Molly thought about the empty rooms waiting for her at home. There was a Chinese take-out menu lying on the kitchen counter. She'd ordered an old Cary Grant–Audrey Hepburn movie, which was resting on a table next to the TV.

"I have to get back," she said. "I have plans tonight."

After they said their good-byes Molly turned around, headed to wait for the bus to Rittenhouse. She pulled her scarf tighter around her neck and watched the cracks in the sidewalk, careful to avoid the tree roots that had broken though the surface. Doubt filled her mind like water seeping into the compartments of a sinking ship. Molly knew what she was steering away from. What she didn't know was what was ahead of her, and if she could stay afloat.

"Molly . . . here! Let me get that for you!"

Jenny rushed up the wide stairs that led to the front door of Molly's rented brownstone just as Molly lost her grip on two of the full grocery bags she'd been trying to shift in her arms.

"Damn it," Molly breathed. Jenny stood beside her as they watched the bags hit the edge of the steps and burst open like romaine-filled piñatas over the concrete sidewalk. At least fifty dollars in wasted produce scattered around Molly's parked car. With an angry swipe of her hand, Molly pushed back the long bangs that had fallen over her eyes.

"You know you're too stubborn, right?" Jenny turned her gaze away from a pigeon pecking at a smashed banana to look at Molly. "You're not at the gym, girl. No need to balance all that weight like you're Jillian Michaels."

"But she has such good arms," Molly said. She was shivering. The sun peeking through the few clouds overhead did nothing to warm up the bitter air sitting over Rittenhouse Square this Sunday afternoon. Jenny skipped down the stairs to pick up a shattered wine bottle and deposited the pieces into a nearby trash can.

"It looks like someone murdered Veruca Salt on your door-step," she called.

"The grape girl from *Willy Wonka*? That was Violet Beaure-gard," Molly said. "Never did like Veruca Salt—the character *or* the band."

"Trust me, I know," Jenny said, and climbed back up the staircase. "I brought wine, anyway. We need to talk."

Molly sighed. "I was afraid you were going to say that."

She fished her key out of her pocket and opened the heavy, mahogany-stained door. Molly's brownstone was a stylish, min-iature version of the other row houses nestled in the Rittenhouse Square neighborhood. Her real estate agent had tried to regale her with all the benefits of getting a smaller home. She'd said there'd be less cleaning to do and a small dining room was a great excuse to bow out of hosting big family dinners, but Molly had just shrugged her shoulders. What had actually sold her on her home was the simple act of walking through the front door. The house was sweet, quiet, and bright, with a large white-framed picture window in the living room that illuminated the whole first floor all the way back to the kitchen. It fit her. There were rumors that the current owner would soon put the house on the market, and Molly wished more than anything in the world to be able to purchase it herself.

Had wished, she corrected herself. Back when she thought there would be another person to help with the mortgage.

"So, what's going on with you, Mol?" Jenny tossed her vintage handbag onto the couch and took a bag from Molly. Her hair, pulled back by a red-and-gold scarf she'd folded into a headband, tumbled around her shoulders like ribbons curling on top of a gift. "I don't hear from you for a couple of weeks, and I can't find you at work anymore. It's like you've gone underground. You have me worried."

"I'm sorry." Molly followed her into the kitchen. "I just . . . I'm not dealing with this very well."

She set her bags on the counter and reached into one for the chocolate chips she'd opened on the way home.

"Any of it," she added.

"Three years is a long time, Mol," Jenny said. Her voice was soft. "Long enough to justify you falling off the planet for a while and then resurface wearing pants with holes in them."

Molly winced and smoothed down the soft cotton of her yoga pants. "Be nice. They're comfortable."

She knew she was going to have to tell Jenny the real reason she'd started wearing clothes with elastic waistbands in public. She needed to say it: that they were the only pants that fit around her thickening middle. Molly had put it off for too long, and now she braced herself. She needed to face this pregnancy, face her fears about what was coming next, and she needed her friend to help her do it. She was having a baby. A thrill rippled along Molly's nerves, surprising her. It had happened, just like that. She was going to be a mother.

Molly had heard acquaintances in recent years talk about

how hard it was for them to want a baby and not have one. She'd
listened to the women talk about how obsessive the desire was,
about how the absence of a baby in their lives and the act of
going through each day without getting pregnant was all they
could think about. But no one had ever told Molly that getting
pregnant without trying could render her just as preoccupied,
just as fixated and unwilling to live her life like usual. It had
made sense to keep news of the pregnancy to herself until she'd
waded through enough of the muck to know how deep it was.
This was a secret that was going to divulge itself whether Molly
shared it or not. But a secret you never planned to know in the
first place can be the easiest kind to keep.

Jenny wandered into the living room with an open bottle of
wine and two glasses. She scrolled through Molly's iPod until
she found Billie Holiday, and Molly sank down onto a small
ottoman beside her. "Foolin' Myself" started playing from the
surround-sound speakers, Holiday's slow vibrato weaving in and
out of their conversation. Molly looked around at her serene,
beautiful house. The living room walls were painted an earthy
gray-green, and she'd tossed some bright red pillows from IKEA
on the sofa for color. With last year's holiday bonus from Shulzster & Grace, she'd been able to pick up a funky floral-patterned
armchair that had been on sale at a furniture boutique in Old
City, as well as a couple of small cherry-wood tables. A brick gas
fireplace held court over the sitting area, grounding the space.

"Do you know what I remember most when I think about
New Year's?" Molly pressed her lips together. "I remember how
shiny Scott's hair looked."

"What?"

"It must've been the gel, or whatever product he uses now,

but that's what I keep thinking about. How wet his hair looked, and how it had these deep ridges from where he'd combed it."

"Okay," Jenny said. "That's what you're picturing? What about that big, shiny diamond he was waving in front of you?"

"That thing was huge," Molly said.

"That thing makes my diamond look like Dan took a jimmie off an ice cream cone and stuck it on my finger." Jenny laughed. "I can't believe you refused it. I think that was the first time I've ever seen you do something so . . . unexpected."

Molly shook her head. "I can't, either."

"So, that's it? You go along, dating him for longer than some people are married, then bail when he actually *does* want to get married?" Jenny took a sip of wine. "You're a piece of work, Sullivan."

"I know, right? It was so weird, like my gut finally decided to speak up," Molly said. "I saw Scott kneeling there and my brain just went, 'Nope. No. Can't do it.'"

She bit the inside of her lip. "And the timing was terrible, considering—"

Molly heard the words come out of her mouth and gulped. No time like the present, she figured, and eyed Jenny for a reaction.

"Considering what?" Jenny asked. "Considering that you'd been with the guy forever and we all thought you'd end up marrying him?"

She hadn't caught the hint. Molly lost her nerve.

"You didn't really think I'd marry him, did you?" Molly asked. She watched Jenny swirl the wine around in her glass, thinking.

"You fought a lot, yeah," Jenny said. "But you'd been with him for so long that, I don't know." She shrugged her shoulders. "It seemed inevitable."

"That's just because he's gorgeous," Molly admitted.

"Can't argue with you there, sister," Jenny laughed. "It's almost a shame. You two would've made really good-looking babies."

Molly suddenly felt faint.

Later, over a dinner of Thai takeout around the butcher-block island in Molly's kitchen, Jenny shifted topics to the changing atmosphere at Shulzster & Grace. There were rumors of staff cutbacks, and while Molly had worried that specialists like her would be let go first to save the firm a huge chunk of their revenue, Jenny had heard that her marketing department would be cut in half, moving the graphic design work out to inexpensive freelancers. Molly took small bites of her pad Thai as they talked, willing herself to keep down the waves of nausea in her stomach. Jenny and Dan had just started making the loan payments for Dan's master's degree from Temple, and even with Dan pulling in coaching jobs on the side, the Philadelphia School District wasn't quite able to shower its teachers in money. Neither Jenny nor Molly could afford to start over in their careers almost ten years after they'd begun.

Molly looked at the bar stool beside her, the place where Scott always sat when they ate, now empty save for an extra napkin folded with care on the seat. Through the window she could see the bare tree that rose from the frozen soil of her tiny, fenced-in backyard. One brown leaf still stuck to the branches, as if refusing to let go.

Not even a month had passed since New Year's Eve, but life as she'd known it had screeched to a stop. The confusion that haunted her days was chipping away at the shell she thought she'd been so careful to create. She didn't like this lost feeling, but she didn't know how to shake it.

Molly's calendar on the weekends was blank now, the hours long and empty. There were no more parties, no exquisite eight-course dinners at Le Bec Fin or soused late nights tasting the pricier offerings at Tria Taproom. She'd spent the last two Sundays sweeping minuscule crumbs off the kitchen floor, thinking about the mornings just weeks earlier when she and Scott would sleep in, then take a lazy walk arm-in-arm down to the Square for a brunch of oysters and ten-dollar Bloody Marys. Last night, Molly had caught a 76ers game on TV, and it was a strange feeling to see the arena but not be there, to see the box above center court where she and Scott used to watch the games. She worked very hard to not think about the plane tickets he'd given her for Christmas. They'd been set to spend Valentine's Day on a resort in Los Cabos, Mexico. Last year at this time, they'd been zip-lining in Costa Rica.

And this year? Molly thought. Through the window she could see the lone leaf on its branch, trembling in the wind. This year, she'd chosen to trade the charming boyfriend and tropical boat drinks for cable TV and ginger ale. Molly's stomach flipped, and she put down her chopsticks.

"We saw a gorgeous house for sale last week, Mol," Jenny was saying. "Three bedrooms, a cute yard, and far enough away from my parents' house that we would never have to visit."

Jenny had never forgiven her father for carrying on an affair years earlier, leaving her and her mother staring at each other in shock in a silent house. Molly knew the feeling of betrayal had only worsened when her mother welcomed him back home months later, once he finally ended the relationship. Molly sometimes thought Jenny blamed her mother the most, for moving forward and pretending that their family had never been ripped apart. Jenny hadn't forgotten. She also refused to pretend.

Molly got up to get a glass of water. Her wineglass remained untouched on the island.

"I wanted to see what you thought of it," Jenny said. "Though with the layoffs possible, I guess we need to hold off on buying anything."

Molly groaned in sympathy.

"I guess that would make sense. For now, anyway," she said. "But that sucks, Jenny."

Jenny was looking at her plate. "Being a grown-up is kind of hard sometimes, isn't it?"

"I'll say," Molly replied, looking at Jenny's empty glass. She heard the last notes of another Billie song trail off, accompanied by the forlorn wail of a saxophone, and in the quiet of the moment that followed, knew what she had to say next.

"Um, Molly?" Jenny hesitantly broke into Molly's thoughts. She was pushing the remnants of her curry around on her plate. Molly noticed that her fork was shaking. "There's something else I wanted to talk to you about, too, but I wasn't sure how to bring it up."

A weight like a rock dropped into Molly's belly. She held her breath and waited.

"Dan and I have been trying to have a baby."

Jenny said the words to her plate. Her shoulders were slumped forward, making her back curve like the rounded part of a question mark.

"But we can't," she said. "Have a baby, I mean."

Jenny looked up at Molly, meeting her eyes.

"We can't get pregnant."

Molly stared at her best friend's face. A kind of paralysis took hold of her body, making her legs feel wobbly. She couldn't move, couldn't breathe, could say nothing in response to the honesty of one of the dearest people in her life. Molly watched Jenny talk, heard her speak of fertility windows and thermometers. She let her reach out, listened to Jenny confide in her, and stayed quiet and removed. Molly felt like she was standing in the shadows of her secret, stuck there, because now she knew that if she stepped out into the light Jenny wouldn't be able to look at her.

"Sorry, Mol," Jenny was saying. Her voice was cloudy. "I hate to unload on you after everything you've been going through, but I had to. I couldn't imagine keeping something like this from you for any longer."

Molly forced herself up to take a box of tissues from the pantry.

"Why didn't you tell me before this?" she asked. "Before everything with Scott? I could've been there for you."

Jenny pushed her curls back off her shoulders in a self-conscious gesture. "Because I didn't want to make too much of a big deal about it. I didn't want to put more pressure on myself than there already was." She shrugged. "It's like, if I didn't talk about it, didn't acknowledge it, even with you, then it wasn't a problem." Jenny laughed. "You probably think I'm nuts."

Molly placed her hands in her lap to hide their trembling.

"So what now?"

"I don't know. I think we have to see a doctor," Jenny replied. "I keep picturing myself sitting on our bed, holding our baby in my arms, but it feels like it's just a dream. It's like we've been wasting weeks—months—waiting for our lives to start, if that makes sense."

"How long has it been?" Molly asked.

"Almost a year."

Molly's spine was so tense it felt like it could splinter apart.

"And each month that goes by has me riding on these huge hopes, and then they go crashing down just as quickly," Jenny continued. "It's like we're stuck on a Tilt-A-Whirl gone bad."

Molly cleared her throat. "Those things are awful."

Jenny took a long swallow of her wine and looked over at the full glass resting on the table beside Molly's plate.

"Hey," she said. "Why aren't you drinking?"

Molly stared at a spot of the red liquid that had fallen onto her goblet's stem and reached to wipe it away. Her glass had remained full while Jenny's was filled and emptied, filled and emptied again. All Jenny wanted was a simple drink, and here Molly sat, drowning in more than she'd wanted in the first place. She shook her head and stood up.

"I suddenly don't feel so well," Molly told Jenny, and emptied her glass into the sink.

CHAPTER THREE

February

If She'd Said Yes

Molly trudged up the stairs to her front door. She was panting a little despite her best efforts to muscle her way along, tugging the plastic grocery bags with a numb hand while she searched her coat pocket for keys with the other. Rittenhouse Market had been packed with office workers looking for comfort food for the bitter weekend ahead. Molly hadn't had the patience for them, the women shoving their carts down the narrow aisles like they were all on deadline, the men shouting into their cell phones with their bets for Sunday's Flyers game. It was all too chaotic. Confusion was swimming through her head like a school of angry fish, and she needed to contain it, needed a moment long enough to sort through it all.

Molly had been naked just two hours before. She'd been naked and shivering and mortified to be lying on a cold exam table while her new obstetrician inspected her insides and pushed around on her belly. All Molly wanted to do was announce that this wasn't how she'd planned on having kids. She stifled the urge to insist that she had a good job and came from a solid family. She did mention, though, working it into casual conversation, that she had a fiancé who couldn't get out of work for the appointment, but he was supportive and excited and they were going to get married and really, it was all okay. It was all going to work out. And then she lay back, stared at the pockmarked ceiling, and winced.

The doctor had told her the baby was the size of a lime. It already had ears that were perfect miniature versions of what they would look like in adult form, and toes that curled. Molly couldn't stop thinking about those little toes. She was going to get to buy packs of tiny socks. *Socks,* she thought. A flood of joy surged up from Molly's chest, catching her off guard. The fear she felt at this adventure that was still unknown and unplanned seemed natural. The joy, though—the sheer thrill that bubbled like a fountain from the depths of her, the giddy awe that would spring up every time a weekly email from BabyCenter.com popped into her inbox—wasn't what she'd expected at all. Happiness over something so frightening was a tricky feeling, and more delicate. The happiness, she knew, could slip away.

Molly paused at the top of the staircase with one arm still in her coat pocket, shuddering in the cold wind that whipped down the narrow tunnel of her street. She remembered the call from her mother she'd ignored that morning and knew she couldn't put off talking to her parents much longer. She was thirty years old. She had a job, was independent, and had been living on her own for years. She knew she should be able to ignore the pit in her stomach when she thought about the conversation they needed to have. She just didn't know how to do it. Her parents had struggled so much to build a life for their children. There had been nights of hot dogs and canned beans for dinner, hushed arguments over money, strict rules about her homework and summer jobs and research for college scholarships. They'd done their best to ensure her future while still being a part of her present. Molly brushed a pile of rotting leaves off the stoop with a little too much force. She couldn't bear the idea of looking her pop in the face and telling him she got knocked up.

She located her UPenn keychain deep in an open bag of chocolate drops and managed to push open the heavy wood door to her brownstone. In the dim light, Molly saw her fiancé sitting on the living room couch with a remote in his hand, fascinated by the din of shouts and lasers blasting from one of the cable movie channels.

"Um, Scott, can I have a hand here, please?" Molly dropped the bulky packages out of her right hand and slid the handbag off her shoulder. "I'm drowning in plastic and Hershey's Kisses."

"Hmm?" Scott hopped up, his eyes still fixed on *The Empire Strikes Back*. He glanced at Molly, then at the bags at her feet. "Hey, what are you doing with groceries? I ended up getting out of work earlier than I thought and texted you. I could've gotten those."

Scott moved toward the sacks of food piled up by the door, but was so focused on the movie he slowed to watch it. Molly, shivering, tried to scoot out of her heavy wool peacoat. The silver buttons popped from their enclosures as if relieved to be free of her bloated midsection. Her lime-baby took up more room than she would have expected.

"Just leave the bags there for now. Take a load off." Scott nodded toward the couch, his eyes still on the AT-AT marching across the television screen. "I'll get them after this is over."

"No, there're milk and eggs somewhere in there. I'll put them in the fridge." Molly sighed and opened the door to the entryway closet to hang up her coat, smoothing it before tucking it in between Scott's collection of wool coats and ski parkas. She hadn't seen Scott's text until she was in the checkout line, or she would've come home. She couldn't wait to unzip her pants.

She dragged a couple of the plastic bags into the kitchen. Scott followed her, all the remaining grocery bags bunched into one large hand. Chewbacca was still moaning from the living room. Molly was used to the way Scott would get sucked into a film, but today she was more bothered by the clutter she found on the countertop than his endearing obsession with lightsabers. She had to sweep an empty cereal box and beer caps to the recycling bin before she could place the groceries on the counter. The reusable bags she'd set out so she would remember them that morning still lay piled in a neat stack on the island. Scott set the groceries on top of them.

"Have you given any thought to dinner?" Molly asked. "All I want to do is take a shower and collapse on the couch, so tonight's got to be on you, if you don't mind."

"I'm already on it." Scott was peeking around the corner of the kitchen doorjamb, trying to see what was happening in the living room. His love of science fiction films was part of what drew Molly to him—it was an interest that didn't fit in with his cool-guy persona, and she felt like she'd been let in on a secret, something special that only she was privy to know.

"Oh, and hey, thanks for that cute note you put in my bag this morning. I needed that." She was reaching into an upper cabinet and spoke over her shoulder. "Work killed me today. Ever since they doubled up on my accounts I barely have time to grab a sandwich in the afternoon. I swear, when Bill's not emailing me with questions about this client, he's calling me to ask about another. And he needs me to stay late for a conference call tomorrow, so it's a good thing you already made plans with the guys."

Molly paused in the midst of putting some boxes of Tastykakes on a shelf. There was silence behind her.

"Hello?" she said, turning around. Scott was mouthing along with a conversation Han was having with Luke. She laughed. She should've known. "Earth to Scott! I'm trying to have big, important conversations here. Like how I can't go to happy hour with you."

"Sorry, babe." Scott smiled at her and moved toward the living room. "It's been months since I've seen this."

Molly heard the click of the TV as it shut off, and Scott walked back into the kitchen. He placed an empty beer bottle on the counter and sidled over behind Molly as she reached back into the cabinet above her. His long fingers spread themselves across her hip bones, pulling her waist to him before he wrapped his arms around her in a hug that made it impossible for her to do anything else but let him hold her.

"Hey, did Jenny happen to call?" Molly leaned her head back to rest for a moment on Scott's shoulder. "She's supposed to let me know how she likes that new temp job at the bank."

"No, no word." Scott kissed the back of Molly's head, then straightened up to open the refrigerator door, holding it wide while he stared at its contents. "Nothing on the voice mail when I got home, either." He reached inside, pulled a container of Greek yogurt from the back of a shelf, looked at it, then put it back.

"I'm worried about her," Molly said. She taped the bag of Kisses closed and shoved them to the back of a pantry shelf. "She loved her job."

"Molly, you freak out too much." Scott nudged her shoulder

with a loose fist until she allowed a smile. "Don't be weird. She'll be fine."

Molly smirked. "I'm not freaking out. I'm just, you know, mildly concerned." Scott shot her a look of doubt and yawned.

"Come on. First not being able to have a baby, then getting laid off?" Molly said. "I'm not sure how much more Jenny can handle."

There was a pause while Scott leaned against the counter, watching Molly organize her bottles of prenatal vitamins. "How was your appointment?"

"It went well." Molly managed a chuckle. "I'm getting excited. My doctor's cool, but she's got this funny sort of hippie vibe going on. I haven't figured out yet if it'll be relaxing or the most irritating thing I've ever encountered. I can just hear her now when I'm pushing the baby out: 'Heeey, mannn, I see the heeaaad. Whoooaa. It's sooo cool.' She'll be passing a joint around instead of a cigar."

"Hey, I'd be down with that." Scott fished an open box of Oreos out of a grocery bag and shoved one whole into his mouth. His evening stubble had begun to appear, darkening the sharp angles of his jawline. He was still wearing his button-front shirt from work that day, open now at the collar, tucked into his flat-front dress pants. He continued to talk around a mouthful of dark crumbs, not seeming to notice the pieces falling out as he spoke. "Anything to help me tune out all that nasty stuff."

Molly looked at Scott from the side of her narrowed eyes. "I know you get weirded out, but it's okay to come to these appointments, you know. Nothing that disgusting happens." She took a cookie from him. "I got to hear the heartbeat today. It's so fast it doesn't seem real. You should go next time."

"No way, gorgeous, that stuff's not for me." Scott grimaced. "I do not need to know what goes on down there."

"Are you kidding me?" Molly snorted. "What are you going to do when I give birth? Hide in the bathroom? Or just wait out in the hall till you hear the baby cry?"

"I won't hide in the bathroom, as appealing as the idea sort of sounds." Scott took a swig of a new beer he'd taken from the fridge. "Especially if your doc really is generous with her ganja." He opened a drawer in the island and started digging through a stack of take-out menus. "But I'm staying up near your head. I don't want to see blood and stuff. Other dudes have warned me to steer clear. I've heard the stories."

He looked up to grin at her. "It's your happy land, Mol!" he said. "Gotta keep it that way. Ignorance is bliss, you know?"

"Well, you have about seven and a half months to change your mind," Molly said. Her voice was light. "Because if you keep up that attitude, my happy land's going to be revoking your visa."

Scott rolled his eyes, but he was smiling.

Molly shoved the last of the bags into the recycling bin. "I've got to go shower. I feel gross."

Scott dropped the stack of menus on the countertop and turned to Molly, cocking his head to one side. He jerked his head in the direction of the stairs, one side of his lips pulled up into a suggestive smirk.

"No, you're not coming with me." Molly laughed. "I've been groped enough today. Besides, you're in charge of dinner, remember?" She gestured toward the pile of menus Scott had spread out before her.

"Well, what's baby Berkus in the mood for?"

Molly had been taking off her scarf and sweater as she moved out of the kitchen, but came to a stop. She turned to face Scott.

"Baby Berkus?" She laughed in surprise. Her hands were still clasping her scarf. "Don't you mean Baby *Sullivan*-Berkus?"

Scott moved his hand through his hair, and Molly marveled for a brief moment, as she always did, at the way his hair still managed to stay perfect after he did that. Then she noticed that there was a piece of Oreo filling clinging to one of the short hairs on his chin, and she dropped back into reality.

"What?" she asked.

"Baby Sullivan-Berkus? You're kidding me, right? You want to give our kid a hyphenated name?" Scott took a slow gulp from the bottle in his hand. "When did this happen?"

"I thought we'd agreed." Molly felt the muscles in her face wrinkle up in confusion. "Back when we first started dating, we talked about it. I even remember the night—you'd taken me ice skating at Penn's Landing because I'd never been. You liked the thought of two becoming one, and all that. You said you were okay with me keeping my last name if we got married."

"Yeah, I said I was okay with it," Scott said, "not overjoyed. But our kids? I didn't think you'd want to hyphenate their names, too."

He stopped and took a breath. "Look, I love all of your independent, I-am-woman-hear-me-roar spunk. But let's get real here."

Molly raised her eyebrows.

"It kind of hurts, I gotta say, that you won't want to take my name, but I won't try to change your mind. When it comes to our kid, though, I just . . ."

Scott paused, then shrugged his shoulders.

"Look, do what you want with your name, Molly. But you can't mess with my kid's. I'm not down with that."

Molly knew she was about to repeat herself, and also knew that no matter how often she asked, the answer would stay the same. "But three years ago, you were all for it. I thought we were on the same page."

"Well, yeah, Molly, of course I told you that." Scott laughed. "I wanted to see you again."

Molly's mouth fell open before she could catch herself. Scott wasn't laughing anymore.

Scott took another swallow of his beer, his eyes locking with Molly's over the bottom of the raised bottle. "Can you even imagine what my parents would say to that? I can hear my mother now, complaining about how she'd be mortified to show her face at the club ever again."

Molly took a deep breath, trying to collect her thoughts. She hadn't meant to start an argument. But a shift had occurred somewhere without her realizing it, and she needed to figure out where they—or at least, one of them—stood now. To know that her pride in their identity as this super-modern, forward-thinking couple was really just based on a couple of quick assurances from an eager Scott was more embarrassing than she wanted to admit, or get used to.

"Scott," she said. "This baby is going to be both of ours. You can't ask me to just not give our child any part of myself—my name is my heritage, and I want this baby to have that."

"Molly, your last name is Sullivan, not McShaunnessey-O'Connell-McBoyle." Scott ran his hand through his hair, rubbing the back of his head in a quick, jerking movement as he did. "And didn't you say Immigration changed your ancestors' name, anyway?"

Scott's voice had gotten louder, and they both heard his

words ring through the air around them. When he spoke again, his tone was soft, and he looked at her with eyes that were narrowed, and almost pleading.

"Are you telling me that I can't have a son carry on my name?" he asked.

Molly stayed quiet.

"Or what if this baby's a girl, Molly? What if she gets married one day and wants to hyphenate *her* last name? You want our poor kid to be Mrs. Sullivan-Berkus-Smith?"

"Have you ever thought that maybe our girl will keep her name if she gets married?" Molly was sputtering.

"I want us all to be a unified team, Molly," Scott said. "That's not a lot to ask. I want her teachers to know we're both her parents, that we're married. I want people to hear of us and know right away that we're a family. The *Berkus* family. What's so wrong with that?"

Molly blew a breath of air, hard, through her lips. One hand was covering her swollen belly. She felt disoriented for some reason. Her feet wobbled on the ground beneath her like it was the deck of a boat she'd boarded by accident. She looked up to meet Scott's eyes.

"Why should you get to choose?" she asked.

Scott was watching her. "Why should you?"

There was a silent moment while his question lingered, unanswered.

"Look," Molly said. "We don't have to talk about this anymore right now. I get your point. But I'm really surprised."

She picked the scarf up from the floor. "I'll go take my shower, if you can order dinner. Please? Anything that's just . . . easy."

"I'll get that curry you like, with extra summer rolls just for you," Scott said, and placed a take-out menu on the island. "Easy."

He met Molly's eyes and smiled, just one corner of his mouth turning up in a gesture that was almost rueful. Molly shuffled out of the kitchen and climbed the stairs.

Once she was standing under the faucet of her shower and felt the hot water cascading over her, scouring away the dregs of the afternoon, Molly let herself replay the discussion in the kitchen. When they first started talking about their future together, in the midst of the heady fog of a new relationship, Scott had been as gung ho and adamant as she about last names. He had seemed so bold to her, so excited to set a standard, even in the face of tradition. It attracted her to him even more. But that was early on in their courtship. That was when there was still a chance that she could walk away.

Molly shook her head back, allowing the scalding water to wash over her face. The soap stung her eyes, but she stayed there, inhaling the steam, letting the water run where it wanted.

A claw of fear had begun tugging at the back of her brain, releasing a trickle of doubt that was now coursing through her veins. She could tell herself that the baby's last name wasn't the real issue. But she couldn't shake the feeling that she'd signed a contract only to keep discovering more fine print she hadn't noticed before, that she'd agreed to make payments on something and was just realizing now that the interest fees were going to bankrupt her. Molly wet a washcloth, rubbing it over her skin, and felt the tiny bulge that protruded right below her navel. She wondered if the baby could hear them, if he or she was a witness to the world it was about to join. It's the youngest of us who are always the ones hardest hit in a war between two grown-ups, she thought. Molly feared the strength of the ammunition that could be created by her and Scott's failings.

The sparkle of the diamond on Molly's left hand caught her eye. She'd forgotten to take it off before her shower, and now it was covered with an oily film from the soap bubbles. She tried to wipe the steam off of the gems and held her hand out to get a better look at them. She couldn't imagine how much the ring had cost Scott. He'd been so happy with it: the setting showcased a round center stone, about two carats big. On either side of the diamond rested three smaller stones of blue topaz—because he'd proposed in December, he said, though Molly suspected he'd thought it was her birthstone—in decreasing size. It was a cumbersome, heavy ring that seemed to get caught in every knitted sweater and doorjamb her hand touched. She liked to keep it off of her finger, tucked away in its black silk-lined box, when she was home, but Scott got hurt when he didn't see it on her. Molly turned the ring around on her finger and rinsed off the bubbles.

She felt badly about her quiet reaction to the ring when he'd first proposed, but her first thought when she saw it had been *Does he know me at all?* It was a ring for royalty, not for a middle-class girl from the outskirts of West Chester. And certainly not for one who still wore the white gold earrings she'd bought with her babysitting money when she was fifteen.

Molly stood in place as the water turned cool, the last of the soap bubbles swirling into the drain. She didn't know why she was surprised. She thought about the expensive watch Scott wore with pride, the red Porsche he leased with help from his parents. Scott was the first to have the newest phone, the best tablet, the TV with the flattest screen. Even his sunglasses had the designer's name splashed on the temples. It was all that he had been raised to know. Molly looked at the huge ring on her hand and swallowed hard. It was jewelry for a different type of life. She guessed now she'd have to look for a yellow wedding band to match it.

Molly wrung the water out of her heavy hair and stepped out of the shower to plug her phone into the small speaker set she kept in her bathroom. She turned on Tori Amos, letting the swell of the piano in "Girl" envelop her as she toweled dry. It'd been a few very long weeks. While Jenny was loading her belongings onto the office elevator, Molly was being asked to take over some of the responsibility for the marketing department. There was no pay increase for the extra work, but it meant she could keep her job. Her workload had doubled, and she found herself trying to fend off rumors of her pregnancy, juggle all of her new tasks, and get through an entire workday, all without falling asleep mid-step. But the new duties also meant the door to advancement had cracked open just a little wider. She didn't want word of an impending maternity leave getting in the way of a chance at the next opportunity. Molly had worked to be at this exact spot in her career by now, even if it was a lot busier than she'd anticipated. Molly could do busy. She just couldn't do chaotic.

As Amos' vibrato filled the room, Molly closed her eyes and reviewed her to-do list. She wanted to help her best friend find a new, good job. She needed to manage her assignments at work and come to some sort of truce with Scott. She also had to have a baby, tell her parents about that baby before it was born, and get married at some point. Molly opened her eyes and looked at herself in the mirror. Her cheeks were flushed a healthy pink from the shower, but they couldn't hide the swollen skin and dark circles under her eyes. She wondered, just for a moment, if joining her life to another person's had to mean handing her life *over* to that person. Molly was afraid of how much of herself she would have to siphon off in order to create this new family with Scott, and if she could expect any of it to ever be replaced.

The noise of this worry pulsated in her brain along with the music, and through the din, Molly heard the doorbell buzzing. She would figure that part out when she could, she knew. The smell of green curry wafted under the closed door of the bathroom, and Molly felt her stomach roll over with sudden hunger. She would deal with her problems one at a time, as she always did. But first, Molly decided, first she was going to get dressed and eat some dinner.

"Molly, come on. We have to do this." Scott was tugging Molly's hand through the doorway of the Rittenhouse hotel.

"No, we don't," Molly said. She looked back over her shoulder at the dark evening outside. The valet was speeding away from the curb in Scott's Porsche. "But you know what we can do? A movie. Popcorn. We can go home."

She pretended to turn around and start back toward the door. "I have the original *Rocky* on DVR. You know you want to."

Scott smiled down at her and placed a hand on her back to ease her through the expansive entrance of the building. He loved this sort of event, Molly knew. Scott's parents had convinced the pair to have an engagement party, even though Molly had threatened Scott with streaking naked through City Hall if he made her agree to it. No one, not even their parents or Jenny, knew what was hiding under the folds of the A-line dress Molly was wearing tonight, and a huge fete thrown by one of the wealthiest of Philadelphia families was not where either one of them wanted to announce their surprise plus-one.

Molly concentrated on the floral pattern woven into the thick rug of the lobby floor, absorbing the uncertainty spreading through her as she stepped across it. Molly looked up at Scott, who strode beside her with the confidence of a man used to crowds parting for him. His hair had been combed back from his clean-shaven face with precision. The aroma of the expensive cologne his mother had given him for Christmas hung around him like the fog that precedes a frost. As they walked, Molly felt the fingers of his large hand reach around hers. His eyes swept the expansive rooms around them, making sure they were noticed as they entered, calculating the impact he had on those who saw him. When he looked down at her, his green eyes locked on to hers with intensity, and Molly felt her cheeks go warm as a smile broke across her face. She turned away from him and looked ahead once again, waiting for her pulse to slow down.

Berkus parties were always a little uncomfortable at first for Molly, but tonight she felt like a kid standing on the side of a pool before one of her early swim lessons. She knew that she had to jump in—her parents wouldn't let her get out of learning, no matter how much she hated the water—but she knew the water would be icy-cold, and she was terrified of the dangers she couldn't see. So she'd stood on the side of the pool, afraid to surrender her body to the chill, wishing they could've just signed her up for soccer camp instead. Right now Molly felt like she was looking around for a life vest. Someone was going to have to shove her in.

They had reached the grand double doors of the ballroom, and before Scott had a chance to open them, Molly paused outside to pat down her metallic gray dress.

"Okay," Molly said. "Let's get this over with before I pop a zipper." She took a deep breath and held it for a moment. "Oh,

God, Scott," she spoke again with a start. "Jenny doesn't know, either. Remember that, okay? Please, just try not to get all chatty with the baby talk once you've had a few beers."

"What baby talk? And what do you mean, a few beers?" Scott was smiling, one eyebrow raised. "You act like you don't trust me."

He moved to open the door, but Molly stayed where she was.

"Something's not right, Scott," Molly said. She was lightheaded. "I feel like we shouldn't be doing this."

Scott rolled his eyes. "I know, I know, movie, couch. Let's just make the rounds, keep my folks happy, and you can be in your pajamas before ten. I promise."

Molly pressed her lips together.

"It's just . . ."

"Molly." Scott tucked his finger under her chin, pushing it up just high enough that she had to meet his eyes. The olive green of his irises distracted her, holding her gaze. "We can do this. I'll take care of you. I promise." Scott dropped his hand from Molly's face, tousling her hair with a quick swipe. Molly scowled at him in mock anger and smoothed the strands over her shoulders. Her uncertainty retreated.

"You are so lucky you look good in a suit," Molly said. "If I weren't planning on making you my trophy husband I'd have been in my UGGs by now."

Scott laughed. "At least I'm good for something."

Molly gasped when she stepped through the doors to the ballroom. Huge, arched windows lined the wall opposite them, facing a courtyard lit with hundreds of tiny white lights that shimmered in the cold winter air. Inside, large potted ferns were nestled among small, intimate tables covered in white linen and gold candlesticks. Food was everywhere: on buffet tables placed around the room, on the trays of the wait staff circulating with quiet practice among the guests. Chandeliers hung from the ceiling, sending prisms of soft light dancing along the jeweled watches and polished shoes of Philadelphia society. Scott's parents should have been considered relatively new to this moneyed class, but they worked very hard to make people think they'd belonged here forever.

Scott's mother approached as soon as they entered, her arms held wide as she leaned in to kiss the air beside both of their cheeks. Molly grinned to see her, pleased as always to be welcomed into the well-mannered embrace of Scott's family. Monica was a tall woman shaped liked one of the metal rulers she'd used when she worked as an architect, dressed in clothes crafted with the sharp, tailored angles she once designed into her buildings. She held her usual vodka tonic, garnished with a twist, in one hand. In the other she held a clutch made from a skin Molly could only identify as exotic and reptilian. Molly felt the small twinge of envy, now so familiar to her, poke at her self-confidence. She tucked her own clutch farther back under her arm.

"Darlings, it is so good to see you!" Monica exclaimed. She stepped back to assess Molly's outfit. "Molly, you look divine as usual. Your hair! And where did you find this dress?"

Molly smiled and shrugged. She thought it best not to announce that she had found her dress on eBay and was pretty sure it was a Miu Miu knockoff.

"So!" Monica placed her hand on Molly's elbow, giving it a soft squeeze. "You never did tell us—when's the big day?"

Two women, both wearing flashing jewels at their throats,

were passing behind Monica. They overheard the question and
slowed down to listen. Molly glanced up at Scott. He rubbed her
back and shrugged, waiting for Molly to fill the silence.

"Um," she replied. "I was thinking it might be nice to have
something small this June, maybe? Something intimate and easy."

Out of the corner of her eye, Molly saw Scott raise an eyebrow and hurried on.

"The backyard of my parents' house would be beautiful during the summer. We could have the wedding there." She heard
the hope in her voice and felt like a child again, pleading.

Molly knew her parents had no extra money to help pay for
a grand wedding. She also knew that her own savings needed to
be set aside for a down payment on the house and supplies for a
new baby. And really, Molly thought, it seemed like a farce to
throw a huge party and wear some extravagant gown when she'd
be so pregnant she'd have trouble just fitting down the aisle.

Monica, though, looked like she'd swallowed the lime from her
drink. Molly saw her friends exchange a quick whisper beside her.

"Nonsense!" Monica threw Scott a sharp glance, and Molly felt
his hand drop from her waist. "You're going to be the daughter I
never had! You're marrying my only son! I *refuse* to hear this jibber-
jabber about a *small* wedding, darling. We'll check into the club.
They should still have something open next year in the spring."

Molly looked down, but didn't say anything. She'd have an
infant by then.

"We'll start looking now at Nicole Miller—that's on Broad
Street—for your dress. Ooh, and maybe we should plan a girls' trip
up to Kleinfeld next month. Does your mother like New York?"

Molly tightened her grip on her purse. She couldn't afford that
kind of dress. And she wouldn't be able to fit into one anyway, she

assumed, if the torn waistband on her maternity tights was any indication of how much weight she'd have to lose before then.

Before she could figure out how to respond, Scott spoke up, one hand ruffling the back of his hair.

"Man, Mom, calm down." He was laughing. "Let us enjoy this party first, okay, before we start planning another. We can talk about it later."

Monica muttered her protest, but took a sip of her drink and fell quiet. Molly leaned into Scott, grateful, and breathed a sigh of relief. She was glad to see Scott's father pick that moment to work his way through the gathered crowd.

"Hey, Dad." Scott stuck out his hand to shake as his father joined them. Edward was a short man with a slight paunch over his belt. He patted the thin strands of gray hair that remained on the sides of his smooth head while he looked around the room, assessing the progress of the party. He took a sip from a glass filled with light beer.

"Did you eat yet?" Edward's North Philly accent pushed the question into two words: "Jeet yet?" Even though he stood right beside Scott's mother, he didn't touch her.

"Sweetheart," Monica answered him, "they just got here! They still haven't said hello to your partner or the girls from the club." She waved her hand as if scattering flies and took a sip of her cocktail. "They'll have time for that later."

Molly felt her shoulders drop and looked longingly at a tray of gourmet deviled eggs as they floated by on the arm of a tuxedoed server. The hunger pangs of pregnancy did not agree with a Monica Berkus party.

"Eh, you heard the little lady, Scott." Edward jerked his head in the direction of some men, all dressed in black suits that were each just a variation of Edward's. They were huddled on the other side of the dais, where a small band was playing a whining cover of "Ain't Too Proud To Beg."

"The Flyers talk was just heating up," he continued. As usual, he spoke more to his son's tie than to his eyes. "That game yesterday was just embarrassing, wasn't it?"

He led Scott away, and Monica was in turn engulfed by a larger circle of women with similar blond hairstyles, speaking with laughs made smooth by easy years of too much liquor and very little financial struggle. For a moment, Molly found herself alone before the next wave of well-wishers swept her away. She spotted her parents sitting at a table with her cousins, trying to catch her eye between the people who swarmed her. Molly could see that her father had trimmed his beard with care for the occasion. She wished her mother, wearing a familiar cap-sleeved blue dress, had sprung for a new outfit. Molly turned to hug the shoulders of an old coworker. She would have to say hello to her family a bit later.

An hour later, Molly spotted Jenny sitting alone in front of an abandoned plate of picked-over hors d'oeuvres. She dropped into the chair beside her with a heavy sigh and set down a short glass she'd asked the bartender to fill with sparkling water and lime.

"Hey," Molly said. She reached in front of Jenny to snag the last chocolate-drizzled bacon bite and shoved it into her mouth. "At least we always know the food is good at these things, right?"

Molly nodded toward the band, which was stepping down to take a break. "Even if the music is enough to make you ask for a doggie bag."

She looked at her friend, whose expression was despondent

enough to make Molly think the band had been worse than she'd thought.

"Jenny, are you okay?" Molly asked. "Has something changed from the last time we talked?"

"What, with the job or the baby?" There were faint circles under Jenny's eyes.

Molly didn't say anything. Jenny's question was her answer, and she knew not to press. Molly leaned forward to hide her stomach. At this rate she'd never be able to tell Jenny her news, but the longer she waited, the more hurt Jenny was going to be. *Not good,* Molly thought. So little of it was good right now.

"I gave your name to some of those headhunters I used to work with," Molly said.

"You're awesome." Jenny sighed. "Thank you. This temp gig is so boring I actually organize paper clips to keep myself occupied."

Molly cleared her throat.

"Well, they mentioned that there aren't many jobs out there right now," Molly said, "but they're looking." She watched Jenny's face for a reaction. "Apparently a lot of the companies are going the way of S&G and downsizing."

Jenny nodded. To Molly it seemed like she was a balloon that someone had left behind at a party, half exhausted of its helium, just drifting along.

Molly took a good look at her friend. She was wearing a ruby-red minidress with a large vintage-looking floral pattern and had paired it with black tights and platform heels that added a solid six inches to her tiny frame. Jenny was prepared for a party as she normally would be, all shimmering eye shadow and curly hair and big gold earrings, but her posture sagged. The vibrant color of her dress only made her seem paler.

"You know what's funny?" Jenny said. "Lack of money aside, this would actually be the perfect time for me to get pregnant."

Molly sucked in her breath. She felt her face grow hot and glanced across the room at Scott, who was talking with a friend from his prep school days. An empty drink was in his hand.

Jenny didn't notice. "Think about it. No need for maternity leave, no worries about somebody coming along to take my job."

She paused again. The women sat in their seats at the empty table, watching the party go on in front of them. Molly heard Jenny take a deep breath.

"It's me, Molly." Her voice was quiet, and when Molly looked at her she saw tears in her friend's eyes. "The doctor said it's me. It's my fault I can't get pregnant."

"Oh, Jenny, it's not your fault. It's no one's fault." Molly said the words, but she was starting to feel like she was to blame a little. Because she knew that soon enough, she'd be adding to Jenny's pain, too. She had the vague feeling that she was letting her life start to unravel, but wasn't quite sure how to begin tidying it back up. This was a first for her, and Molly thought that it had better be the last. "You guys will get there. It'll work out. It always does."

"I hope you're right, Mol," Jenny said. "Thank goodness for you and Dan, though. They say you marry your father, but I'm so glad I escaped *that* particular two-timing impulse. I swear, if I didn't have him, and if the Delaware River weren't so polluted, I probably would've jumped off the Ben Franklin Bridge by now." She looked sidelong at Molly, waiting for her laugh.

But Molly wasn't laughing. "Didn't you always assume that your twenties were supposed to be the toughest part of your life?"

she asked. "I was under the impression that once you turned thirty your life kind of settled down a bit."

"Yeah," Jenny said, "but whoever told you that rumor *lied*. And I'd like to have a little chat with the jerk myself, if I ever find her."

Jenny shook her upper body in a quick movement like she was shaking off a bad dream, sat up, and looked around the room. "Enough with the boo-hooing. This is your party! And it's a good party, despite your grandma Norah yelling at Dan earlier for not using a napkin when he eats."

Molly broke out into a laugh after all. "What?! She did that to him, too?"

"Oh, yeah. And reminded him to use a fork instead of his fingers."

They were still chuckling into their glasses when Dan came over to join them. Molly saw Jenny light up to see him, as always. Dan was the perfect complement to Jenny's fair, blond looks. He was about as tall as Jenny when she wore her heels and had a penchant for wearing Dr. Martens that added another inch to his height. He'd taken to wearing a wallet chain when they were living in some of the rougher neighborhoods around Temple during grad school and had never really shaken the habit, even though he was thirty-one and now taught in one of the nicest schools in Chestnut Hill. He didn't look much older than the kids in his classes. His dark black hair was short and slightly spiked, and he had almond-shaped eyes that were a deep, dark brown. Molly thought Dan was one of the most genuinely kind people she'd ever met, which may have been one of the reasons why his students were so quick to trust him.

"Man, Molly, if your big day's half as nice as this party, I'd skip my own wedding to be there." He shoved a bacon-wrapped scallop into his mouth.

"No, you wouldn't, Dan." Molly laughed. "You showed up four hours early for your own wedding."

"I was excited." He winked at Jenny. "I'm just saying—this is some top-notch stuff. Did you know they have restroom attendants here? There was a guy in the bathroom handing me towels *and* breath mints *and* a dish. Not quite sure what the dish was for, but I thanked him for it anyway."

Dan gestured with the small plate, which was now covered with crumbs and cocktail sauce. "I guess they keep extras in there in case they run out by the hors d'oeuvres."

"Dear, dumb husband." Jenny patted Dan's arm. "I don't think the attendant was handing you a dish so you could stuff your face."

Dan looked from Jenny to Molly.

"He wanted a tip, Dan," said Molly. "He was asking for money."

"Oh, damn it," said Dan, scraping some bacon and scallops from his plate onto a napkin. "That's why he got so salty when I left. I gotta go give this back to him."

Before Dan had a chance to go, Scott strolled up, a half-empty glass in one hand and what looked like a refill of scotch in the other.

"Great party, right?" He gestured broadly to the rest of the room, sloshing a little of the liquor onto Molly's good boots. Out of the corner of her eye she saw her parents watching them.

"Molly, aren't you so glad now that my folks convinced us to have this thing?" Scott lowered his voice into a loud whisper. "And you'd be so proud of me! I haven't mentioned one word about the *baby*," he said, rubbing her belly, "to anyone!"

"The *what*?" Jenny and Dan stared at Molly, mouths open.

"Oh, shit," Scott said. He swayed a little on his feet. "Sorry, Mol."

They'd attracted the attention of a couple of second cousins who were standing at the bar nearby.

"You're pregnant?" Jenny's voice was low, almost a hiss. Molly had never seen her friend's eyes so wide. "The whole time we've been talking about babies, and you haven't said a *word*?"

"She didn't want to tell you," Scott said, his voice louder than the rest of theirs. Molly realized he was trying to smooth over his mistake. "'Cause she didn't want you to get upset that she was going to be hatching her egg before you had a chance to lay yours."

Well, Molly thought, *that didn't work.* Dan, for a brief moment, looked like he might punch Scott in the nose.

"Scott! What are you doing?" Molly whispered, brushing his hand away from her stomach. She glanced at Jenny, who was standing still in front of them, her face ashen. "How much have you had to drink?"

"Oh, hey, baby, let's relax about it, okay?" Scott's expression was earnest. "It's the twenty-first century. People don't care." He gestured to Jenny and Dan before looking at Molly again. "So you're already knocked up! What are you really worried about? The seal is broken! That ship has sailed! We should be proud of ourselves. Ya know what I mean?" He held his hand up for a high five, and when Molly just glared at him, he turned to Jenny, then Dan, with his outstretched palm. Both stood in silence, drinks in hand, and looked at him.

Molly felt a sudden flood of embarrassment rush through her, starting at her swollen feet in their stained boots and welling up in her body until it washed over her face. She closed her eyes, as if the scene would go away if she couldn't see it.

"Scott, just stop," Molly said. She could feel the heat simmering across her face. "Jenny, I wanted to tell you, every day since I found out." She looked from Jenny to Dan. "I just didn't know how."

She saw her friends share a glance of understanding. Jenny would've done the same thing, she knew. Molly started to speak, but Scott was still talking, the consonants of his words starting to lose their edges.

"Dude, I think I'm wasted." He smacked Dan on the arm with the back of his hand and turned to the women. "Though, you want to talk about wasted, you shoulda seen Dan that night the boys all went to Finnigan's Wake to celebrate me sealing the proposal deal with you. How many shots did you do, Dan? Five? Six?" He elbowed Jenny's husband and laughed.

Dan blushed and glanced sidelong at his wife. Jenny looked like she was ready to head to that bridge she'd talked about.

Scott leaned toward her. "You should be proud of your man, Jenny. He acts like such a goody two-shoes, but he can really throw it back."

Dan was rocking back and forth on his heels. Molly saw him look toward the restroom as if he couldn't wait to get that plate back to the attendant. Maybe he'd give a tip along with the dish this time, she thought.

Scott was still talking.

"Yeah, Dan, and how many drinks did you buy for that chick you were talking to all night? I saw you disappear, you know." Scott clapped his hand on the shoulder of an uncomfortable-looking Dan and took a gulp of his scotch. Jenny turned to her husband. The color of her face had shifted from pale to crimson.

"Hey," she said. "I tried calling you a hundred times that night. What is Scott saying?"

"Jenny, he's drunk. He doesn't know what he's talking about," Dan said.

"Yeah, I'd hope so. But you never told me why you didn't return my texts. Is this why? Because you were with some other girl?"

Jenny had once said that the worst decision her mother had ever made wasn't in marrying her father—it was in staying with him. Molly held her breath and waited for Dan to speak.

"Jenny, it's not how it sounds—" Dan protested. "I think the liquor's making Scott a little rammy. We've all had a rough night."

His worried eyes were now glaring at Scott.

"Then what happened, Dan? When you left with her? What happened?" Jenny's spoke in hushed, urgent tones. She was shaking and didn't seem to notice that she'd attracted some attention in the room. "Wait—you told me you spent the night at Scott's. Did you not, then? Where were you?" Jenny's voice got shrill. "What is going on here?"

Molly swallowed hard.

"Jenny, I—" Dan began.

Jenny was starting to cry. "I waited up for you all night, freaking out because you hadn't called me. We *never* do that to each other. I checked the city police's website to make sure there weren't any accidents or shootings or kidnappings. You don't even know all the stuff I was thinking could've happened to you. I called your freaking *sister* to see if she'd heard from you. Your *sister*! I HATE your sister!"

"Whooaaa." Scott's eyes widened and he clamped his mouth shut. He looked from Jenny to Dan and back again, arms limp at his sides, holding the empty glasses. Molly stood stock-still, almost afraid to move lest someone tell her that what was happening was actually real. Jenny and Dan were the most rock-solid couple she knew. It had to have been a misunderstanding.

Jenny didn't acknowledge the tears spilling down her cheeks by wiping them away, and instead stuck her chin up in the air and blinked hard.

Scott spoke. "I . . . I didn't mean to . . ." His voice cracked.

Dan glared at him and moved toward his wife. Her arms were crossed over her chest, and she took a step backward.

"Jenny, come on. You know me well enough by now—"

"Dan, apparently I don't know anything anymore. Not when everything is turned upside down."

She glanced at Molly. Molly dropped her gaze to the floor.

"I can't do this. Not one more thing." Jenny shook her head. The tears fell uninhibited now. "You, Dan," Jenny said. Her voice was a whisper. "You, too?"

Dan didn't have a chance to respond before Jenny strode out of the room, leaving them staring after her in a stunned silence. He took off after her in a jog, and Molly stood beside the space they'd left, watching one more piece of the puzzle fall away.

CHAPTER FOUR

March

No

"So, I guess that's that, then?" Molly's father took a sip from his coffee and placed the mug back on the coaster.

"Yeah, I guess that's that. For now, anyway," Molly said. She swallowed a mouthful of her decaf, wincing as the hot coffee scalded her tongue, and ran her fingers around the lip of the mauve-colored mug. It was the same cup she used whenever she visited her parents. In fact, Molly realized, it was the same cup she'd used every day at home since she'd been a teenager. Molly stared at the mug. She never had been good at dealing with change.

Her mother stood at the kitchen sink, fingertips braced on the edge of the counter. She was looking out the window, her thin frame silhouetted against the slanting late-winter light shining through the clear panes. Her cotton button-front shirt was rolled at the sleeves up to her elbows, a carryover from the days she'd spent sitting at the table, hunched over the papers she graded with a calculator and red pen. She was a small woman, but years of managing twenty-five high school students at a time had created a determined fire inside of Emily, a way of focusing her attention that Molly found both enviable and intimidating.

Emily turned around. "Well, Molly." She rubbed her hands together, their dry skin making a rasping sound like sandpaper that's been worked over too many times. "This isn't quite the order that we had wanted you to do things, is it?"

Molly's mother met her eyes, holding them until Molly grew uncomfortable and looked away. Her father remained quiet, but his gaze never left his daughter, either. Molly knew they were both trying to see through her somber demeanor, wanting to get past their own disappointment to the root of what was hurting her the most. There were good parents who were fixers, Molly knew. But better parents nudged their children in the right direction and let them do the rest.

Molly could hear Fleetwood Mac playing from the stereo in the living room. "Bleed To Love Her" was one of her dad's favorites.

"No, Mom, it isn't." She didn't shift her gaze from her mug.

Emily bit her lower lip, then turned to her husband. Jack didn't take his eyes off of Molly's face. For a moment, the air in the kitchen was still.

"Are you keeping the baby?" Jack asked. The question, like most of Jack's, was to the point.

"Yes, yes," Molly said. "Anything else wasn't an option, you know that." Whether it was perfect timing or not, Molly had always seen herself as a mother. As it happened, so did the universe.

"And what is Scott's role in this? Besides the obvious, I mean?" Emily asked. Molly cringed. Emily had tilted her head to look at her daughter, her gray-blue eyes steady and dry.

"Scott appears to have washed his hands of the whole deal, Mom, because I haven't heard a word from him since I told him about the baby. I hurt him pretty badly, so it's either that or he's in denial." Molly shook her head. "I don't know. And at this point, I can't worry about him. I'm on my own, baby or no baby."

Jack cleared his throat. He was a burly grizzly bear of a man, with a full gray beard and large hands. He had a penchant for faded jeans and flannel shirts, and always seemed to carry the vague scent of pipe tobacco about him, even though he didn't smoke. It was hard to ignore him when he was in a room, even if he remained silent, but on the rare occasion he spoke up, people stopped to listen. Molly looked up to meet his eyes now and swallowed, hard.

"Well, Molly, Scott's a rat bastard if he's not going to support this baby. That's obvious."

"Way to help, Pop."

"Let me finish." Jack leaned forward to tuck a finger under Molly's chin, just like he used to do when she was a little girl. "But that doesn't mean the child's not going to be taken care of. You know that."

Molly nodded, but her mouth felt dry.

"It'll work out, Molly. It always does."

Jack sat back in his chair and thumped both of his hands on the tabletop with a definitive *whack*.

"Well, then, Emily," he said, and his mouth broke into a smile that exposed his small snaggletooth. "I'd say it looks like we have a grandchild to get ready for." Jack picked up his coffee and gave Molly a wink over the lip of the mug. Molly allowed herself to relax just a bit.

Emily shook her head as if she'd snapped out of a trance. She, too, broke into a smile, though hers was more hesitant, forced.

She tucked her hair, which hung in a sweeping gray line to her shoulders, behind one ear.

"Why, then, I suppose we do!" She began moving around the kitchen, hands busy, smoothing dish towels on their bars and straightening the ceramic flour jars on the countertop.

"Do you know the sex of the baby yet?" She asked the question over her shoulder.

"No, Mom." Molly felt her chin jut up. "I want it to be a surprise."

Emily threw a wet dish towel onto the linoleum countertop with a slap.

"A surprise! Haven't we had enough of those for a little while?" Her mother forced out a low, scraping chuckle that ended with a cough.

Jack gave Emily a sharp look. She shrugged and kept moving, now clearing the pie dishes from the table.

"Oh, all right. So we don't know if it's going to be a boy or girl. But you do realize that people are going to give you a lot of yellow and green clothes, Molly."

Molly nodded.

"I just hope you're ready for that baby to be dressed like a sick duck."

Jack stood up and patted his daughter on the shoulder. "I think I'm going to go work in my shop for a little while, dear." Molly's father owned a hardware store and often did some carpentry on the side. He started to walk out of the kitchen, then stopped, his hand still on Molly's shoulder. He leaned back to look at her.

"This baby is going to be loved, kiddo. Don't mind your mother's huffing and puffing." He chuckled as Emily swatted him on the rear with the dish towel. He dropped a quick kiss onto the top of Molly's head before walking out to the garage.

Molly closed her eyes. She could hear her mother chattering away, but she didn't catch Emily's words. She breathed a silent sigh of relief—it was over, that step was finished, it was time to move on—and opened her eyes to answer her mother's repeated question.

"I don't know for sure, Mom, but I think Jenny will probably throw me a shower. Do you want me to give you her number?"

Molly dug into her bag for her smartphone. From the living room, she could hear the dejected, driving bass line as the next song on the mix began, and she recognized "I'm So Afraid." She turned her attention toward her mother.

A few weeks later, Molly stood in the fitting room of a maternity store on Walnut Street, turning left and right to judge how her slight bulge of a stomach looked under a new tunic shirt. She squinted at her profile in the mirror, the bottom half of which was obscured by sticky-looking handprints on the glass. The walls of the plain white cubicle were built too close together for anybody with a belly poking out over her pants. An odor of old apple juice and spoiled milk hung in the air like smoke after a fire. She squirted some sanitizer onto her hands from the large bottle she kept in her bag and rubbed them together, assessing the pregnant body she saw in her reflection. Her hips were already wider. Her small breasts had started to bulge over the top of her bra cups like the chocolate cupcakes she brought home from Brown Betty each weekend. Her pregnancy was moving forward like a bus pulling away from the curb, speeding up before she could reach its door.

Molly took off the bright pink shirt and reached for another in

a larger size. She wished Jenny were there with her, giggling over
the elastic waistbands and intimidating nursing bras with all their
snaps and strange flaps. Jenny had been very quiet since Molly told
her the news. She and Dan had just had a huge fight—strange for
them, under any circumstances—which Molly didn't know about
when she'd decided to share the news of her pregnancy. Molly
cringed at the memory of Jenny's tears, her silent nod of acceptance
as she sat on the stool across the kitchen island from Molly. They
were very careful with each other now, more tentative in their
conversations than they'd ever been. Molly needed her friend just
as much as she knew Jenny needed her. But it should be Jenny here
trying on the maternity clothes, not Molly, and they both knew it.

Neither friend said it, of course, but the knowledge sat there,
big and raw and ugly. That it wasn't right that Molly was starting to feel excited, that she was the one who got to be curious to
meet the person growing inside her. That Molly should be
amazed by the way her body was shifting, or be the one to wan-
der into her kitchen at two in the morning because she craved
marshmallows in peanut butter. It was supposed to be Jenny.
Molly couldn't keep the guilt from working its way into her
consciousness, like the buzz from the sugar she'd get after the
late-night binges. Jenny should be the one trying on the too-big
maternity top: Jenny, with her good husband, and her financial
planning, and all of their hopeful trying. Not the single woman
with a workload too big and a wallet too small to carry. Jenny
had had some sort of breakdown after that day in her kitchen,
fleeing her life with Dan for her parents' house in the suburbs.
She hadn't been back to the city since.

There's a happiness to be found in bad timing, Molly thought,
if only we can allow ourselves to lose control just a little. It's

hard, too hard, to do that, though, and, like Jenny, Molly was afraid. But she also knew, just as she'd known she was going to raise this baby herself, that sometimes—just sometimes—being in over your head gives you a chance to learn how to swim.

Molly just wished she weren't so scared.

She looked at herself in the mirror again, her belly like a deflated beach ball under her shirt. She twisted the tunic over her head with so much force a stitch popped, then pulled on her own shirt, avoiding her reflection. Monica probably would have insisted she be here, too, she and Jenny jockeying for space in the dressing room with her. Molly would've had a pile of complete outfits set aside and purchased already. There would have been designer jeans, and dresses for every trimester, and a complete lingerie collection of underwear and tights, already packaged in shopping bags, ready to make their appearances on Center City sidewalks and Chestnut Hill cafés. The occasion would have been a celebration. Molly sat down for a moment in her too-tight bikini briefs. She clutched the discarded shirt and told herself not to cry.

"Everything going all right in there?" Molly heard the sales-girl's chipper voice hop around the corners of the dressing stall curtain. She yanked on her jeans and grabbed her small pile of items to be purchased, hefted her bag onto her shoulder, and sidled out of the room, struggling for a moment with the curtain as it wrapped over her protruding middle.

"Oh!" The girl jumped back, giggling.

"I didn't expect to see you just"—she waved her fingers like a jazz dancer—"*pop* out like that! Did you find everything you need? Did it all fit well? Oh my gosh, it must be so exciting to go shopping for maternity clothes for the first time."

Molly tried to interrupt her, but the girl kept talking.

"This is your first time, right? I mean, you're barely showing! I can't wait till it's my time to be pregnant."

"Well—" Molly started to say.

"I mean," the girl laughed, "a lot of years from now, of course. I don't need to be giving my parents a heart attack or anything. God, they'd kill me."

The teenager wrested an armful of clothes from Molly's grasp and moved over to the register. Her straight, blond hair swung back and forth over her shoulder blades as she moved. Molly ran her fingers through her own hair, securing it into a loose bun on the back of her head with an elastic band. She was very aware of the years that separated her from this young woman. She wondered if the girl was even old enough to be going to prom this spring. She wondered when she'd turned so crotchety.

The clerk was telling a story about her boyfriend as Molly handed over her debit card, but Molly couldn't concentrate on the monologue. She had scheduled a lunch with her mother for that afternoon, and it was going to be the first time she'd seen her since her awkward announcement.

Molly hadn't spoken to either of her parents recently, except for a brief conversation with her father when he called to tell her that WXPN radio was running an old Stevie Nicks live show. But her mom had called her Thursday to ask if she could come into the city to meet Molly for lunch. Molly didn't know what to expect, but she suspected this wasn't a casual lunch date. She couldn't imagine Emily chatting about nursery design or where to register for gifts. What Molly could brace herself for, though, was for her mother to show up with a PowerPoint presentation on why Molly should give the baby up for adoption, or to gypsies, or maybe drop her off at a convent. Molly liked to be one step ahead at all times, but Emily usually had the whole year planned out. Molly's stomach felt queasy under the swell of her abdomen. This pregnancy was becoming more complicated by the day.

"So, do you want a girl or a boy?" The salesgirl was still talking as she handed Molly the stuffed bags over the counter. She hadn't stopped smiling once since Molly stepped out of the dressing room. "I'd totally want a girl, just so I could put her in all those cute little pink skirts I keep seeing. You know, the ones with the tutus? I want my perfect little princess. Not now, of course! My boyfriend would die. But one day. What does your husband do? Will you stay home with the baby, or keep working? He must be so thrilled to be a dad, right?"

The girl stood there, smiling, on the other side of the counter. Her eyebrows were raised, waiting.

Molly jammed her wallet back into her purse.

"Um, actually," Molly said, standing back up straight, "there is no husband. I'm not married. Don't have a boyfriend, either, for that matter."

"Oh." The girl breathed in, her eyes as wide as the hoop earrings she wore. "Uh. So. Huh." She looked around the store, then at the register, and shifted a pen to the other side of the table. The smile was gone from her face.

"I'm sorry." Molly was quick with her words. "I didn't mean to be rude.

"I am excited for the baby," she continued, "but I'll most definitely still be working once he or she comes. It's what happens."

The girl looked up, her tweezed eyebrows furrowed together. "What happens?"

Molly gathered her bags together, then met the teenager's eyes.

"It's what happens when you date the wrong guy, get pregnant by the wrong guy, and somewhere in there decide that he's never going to be right enough for you to ever marry. It's what happens when you suddenly hear the words 'single mother' and know it describes you, too." Molly shrugged, and smiled. "So think about that on prom night, okay? Have a good time. But, you know. Don't do anything I wouldn't do." Molly gulped. "Now, I mean. Don't do anything I wouldn't do now."

She hurried out the door, leaving the salesgirl staring after her, mouth open, hand already reaching for her cell phone. Molly quickened her pace, the large bags banging her knees with every step. She had a lunch date to keep.

A short while later, Molly swung the door open to enter Caribou Café, a chic French bistro on Walnut Street. Her mother rarely came into the city anymore, preferring to stay close to the comfortable—and affordable—pubs and diners of West Chester, a university town with its own restaurant scene filled with familiar faces and the occasional cluster of college students. Emily must have been desperate to see her, Molly thought, to brave the unfamiliar one-way streets and parking garages of the city on a busy spring Saturday. With a pang of guilt, Molly had made reservations at Caribou, feeling that she at least owed her mother a nice lunch. Emily had spent a couple of years studying in Paris before she'd met Jack, in a whole other gutsy, more worldly life. Molly had never had a chance to experience an adventure like that before meeting Scott. A splurge on a Parisian-style bistro meal was the best she could do, and it made her feel young somehow.

She paused at the entrance of the restaurant, pushing her aviators up to rest on the top of her windblown hair. It took a second for her eyes to adjust from the sharp glare of the early spring afternoon to the hushed tones of the intimate, narrow restaurant. Molly spotted her mother sitting at a two-top against the railing on the second floor, ramrod-straight in the plush burgundy chair, watching the door. Molly took a deep breath and began to work her way in between the tables and up the dark wood stairs, holding the shopping bags ahead of her like the prow of a ship cutting through water. The walk had made her so ravenous that she felt dizzy and had to hold on to the rail as she climbed the steps.

"Hey, Mom." Molly leaned down to kiss her mother's cheek before sinking into her seat. Emily smelled like the powdery scent she dabbed behind her ears on the most special of occasions.

Emily took a long look at Molly, and then the shopping bags. "You've been busy! A Pea in the Pod?"

"Yeah, it's a maternity store." Molly patted her stomach, where her cotton-and-spandex shirt was stretched across her belly button. "I thought it was about time I got out of my denial and into some pants that fit."

"Well, that's nice, I suppose," Emily replied. She patted her hands across the napkin in her lap. "But why didn't you tell me you were going? I'd have come in early to go with you."

"I didn't want to bother you," Molly said. She looked at her mom, confused. She hadn't thought to ask her mother, who'd much rather thumb the pages of a book than hangers full of clothes. Monica had always been her shopping buddy. Besides, she didn't want to let on how little she could afford to get. Her parents were already worried enough about her. She didn't need to know that each of the outfits in Molly's bag had come off the clearance rack.

"Well, next time let me know," Emily said. "I feel like I've missed so much of your pregnancy already, considering how late you told us."

Molly pressed her lips together. Her stomach growled in defiance.

"But now I'd like to get you a few things." Emily looked at Molly with eyes that were soft, then smiled. "My daughter's having a baby. My *baby*'s having a baby."

Molly took a second to take in her mother's posture. She knew that Emily's retirement pension was needed to help cover the increasing overhead at Jack's store. Her parents couldn't afford any extra costs right now. Molly thought about Monica, whose wallet was filled with so many credit cards it made Molly anxious. She'd never seen her so much as glance at a price tag.

"Okay," Molly said. She paused, contemplating her mother's sudden interest in bonding activities. It seemed that impending motherhood could stir change that spread well beyond just the woman awaiting her child. "I'll call you next time, and we'll go out. Maybe King of Prussia mall, next month?" Molly patted her midsection. "The way I'm eating, I'll be out of these clothes before I have a chance to take off the tags."

Molly signaled the waiter to let him know they were ready. If she didn't order lunch soon, the restaurant would be in serious danger of her gnawing away at the table, bleached linen tablecloth and all. The double cheeseburger she'd wolfed down at McDonald's before clothes shopping was a distant memory by now.

In the restaurant below them, business lunches took place at some tables, and mothers sat at others eating crepes with one hand while feeding babies with the other. Emily looked over at Molly.

"How are you, Molly?" she asked. *"Really?"*

Molly blew out a deep lungful of air.

"Excited. Terrified. You know, the usual." She tried to chuckle. "I'm worrying about everything. Whether to breastfeed, and if I do, how it'll go. If it'll hurt. What it'll do to my boobs."

Emily shrugged and nodded. She knew.

"I can't wait to meet this person, of course. BabyCenter says she—or he—is the size of a green pepper already. But then I start thinking about sleep deprivation and discipline and not, like, accidentally poking her in her soft spot, and I freak myself out all over again."

She laughed, but didn't say the rest. That she was worried about doing it on her own. Without Scott. Without a partner. Without somebody there to tell her if what the hell she was doing would be the right thing or not. Molly asked herself sometimes how she was supposed to raise a child when it often felt like she wasn't quite all the way grown herself. She wondered if all adults felt like she did—like they were pretending at this grown-up game, waiting to be discovered in society's biggest charade.

Molly's stomach growled again, and the sound was loud enough to make her squirm in her seat. She looked around to make sure no one else heard the gurgle. More than fear or anticipation, Molly was consumed by hunger, and right now she was feeling so famished she would consider eating the menu in front of her. She wondered if she had any Tootsie Rolls left in her bag.

"Look, Molly," Emily said. "Scott's that baby's father. He needs to provide for his family. Support you and the little one. It's not right that you should be on your own in this."

A mother knows her daughter's mind. Molly sighed.

"Mom, I'm not on my own. I have you. And Pop. And you know Jenny and Dan are practically going to move in once the baby's here. I have a solid support system. You don't have to worry.

And financially, I'm okay." She swallowed down the small lie. She had always taken care of her bills, but was embarrassed that she had gotten used to Scott treating her to all the rest. "It'll be fine."

Molly glanced around again, considering whether it was worth making a scene to find a manager.

"But you may have to bail me out of jail, because I'm going to snatch somebody's food off of his plate if I don't get some bread on this table." She craned her neck to the rear of the restaurant. "Oh my gosh, where is he?"

Trying to ignore her angry, empty stomach, Molly filled her mom in on the situation with Jenny and Dan, and how Jenny had moved back in with her parents in Cherry Hill. A waiter strolled by the table and dropped a basket of rolls in between them before taking off again. Molly groaned with both relief and exasperation.

"But why would she do that?" Emily asked. "I thought they were trying to have a baby."

"Yeah, but that's the thing," Molly said. "She's put so much pressure on herself to be perfect, and I think what Scott implied was enough to be a breaking point for her. You know how scared she is of becoming her parents. I think she already needed some distance, and this just pushed her right into it."

"Do you think?" Emily asked.

"That he cheated?" Molly shook her head. "I don't know, actually."

Her mother laughed. "It's Dan, Molly. Do you remember that time we were all down the shore?"

Molly remembered. It was the first summer after she'd met Jenny, when the three of them stayed at the shore house Molly's parents had splurged to rent in Avalon. On the beach one afternoon, Jenny had stepped on a tiny jellyfish and reacted with such pain, anyone would've thought she'd been bitten by a shark. Dan had rushed to her side and carried her all the way to the lifeguard stand for first aid. He'd been so concerned about her, brushing her hair from her face as she cried, and all the lifeguard needed to do was give Jenny a Band-Aid and advise her to take some aspirin.

"That's exactly why I let Scott go, Mom," Molly said. "I could never imagine him worrying over somebody like that. All that concerns Scott is whether somebody is caring for *him*."

She thought back to a temper tantrum Scott once threw when he couldn't get tickets to a revival of *The Godfather*.

"I don't need two babies to take care of." She was quiet a moment longer. "And I don't want my child being raised by somebody who grew up thinking his housekeeper's name was 'Mommy.' Scott has no idea how to be a parent. I don't want my child to grow up wondering why her daddy doesn't care enough about her."

Emily pressed her lips together. "But she's going to wonder that, anyway, Molly, without a father in her life."

Molly swallowed.

"I realize that."

Molly wondered if it would really be that bad to sneak a few sips of her mother's wine now that she was out of the first trimester. A small glass might not hurt, possibly.

"Have you stopped to consider that maybe a poor father might be better than no father at all?" Emily asked.

Molly nodded. "Of course. I think about it a lot. But, Mom, you're forgetting that Scott hasn't offered to *be* a father now that we're not getting married. Should I have to marry him just to get him to step up? What's he going to do, suddenly decide he's got some recessive paternal instinct that's just dying to express itself because he has a ring on his finger? Come on."

Emily didn't hurry to respond. Molly's thoughts were scrambling now, scratching at her common sense like the hunger pangs clawing at her stomach. She knew she was right. She knew she hadn't made a mistake breaking up with Scott. She just wondered if she was the only one who thought that way.

"Wait. Does Pop agree with you?" she asked. "I can't imagine that he'd be okay with me marrying Scott. Pop used to call me after Scott drove me home from your place just to make sure he wasn't still there."

Emily cleared her throat. "I can't speak for your father. You know him. He sets his own mind on matters like this."

That told Molly nothing. She nodded in acknowledgment, but what she really wanted to do was bang her forehead against the table.

"We just . . ." Emily hesitated. "We wish circumstances were different, that's all." She sighed, and leaned over to rub Molly's arm. "I'm sorry, honey. I shouldn't say that, not now. I just never thought that when it came time for you to have children you'd be doing it alone."

Molly's memory fell back to a Saturday morning a few days after her first date with Liam. She'd walked over to Reading Terminal Market in search of steamed crabs. A friend from college was coming in that night from the Midwest, and Molly was intent on making a meal she could only find fresh on the East Coast. Molly stumbled into the market early, sweaty from the trek, her hair in a wild bun on top of her head. She was wearing the baggy sweatpants she'd pulled on straight out of bed. She hadn't felt like putting on makeup before she left the house, and it was a decision she regretted as soon as she saw Liam standing in line at the seafood counter. But his face broke into a grin when he saw her, and they spent the rest of the morning together, wandering around the city with coffee in their hands, talking. Molly, in her ragged hoodie and old running shoes, never felt prettier than when she was with him that day. After that, her best moments with Liam were the ones that unfurled on their own, without pretense.

It had all been so uncomplicated.

"Yeah," Molly said. "Neither did I."

Molly knew that her child hadn't been conceived out of love so much as out of her need to make everything okay, of a hurry to patch up the relationship and move on, but it wasn't the baby's fault his parents had messed up, or that his dad now didn't seem to want him. Molly was determined to make sure this baby was raised with so much love that it wouldn't matter in the slightest how he got there, or who made him. She owed the child that much.

"Mom, the bottom line is that even if I wanted Scott back in my life—which I don't—he doesn't want to be there. Not everyone can have what you and Pop do. Scott proposed *before* he knew I was pregnant, not after."

Emily smoothed the napkin again in her lap. Molly fought the urge to snatch the cloth from her mom's legs and throw it over the balcony. Her appetite was roaring with a growling vengeance. She had never been this hungry, not even that time in college after she'd heard a speech from PETA and made it almost four weeks as a vegan.

"Mom, you're not listening." Molly's voice grew harder. This lunch was going to be more painful than that entire month by far.

"Scott completely freaked out when I told him. He acted like his world was ending, and then . . . he shut down. It seemed like a switch just shut off in his heart. It was almost like it was suddenly perfectly fine that I didn't want to marry him now that it meant there would be three people on our honeymoon."

Emily blinked hard once, and lifted her water glass to her lips.

"Why else do you think I haven't talked to him in two months?" Molly said. "He wanted me, but only me—nothing more. Not exactly father-figure material, right there." Molly was shaking. "So yeah, no dad at all is better than having a disinterested one."

The restaurant had gotten very noisy. Molly fingered the edge of her menu, which was still lying open in front of her, and waited for her mother to respond. Her throat was dry, and she could taste the vague burn of bile climbing from her empty stomach. She needed her mother to see that she was going to be able to do this. She had to convince her parents, and then maybe she'd be able to convince herself.

"Okay. Okay." Emily tucked her hair behind her ear. "I'm sorry. He's a rat bastard and your dad is right. I get it."

Molly had to smile at her mother's vocabulary. She rarely heard her mother swear.

"He's not a *rat* bastard," she said. She was surprised to hear herself defending him. "I think he's just immature. And probably a little spoiled."

Mother and daughter were silent for a moment before Emily spoke.

"Molly, you have your reasons for doing what you do," she said, "and as long as you're following your gut, that's no other way to go. But there's a baby now, and that baby needs more stability than a single mother might be able to offer.

"We'll just have to figure something out," she continued. "What we lack in finances we have in smarts, right?"

Molly, alert and still, watched her mother like a rabbit who'd just been spotted by a dog. Emily leaned forward to look her daughter square in the eyes. Molly didn't like what she saw.

"I have an idea."

"What do you mean?" Molly felt a knot of fear form in her stomach. The ache there was more than hunger now, more than what another cheeseburger, even with fries, could shove out of the way.

"Well, your father and I had a good talk, and because of the circumstances"—Emily took a deep breath—"we'd like you to move back home."

Molly's mouth fell open. What she wouldn't give for that glass of wine right now, Molly thought. Or the whole bottle.

"I'm sorry," she said. "You want me to do what?"

"Your father and I don't want you doing this on your own. We want you to move back home. Like I said, it's just not right for a young person like yourself—"

"Mom, I'm thirty years old. Women are becoming single mothers every day, often by choice. I'm hardly an anomaly."

"I said nothing about you being a woman, Molly. Relax. I'm talking about you—a person, a parent—raising a baby in the world alone when she doesn't have to."

Molly began to protest again, but Emily cut her off. "Have you thought about child care yet?"

"Yeah, a little," Molly conceded. When she'd discovered how expensive day care was in the city she'd gotten disheartened and taken a break from her research.

"So you probably know that it will cost you so much money that you'd practically need a part-time job to pay for the day care for the full-time job."

Molly couldn't disagree.

"So, we've decided. Since I'm retired now and your father's home practically all the time anyway, we want to help out, and this is a way we can do so. Your brothers have been out of the house for years, so you move back home, and the baby can have either Patrick's or Johnny's old room. The train's just a fifteen-minute drive from the house. Yes, your commute will take a little longer—" she said.

Molly interrupted. "An hour longer."

"But you'd have child care you could trust, and you certainly can't beat the price."

Molly closed her mouth. Emily sat back in her chair and placed her hands in her lap, somehow looking both resigned and triumphant. She was not fiddling with her napkin now.

Molly sat still in her seat, shock making her immobile. She hadn't even considered moving out of her house. When she'd briefly considered her parents as full-time babysitters, she balked because of the long drive they'd have to make to and from the city. Her mom, who'd never played an organized sport in her life, had just thrown her a serious curveball.

The waiter approached, pad in hand. "Hello, ladies. I hope I've given you enough time to settle in. Are you ready to make your selections?"

Emily immediately placed her order for the *soupe à l'oignon*, her perfect pronunciation catching Molly off guard, and a Niçoise salad. She handed the server her menu with a decisive thrust of her arm. Molly frantically scanned the list of entrees, feeling the mounting pressure as both her mother and their server turned their gazes to her, waiting. She hadn't had a moment to look over the menu. She was famished, and confused, and she had no idea what she was going to choose.

CHAPTER FIVE

April

Yes

Molly rushed into the kitchen, her low heels clattering against the stone-colored tile floor. The sound echoed off the stainless steel surfaces of her appliances and bounced around the modest room. Scott was already there, still in his pajamas, making a cappuccino from the gourmet espresso machine Molly had bought after her first promotion at Shulzster & Grace. She'd been on a team assigned to help get the mayor out of his latest scandal—illicit drug use instead of an extramarital affair this time—and her quick thinking to publicize some old photos of the mayor in his tie, sleeves rolled up to the elbows, playing street basketball with some children from an inner city boys' school, catapulted her to the front of the table at the next meeting, and most meetings after that. Molly swiped a Pop-Tart off of Scott's plate on the counter and held it up to him by way of thanks.

"Okay, then," she said. Her words tumbled out in a rush. "I'll see you tonight."

She planted a kiss on Scott's sandpaper-rough cheek and swept her keys off the kitchen island. He was leaning against the counter, legs crossed at the ankles, with his head bent over his smartphone. The trash can on the floor beside him was full, but he hadn't seemed to notice it. Molly took a hurried glance at the clock on the microwave and groaned. The sound was loud enough to make Scott look up from his phone.

"Look at the time!" she said. "I can't keep rolling into work this late. One day they're going to get fed up and make me roll right back out."

Scott pretended to pout in his fiancée's direction before turning back to his hot drink and Sixers scores. Molly brushed her fingers through her hair, using the microwave door as a mirror to loosen the curls she'd just styled around her shoulders. In the reflection she could see Scott straighten at the sight of Molly's hair falling to rest against her back. She heard the clatter of his phone on the countertop right before she felt his hands massaging her shoulders.

"Scott, I gotta go, hon," she said with a laugh, and wriggled out from his grasp. Scott sniffed in protest, adjusted the crotch of his pajama bottoms, and returned to his phone and Pop-Tart.

"Don't forget your tea," he said, and nodded at the insulated travel mug on the counter. "I also packed you one of those chocolate muffins you like. Well, two, actually." He smiled. "One for now, and one for five minutes from now."

Molly blew him a kiss of thanks, tucked the breakfast into her bag, and hurried through her empty dining room toward the front door. This weekday morning was no different from any other. It was just the numbers on the clock that kept changing as she left later and later for work each day.

"Hey, Mol, wait a sec." Molly turned back from the door to see Scott walking toward her, his mouth full, his feet tracking crumbs on the wide planks of the dark wood floor. Stifling a whimper of frustration, Molly waited for Scott to clear his throat. She realized the knuckles of her free hand were tapping against her thigh, the fingers balled into a fist around her phone.

"Can you mail some bills for me on your way to work?" Scott asked. "You walk right past the post office anyway."

Molly felt the morning slipping away from her like water through the loose knot of her fingers.

"Yeah, but here, give them to me quick," she said. "Please. I really have to run."

Scott placed his mug on the side table and leaned over a stack of paperwork to rifle through the papers. Molly saw an empty coaster sitting there, and winced.

"Scott, the coaster. Please." The blinds on the tall front windows were still pulled shut, and Molly watched Scott hunch close to the envelopes in the dark, his body bent at a lazy angle. The gray cotton of his pants sagged down below the back of his designer boxer briefs.

"Hold on, hold on, they're here somewhere. Hang on a second."

He straightened and looked around the room. "That's weird. I thought I put them here. Maybe I left them upstairs." Scott was walking toward the staircase before Molly spoke. Her bag was still on her shoulder, and she started to open the door. She glanced at her phone. Ten emails had rolled in already.

"Scott, I'm sorry. I can't wait. I wasn't kidding when I said my bosses are getting ticked. And I certainly don't want to give them any more excuses to start laying people off." She laughed, but her voice shook. "I own way too many wrap dresses to not have a job to wear them to."

"All right, all right." Scott strolled over to Molly and ran his finger down her flushed cheek. "Though you know it'd be fine by me if you wore nothing but sweatpants and T-shirts all day."

"Yeah, right." Molly laughed. "I'd look really good walking down JFK Boulevard to a client dinner in that."

"No, not at work," Scott said. He dropped his hand and slouched against the rails of the staircase. "I mean here. If you quit your job once the baby came and stayed here full-time."

"Huh?" Molly looked up at Scott and cocked her head. For a tiny moment, she forgot she was in a hurry.

"What?" Scott looked surprised. "You don't need to work. I make enough money to buy this house, to support us."

"Isn't it more your parents' money, really?"

Scott's expression told Molly she'd gone too far.

"Okay," Molly said. The hand with the phone dropped down to her side. "But you haven't bought the house. We're going to buy it together, you and me, both names on the mortgage. And right now it's *my* lease. And I like working to pay for it."

She pointed to his coffee mug. "How do you like that espresso machine I bought? That cappuccino tastes pretty good, right?"

Scott, with a sheepish smile, took an exaggerated gulp from the mug. When he pulled it away from his mouth, Molly noticed that he had a thin foam mustache from the drink. He didn't wipe it from his top lip, and she felt her stomach turn at the sight of the brown foam clinging to the dark stubble under his nose. She felt the minutes ticking by, every one of them making her later to work, but stayed rooted in her spot on the wood foyer. Her phone buzzed with a new email notification. *One problem at a time,* she thought.

"Your mom stayed home when you and your brothers were young," Scott was saying. "What's so crazy about me wanting that for my kid?"

"Because you know I never wanted to be a stay-at-home mom." Molly's quiet voice hid the fear knocking around in her heart. "I worked way too hard and for way too long to get to where I am. I can't bail out now," she said. "This is my career, Scott, not just temp work."

"It's just a job." Scott shrugged. "And I think you should consider quitting it."

He approached her, standing so close that she could smell the bitter coffee on his breath. He took her arm in a loose grasp and kissed her cheek.

"I only want what's best for us, Mol," Scott said. He moved his hand to her belly. "What's best for all of us."

Molly dropped her bag to the floor and put her hands on either side of Scott's waist, pulling him closer to her. Her mind raced as quickly as the second hand on her watch. Scott hadn't really wanted this baby, she knew that, so hearing him talk about the three of them as a family gave her a little more hope.

"But what if I had a better idea?" Her voice was muffled by the rumpled cotton of his shirt. "What if there was a way for me to keep working, but for us to still have a parent at home full-time. If it's that important to you?"

"And what's that? You suddenly learned how to clone your-self?" Scott stepped out of Molly's reach. His arms were crossed in front of his chest, his posture defensive.

"Don't be silly," Molly said. "Look, we can manage our bills on my income if we're careful, and we're going to be on my health insurance anyway once we get married, right?"

Scott didn't respond, and Molly watched his eyes narrow while he waited for her to continue. Molly stifled the urge to hurry and get her thoughts out in the open. She was very aware of her awkward stance by the door, of the constricting clothes that wrapped around her growing thighs and breasts like bandages. She took a deep breath.

"Why don't you consider staying home with the baby? We'd have to give up some of the fun stuff, but we could make it work. I would be able to keep my job, and you could still get what you want."

Scott stretched his neck. He wasn't looking at her. Molly didn't want to scrimp and budget and worry if the next paycheck would come in time to buy diapers. That had been her childhood. She didn't want it to be her baby's, too. But she kept talking, rushing the words. It seemed like all she was doing lately was hurrying to fill up the empty spaces, smooth over the rough patches, cover up the imperfections. She was getting so tired of always scurrying along, tidying up as she went.

"You've said before you just work to pay the bills anyway," she said now. "So why not just focus on the baby?" Molly said the words even though she had never really thought about Scott as a hands-on dad. And even as she spoke, she knew he never had, either.

Scott set the coffee cup down again, this time with a sharp clack on the polished table. Molly's nerves jumped at the sound. Scott seemed to pull himself up to a height taller than his usual stature.

"Molly, don't take this the wrong way, but I'm never going to be a stay-at-home dad." He chewed the words like they were bites of rotten food.

"Why not? You said it was important to you."

"It's important for *you* to stay home, not me."

Molly backed away from him, just a little. "But why?"

She clutched her work bag to her body and stared at Scott's face. His eyebrows were furrowed together, causing a deep vertical crease in his forehead. There was very little breathing room between them. Molly threw her shoulders back and felt herself stick out her chin, up and out the way she used to do when she was a little girl, defying her parents. Her heart was pounding against her rib cage. She was so late.

"Why would you assume I'd be the one to stay at home? Why not you?"

"Because I'm the man, that's why," Scott said. His voice held the same whining pitch as a little boy's. "And men aren't housewives."

"Scott, you sound ridiculous."

He reached behind her to open the door and braced it wide with one hand. "Don't you have to get to work?"

Molly was out on the stoop now, and turned her body in the doorway so that she faced her fiancé squarely, as if seeing all of him directly would help her understand his thinking. He was still standing inside the house, his body filling out the door frame. One hand still held the door open.

"I'm a dude, Molly," Scott said. "And where I come from, dudes don't stay home to wipe noses and butts. And I'm certainly not going to quit my job. It's not the way it works."

He jerked his head up in a sort of half-nod. "How many stay-at-home dads do *you* know?"

Molly couldn't think of one.

Scott shook his head and reached for his discarded coffee cup with his free hand. "That's what I thought."

Molly adjusted the heavy bag on her shoulder. "Of course I don't know any stay-at-home dads, Scott, because I don't know that many people my age who are even parents. But those dads are all over the Internet. I see them in the park with their kids. There's even a TV show about a full-time dad. For Pete's sake, Scott, we watched it together!"

"Molly, I am who I am. You're gonna have to deal with that." Scott leaned down to pick up the newspaper from where he'd thrown it on the floor earlier that morning. It was still in its plastic bag, and it gave off a faint musty odor. "But if you want to talk some more about the stay-at-home *mom* thing . . ."

"Scott, no," Molly said. "Just . . . no."

Scott stared at her, pushing his tongue against the inside of his cheek. Molly was shivering, and she saw the muscles in Scott's face soften when he noticed.

"Molly, I said it already. I only want what's best for our family," he said. "Just think about it. I think you'd be great."

Scott left the open doorway. Molly reached for the doorknob as he sauntered back through the house, his bare feet slapping against the hardwood floor.

"Oh, and hey," she heard him say from the shadows of the living room. When she peered in, she saw he was already splayed out on the sofa in his rumpled pajamas, turning on *Sports-Center*. One arm was thrown over the back of the cushions, and an ankle crossed the other leg at the knee. "Don't forget we have my mom's charity gala tonight, so don't be late coming home, okay?" He spoke to the television. "She said she's sending over a dress for you. It'll be here when you get back."

Molly shut the door behind her with a thud and stomped down the stairs of her row home. She typed out a quick text to her boss as she walked, saying that she'd run into a roadblock on the way to work and would be there soon. She moved with a pace close to running, fighting against the tears pressing against the backs of her eyes.

The buzz of their argument filled her head as she walked. She moved toward Center City, keeping the spires of the soaring Liberty Towers in her sights, as if getting distance from her home could make reality evaporate like the steam rolling out of the vents from the train stations beneath her feet. The sidewalks in her neighborhood were nearly empty of people at this hour, except for the stray college student with an unshaven chin and backpack slung over his shoulders trudging to meet the trolley to University City or Drexel. Molly thought of Scott, who was probably still watching ESPN or playing a computer game at that moment, wasting time until his afternoon appointment. He never hurried. It wasn't in Scott's nature to fill up his time with enough activity to make him late. He was a Ping-Pong ball, rolling through life, headed in whatever direction he was told to go.

Molly dug her iPod out of her bag and stuck the buds in her ears, shaking her head as she replayed the conversation in her mind. Florence and the Machine began to reverberate through the ear buds, and as the hypnotic, low beat of "Heavy In Your Arms" filled her head, Molly clicked down the street in time to the music, glad for the noise. She needed the crisp air from the walk in her lungs and brain. She was desperately late, but she'd run if she had to, second-trimester belly and all. Molly quickened her pace as she neared the intersection.

She didn't want to admit it, but Scott had managed to make

a point that morning. Not the off-base point about how men weren't supposed to stay home—*Excuse me, Don Draper,* Molly thought, *but times have changed*—but she had to admit she did sort of like the idea of one of them being home with the baby. She had never imagined herself as a stay-at-home mom, though, and balked at the assumption that she should be the one padding around the house with a baby draped over one shoulder and an apron tied around her waist. But she'd overheard enough conversations among her colleagues about their misbehaving children, troubles with day care, and horrible sex lives to be worried about how life was going to change in a few months. Nobody ever made the working-with-child life sound feasible, let alone enjoyable. And this morning, Scott had forced Molly to face a decision she didn't want to make.

He had a habit of doing that lately.

A wind picked up with a biting force, whipping around the street corners and slowing her pace. Molly dug her hands deep into the pockets of her coat, her skin stinging as much as her thoughts. The tree-filled blocks of luxury brick row homes and boutique shops had given way to the high rises of apartment buildings, and traffic was now filling the streets, car exhaust contaminating the air in her lungs. She stopped at the corner to wait for the light to change. Florence had stopped singing, and all that filled Molly's ears was the *boom-boom, boom-boom* of the song's closing drumbeat.

She'd once asked a coworker of hers how she did it: the woman worked full-time, had a lawyer husband who stayed at the office long into the night, and was raising three school-aged children who, as Molly heard it, were involved in about every activity a kid could do. When Molly asked her how she managed, the woman had responded, "Autopilot. You just have to set yourself on autopilot and go." And that sentence had stayed with Molly.

Molly didn't want to live her life on autopilot. She was determined to never take for granted the life of this little person growing inside her, and she didn't want this resentment toward Scott to keep growing. He was entitled to want what he did, she knew, but so was she. The person you greet at the end of the aisle on your wedding day is going to be almost the exact same person you took out to dinner on your first date, whether you want to recognize it or not. People don't change all that much, Molly thought. But maybe their expectations do, which is what sends most people staggering after the ring has been slipped onto the finger.

Molly rubbed her hand across her forehead before checking her watch. Another song ended, and, hastening her step, she crossed the busy street.

Emily had been a stay-at-home mom until Molly's youngest brother, Johnny, entered middle school, and Molly had always felt sort of lucky that she hadn't had to go to day care. She would race down the school bus stairs after it dropped her off at three twenty and burst into her kitchen to find a snack and a glass of milk waiting for her. She'd yammer away about the crazy experiment they did in science and the way her friend Becky's new crush had said hi to her in the cafeteria, and the whole time her mother was there, leaning against the kitchen counter, hands resting on the countertop, smiling, nodding. Listening. Their family didn't take beach vacations, and they couldn't afford many restaurant meals or name-brand shoes. But Emily could always be counted on to be there, listening.

When Molly was sick, she could sleep as late as she wanted.

She'd lie in bed with her comforter pulled up to her chin, dozing in and out of a daze of Vicks VapoRub and lemon Ricola. She'd listen to her brothers gathering their school books and her dad showering for work and could hear Emily hushing everyone to be quiet because little Molly wasn't feeling well. Later, her mother would bring her homemade chicken noodle soup and ginger ale, and Molly would lie with her head in her lap to spend a groggy afternoon watching *The Price Is Right*. Because Emily was home, Molly could be home.

She wondered how she was going to handle the intricacies of a daily schedule once her maternity leave was over. What time would she have to wake up? Would she shower and get ready before the baby was up? What if she did try to breastfeed—she'd have to pump breast milk at some point, wouldn't she? And each time she put on her heels and packed up her laptop, Molly knew Scott's irritation would grow. It seemed like all the great opportunities the twentieth-century women's movement created for Molly had evaporated now that her body had a fetal co-owner. She'd read a magazine article one day that told her that she was selfish for working if she didn't have to, but see a talk show the next that decreed full-time parenthood an antiquated notion reserved for religious types and lazy people. Molly didn't know who was telling her the truth.

"Grrrr!" Molly exclaimed out loud. She was in Center City now, dwarfed by the high-rises of Penn Center, and her exasperation attracted the startled gaze of a lawyer on his way into the courthouse. She ripped the buds out of her ears in frustration and tried not to cry. The one time she missed a step, wasn't careful, and this happened. Now she had pants that didn't fit and a creature inside her making her crave chocolate syrup and Pop

Rocks. Molly passed a food truck as she neared her office, and the warm, yeasty aroma of hot dogs and soft pretzels coated with coarse salt wafted on the air. Her mouth watered with a new, ferocious hunger, and she placed a protective hand over her stomach.

There was a person actually growing inside of her, and Molly was determined not to mess it up. Not another step. She wasn't missing another chance to toe the line. *One mistake was enough for this lifetime,* she thought. *Stupid unplanned pregnancy.*

In the same instant she felt guilty for the thought.

"Sorry, baby," Molly said, and patted her belly with a soft hand. Finally arriving at her building, Molly entered the wide marble lobby and got in line for one of the small elevators. She noticed a very pregnant woman exit through another pair of elevator doors and waddle past her. Molly smiled at her as she passed, feeling for a minute like they were both members of some secret girls-only club to which no one else had the password.

Molly had been watching too many DVR'd episodes of *A Baby Story* lately and, as her own delivery date grew closer, was starting to get frightened of realities like "episiotomy" and "forceps." But she was going to get to become a mom. In a few months, she was going to get to meet this baby and have a little boy or girl who would be all her own, and the thought—of a toddler holding her hand on their way to the ice-cream truck, of her child playing with blocks on the rug beside her, of the smell of baby shampoo when she kissed her infant's head before bedtime—made her flush with a kind of thrill she hadn't even known she longed for. But she hadn't imagined that it would happen like this. Not when her career was really taking off. Not before she and Scott had really had a chance to be married for a while. All her dreams of a honeymoon backpacking through Europe were traded for the reality of schlepping the baby to its grandparents' houses in the suburbs on the weekends. Instead of bottles of white wine, she'd be chilling bottles of breast milk. And as for rolling around in the bed of some quaint Italian boutique hotel in Tuscany, well, she wasn't quite sure how anything that involved being sexy and naked was going to happen if she'd have a baby attached to her boobs every hour and a half.

Molly smoothed her hair over her shoulders and buttoned her blazer as the elevator car rose slowly to the twentieth floor. Of course, she thought, if Scott had his way, she wouldn't be working by the time they had a honeymoon, and they might not be able to spend the money on a European vacation anyway. Molly was starting to think that having a baby was going to be more expensive than either she or Scott realized. She had to hold on to her job. It was the only thing keeping her head above the murky waters of uncertainty right now. Scott had to realize that eventually, Molly figured. Maybe.

With a start, Molly realized that she was trying to get Scott to change, too. It's really easy to moralize when you're the one standing at the pulpit.

Thirty seconds later, Molly was rushing through the front door of Shulzster & Grace, taking off her coat, and pulling files out of her bag before she reached her office. Everyone she passed was already at their desks, heads bent over keyboards, phones held to ears. One look at Bill's face told Molly that she should have been one of them. It wasn't the first time this week he'd given her that look, and she felt a pit form in her stomach. Molly dropped her bag and coat on her desk and strode back to Bill's office. Once she entered, she sank down into the seat across the desk from him, glanced at the clock, and, as an apology, gave her boss a little sideways smile.

Bill leaned back in his chair and crossed his arms across his chest. He was a narrow reed of a man not that much taller than Molly, with thinning hair cut very close to his head. He favored gold watches and neckties with huge, unfortunate geometric patterns, but he was fair—tough, but professional. Bill was ten years older than Molly and had been married for twice as long as that. By the number of framed photographs on his desk and bookshelves—fifteen at Molly's last count—he was a man who was content at home, with his soft, kind wife, four children, a dog, and a cat. Molly thought that Bill's life seemed about as all-American as it could get. It was normal, and a tad predictable, but it was the life he'd worked very hard to achieve. She could almost forgive him the obviousness of naming his dog Fido.

Right now, though, Bill wasn't smiling over his blessings in life. Right now, he was pissed off at his star employee.

"Molly," Bill said. "You missed the eight o'clock conference call with the Hooper company. They were looking forward to talking again with the woman who got all of America to 'Hooperize' their online accounts."

Molly slapped her hand against her forehead. "Oh, no. That was this morning?"

Her boss nodded.

"Bill, I'm so sorry. I had it in my calendar for tomorrow. I'm sorry. It won't happen again." She registered the look of disapproval on Bill's face and stammered a little bit. "Oh, come on, Bill, you know this isn't like me! Even Wonder Woman had to lose her golden tiara now and again, right? How—how can I make it up to you?"

"Well, for starters," Bill said, "you could think about starting to show up on time again. And possibly making some of these evening events. And answering your phone when I call you, even if you're at lunch. Just like you used to."

Bill glanced at the open door behind Molly and lowered his voice.

"Molly, there are rumors that you dozed off at your desk yesterday afternoon"—Molly felt her face grow hot but said nothing—"but I'll just assume you were doing some restorative meditation during your lunch break." He clasped his fingers together. "Molly, I'll be honest with you. You're slacking off. This is unlike you. We're in the middle of layoffs, and the big shots are looking to cut corners wherever they can. What are you thinking? It's like you're trying to get yourself canned."

"No! Oh my God, no, Bill!" Molly felt her skin break out into the same cold sweat she'd felt when she'd been speeding down Route 202 and a police car had pulled up behind her, lights flashing. She dug her fingers into the sides of the chair's seat. "I love this job. I've just been going through a slump. And that slump is hereby over, officially, at this very second. I am slump-free. De-slumpified. This, right here"—Molly gestured widely over her head and torso—"is a no-slump zone. I am—"

"Okay, Molly, I get it." Bill shrugged and threw up his hands. "You're back. Good. Now, get in your office. We have a call in three minutes."

"Okay. I'm there." Molly stood up, smoothed her new black maternity pencil skirt over her thighs and started for the door.

"Oh, and Molly?"

Molly turned. "Yes?"

"Be careful. Stay on your game. The bigwigs are especially watching you."

Molly gulped. "Consider me warned. Thank you."

The sun was setting that following Monday, casting a sharp red-tinged glare on Molly's office window. She'd spent the entire weekend holed up in the guest quarters of Scott's parents' home, eating caviar for brunch instead of catching up on work as she'd intended to do. Even as long as she'd been dating Scott, the lifestyle in which he'd grown up still stunned her. She was used to casual Sundays at home, with her dad standing over the stove in his slippers, a coffee mug in one hand while he cooked up scrapple and scrambled eggs to eat before they rushed off to church. At Monica and Edward's house—the Manor, as Molly thought of it—a cook prepared omelets to order when they came together for a lazy, late-morning meal. There were bowls of fresh fruit and yogurt parfaits and French-pressed coffee. At Molly's childhood home, the family wore pajamas to the table and traded sections of the Sunday paper. At Scott's, one was expected to change clothes before eating and remember which fork to use. It was a whole other world, and everything in it sparkled.

Molly had been working double-time today to make up for the lost hours over the weekend, Bill's warning still reverberating in her head. The last beam of sunlight disappeared behind City Hall as Molly closed her laptop and stretched her neck. She was surprised at how many of her clients had no idea how to navigate social media, and she had spent the afternoon creating pages for two of them on various sites. She could be just as focused as her father and just as thorough as her mother. She rolled through the websites now on her phone to assess the positive feedback they'd already received. She decided that she had just enough time to send one more email to Bill before meeting Jenny for dinner. Her eyes felt like they could close any moment, and her back ached. She looked down to see that her feet were swelling a little over her shoes, making the thin heels look like a set of doll's slippers that had been forced on under her heavy ankles. Molly was soon going to have to figure out how to make Target flip-flops work with her new Topshop maternity dresses. She wondered how it would feel to waddle down the halls of S&G to meet a client in a few months. She fished the last chocolate-covered mint out of the bag on her desk and chewed the candy without really tasting it. The company was going to have to lay somebody else off just to afford to expense her business dinners.

Molly felt her stomach rumble at the thought of food. She looked out at the floodlights popping on below the statue of William Penn on his perch above City Hall, illuminating his regal stare over the city, his aloof stance high above the rush of traffic still trickling out through the clogged streets. She thought of Scott, probably home by now, and the empty room on the second floor of the house that would be the nursery. This time next year, a baby would be sleeping in that room.

Molly looked around her office, which was filled with the imprint of her personality: a potted fern kept clipped of all browned leaves, framed diplomas hanging on the wall next to a Sixers pendant, and a vintage, autographed photograph of Lena Horne. She had bookshelves filled with reference binders, photographs of Scott and her nieces, a stuffed doll of UPenn's mascot—the Quaker—all arranged with care and dusted at the end of each week. There were duplicate chargers for her phone and tablet and computer, a drawer filled with individually wrapped chocolate squares and instant-coffee packets, a spare pair of heels under the desk, and an extra coat hanging from a single hook on the back of the door. This room was as much a part of her as her bedroom at home. Molly stood to close the blinds on her window and gathered her files. She slid them into her leather bag, grabbed her phone and her coat, and shut her office door behind her.

Molly was on time to join Jenny at Pattaya, their favorite Thai restaurant in University City. It was a small place, and warm, patronized by college students and aging professors. The women had discovered the casual eatery one night after a seeing an awful independent film at the now-closed Bridge theater. It had quickly become their favorite destination, mainly because it was one of the few quiet places in the city where they could catch up without running into somebody one of them knew. Philadelphia, as big as it was, was a lot like any town: live there long enough, and one day you realize that you recognize at least one person wherever you go. Most of the time Molly found comfort in the predictability. But some days, like those when she was halfway through a pregnancy, with skin that'd exploded like a teenager's and a new tendency to burp without warning, she was just as okay being anonymous.

"Hey!" Molly waved to Jenny, who was at the bar and halfway through a tall glass of what Molly recognized as a Tamarind Dream. To Molly, it might as well have had a red flag in it rather than an umbrella. Jenny hitting the hard stuff this often was like seeing snow fall in Texas in June. It meant something was going very, very wrong in her world.

"Ah, bar stool, blessed bar stool." Molly sighed when she reached Jenny and sank onto the tall chair beside her. "How I've been waiting for a seat like you."

Jenny shook her head and laughed at Molly over the rim of her glass. "Baby weighing you down?"

"I'll say. Cramping my style, too." Molly signaled for the bartender. "Could I have a glass of water with lemon, please? Thanks."

She turned back to her friend and stared at Jenny's drink. "That looks good. Can I at least smell it?"

"Molly, you don't like stuff like this even when you can drink!" Jenny exclaimed. "They don't make a nonalcoholic whiskey and Coke?"

Molly shook her head. "I think that's just called Coke."

The bartender slid Molly's water across the bar. Molly looked from her glass to the colorful cocktail in Jenny's.

"So. I take it things aren't going well," Molly said.

"Not unless you count me going insane at my parents' house," Jenny said. She took a deep gulp from her drink.

"I thought there had to be a reason you were going for the vodka."

"Molly, it's been awful," Jenny said. "I spend my days at that horrendous bank job—seriously, do they really need someone to itemize receipts anymore?—and come home to meatloaf and boxed mashed potatoes on TV trays every night. All my parents do is watch game shows. I think it's the only way they know how to live together, if you really want to know. They don't talk about anything more important than how pretentious Alex Trebek's French accent sounds." She picked up a napkin and began twisting it with her fingers. "Which it totally does, by the way. I've practically moved into the gym in the evenings just to get out of there. And get this. When I *am* home they barely talk to me because they're so afraid of acting judgmental about the situation with Dan, but their silence makes it so obvious that they think I should run back to him with open arms." Jenny paused. "As if they're in any place to give marital advice." The napkin was now lying in shreds on the bar. Molly looked at her friend, who was pushing the pieces of paper into a single pile. Both with the napkin and with Dan, Jenny had created a mess out of something so trivial, and Molly had to fight the urge to sweep her arm across the counter and clean up the jumble of fragments.

"And what do you think about Dan?" she asked instead.

"I think I'm afraid Dan's a cheating rat bastard, that's what I think." Jenny took another gulp of her drink, flinching as the liquor went down her throat.

"Been hearing that phrase a lot lately," Molly mumbled.

"What'd you say?"

"Nothing. Never mind." Molly took a deep breath and twisted on her stool to face her friend. "But, Jenny, he didn't cheat on you. You know that."

"No, I don't. How could I? He didn't exactly explain himself at your party," Jenny said.

Molly groaned. "Jenny, Scott was blabbering all over the place. Dan couldn't have gotten a word in edgewise if he'd stood on a chair and shouted. Have you tried talking to him? I know how you get when you're angry, and you're not exactly the easiest person to communicate with."

Molly paused. Jenny's expression was impassive.

"No offense."

"None taken. I know I shut down, I do. But I just keep imagining him talking to this girl, actually going off with her somewhere dark and doing God knows what. They say you marry your father, you know. I can't get the image out of my head. And then I just get so . . . so *angry* that I hang up the phone when he calls and don't answer his texts," Jenny said. "I don't want to be made a fool."

Molly stared down at her water glass, as if the answers to Jenny's problems could be found in the ice cubes. She'd never known Jenny and Dan to not be attached at the hip—they were as good as Mr. Darcy and Elizabeth, Fred and Ginger. A person didn't think of one of them without considering the other. Some couples were like that, Molly thought. Most good couples, anyway. Molly glanced down at the ring on her left hand and cleared her throat.

"Listen."

Jenny looked up from her drink and cocked her head, waiting.

"Have you talked to Scott?"

Jenny's face flushed pink, making her freckles pop like tiny polka dots against her skin. She shook her head. "He left me some crazy-long voice mail. I *may* have deleted it before listening."

Molly gave her a blank stare. Jenny shrugged.

"I was a little angry."

"Well, I talked to Scott about that night. He said that he just saw Dan talking to that girl, then walk away for a while—that's it. Remember how obnoxious and drunk Scott was at our party? You know he likes to stir up trouble just to get attention."

Jenny snorted. "And you, the one who doesn't like to make waves at all."

She grew quiet, and Molly watched the smile fade from her face. Jenny glanced at Molly's belly like it was a car accident on the side of the road, something she knew was there but didn't want to acknowledge.

"Did you know that not one thing has changed in my old

bedroom at my parents' house since I moved out?" she asked. "My horse show ribbons are still taped to the mirror. I won those in the ninth grade! They even have my old R.E.M. posters up on the wall. And how did I ever think that yellow paint with bright pink curtains was a good idea?"

Molly raised one eyebrow. "You know what I think is a good idea?" She pointed at her friend's empty glass. "Getting away from the Jenny Museum and going back to your husband. Even if it's just because your apartment is better decorated."

"I know," Jenny said. "I know. You're right. And I miss him so much it makes my chest hurt. But it's not going to be the same, Molly. Especially if my Dan isn't really *my* Dan."

Molly flinched. She loved Dan like a brother. She'd never heard Jenny doubt what she had with him.

"I just want somebody to be mad at," Jenny continued. "We've been through hell and high water with this job thing and trying to get pregnant, and then all this stuff comes out about him and some girl? I just don't get it. It was like the last straw on a really big camel's back, and it hit too close to home."

She guffawed. "Literally! Get it? Because now I'm *at* home?"

"I get it." Molly sighed. "And I'm betting that your gut is telling you that it's all in your head. We know Dan too well." Molly dipped her head a little. "And Scott, for that matter. Dan probably didn't do anything worse that night than drink too much."

"So you think I'm being a shit?" Jenny shook her head and started picking at another napkin. "I don't want to be a shit. It's just all so . . ."

"Shitty?"

"Pretty much."

"I think you love him, that's what I think," Molly said. "And

I think you have a lot going on right now, so it's easier for you to hide than face it. But I also think it's too easy for us to feel like our current relationships are going to look exactly like the ones we grew up with."

Jenny sighed. "You know," she said, "I thought that going home would let me just forget it about it for a while, like I could be a kid again, and worry about somebody else's marriage instead of my own. But I guess that's the thing about being a grown-up—you can't run away from your problems when you're the one creating them. Fine. I'll call him tonight. At the very least, my parents will be thrilled to not hear me heckling Pat Sajak anymore."

She looked at Molly with shrewd eyes. "When did you get so much common sense, anyway?" she asked. "Is impending motherhood changing you already?"

"Must be," Molly said. "It's all that marriage-and-babies stress. Making me age more quickly."

Jenny glanced at Molly's belly again. Molly tensed up, and pushed her glass away from her.

"Okay, I have to say it," she said. "This is weird now, isn't it?"

"What are you talking about?" Jenny's voice was light, but she looked at Molly with eyes that belied the brave facade.

"I'm talking about how we're hanging out, just like any other time, but now there's this elephant in the room."

"Nah, you're not that big yet."

"JENNY."

"Fine," Jenny said. "You mean the elephant that's in your belly? Or the fact that there's no elephant in mine?"

"Both." Molly gauged her friend's reaction. "I can't hide it, Jenny, but I sort of wish I could sometimes. Only because I want you to be happy, and I want me to be happy, and I don't want to hurt you every time we get together just because *this*"—she gestured over her stomach—"is happening."

Jenny blew out a gust of air between her lips. "And I don't want you to not be excited just because of my own issues. It's fine. It's going to be great. I'm happy for you, Molly. I'm so excited for you, I swear." She shrugged. "Just don't mind me if I get a little misty-eyed sometimes when I see how cute that little baby bump of yours is. I think I'm more of a mess than I'd like to believe. Shocking, I know."

Jenny cleared her throat. When she spoke again, her tone was brighter. "So, tell me. What's going on with you guys? Still no wedding date, I know. But I hear the second trimester is supposed to be the sweet spot of a pregnancy."

Molly shook her head. Her best friend already knew about the changes in Scott the last few months: how he'd backpedaled on the baby's name, his recent push for her to stay at home once the baby was born. She'd skipped the part, though, about the pit in her stomach that appeared whenever they talked about these things. She hadn't mentioned, either, that when she was with his family she felt like a commoner who'd been lucky enough to meet the prince—a commoner who was learning that she might have to turn her back on her old life in order to step up to the pedestal required of her in the new one.

"Why doesn't Scott quit his?" Jenny was asking. "You actually *go* to your job."

Molly made her voice deep and guttural. "Because he's a *man*, that's why. And *men* don't quit their jobs just to change poopy diapers."

"Damn, Molly." Jenny let out a low whistle. "Who knew Mr. New Money could be so old-fashioned? He knows you love your job, right?"

"I thought so."

"And he knows that your job is paying for that house right now, too?"

"Yup. Pretty sure."

"And he knows that if you give up the work that you love that pays for your life you're going to be absolutely miserable, yes? I know how you are when you're out of a routine. It ain't pretty."

"Downright ugly, if you ask me." Molly laughed. "I know. He came out of the blue with it last week. It's just not something that's on my radar."

"Well, yeah, especially when Scott's got the easiest job in the world. How many times have we stopped by your house after work and he's already sitting around in his underwear?"

"Yeah, I'm sorry about that."

Jenny giggled. "It's okay. Scott may be clueless, but at least he looks good half-naked. You ready to eat?" She looked at Molly's belly again, this time with a smile. "Eh, who am I kidding? Of course you're ready to eat."

Molly placed the cash for the drinks on the bar and pushed it toward the bartender before Jenny could protest. The two women rose from their seats. Molly winced as she placed her body weight on her swollen feet.

As they walked toward the hostess station, Jenny slowed down. The bar area had become crowded since their arrival, and she raised her voice so Molly could hear her over the din.

"So, how did you leave it with Scott?" she asked. "About the job thing?"

Molly shrugged her shoulders. "We're still arguing. But he did a pretty good job Friday morning of making me feel claustrophobic."

Jenny stopped in front of the hostess stand and turned to her. Molly blushed as her friend's eyes moved over her face.

"Claustrophobic?"

"Boxed in," Molly admitted. "Like I have nowhere to go. He seems adamant about me staying at home, and I feel like I'm going to have to give in in order for us to be okay. I don't know. I just feel like no matter which way I turn, I'm going to feel guilty about something."

She stood in place, quiet.

"That's not good, Molly," Jenny said. "You shouldn't have to feel that way, especially not now. Think about how happy you used to be when you were around Liam."

"That was a long time ago, Jenny."

"But the idea of getting married and having a baby should make you feel like you're grabbing hold of the world," Jenny said, "not like the world's got you by the nose."

The restaurant around the bar buzzed with a low noise, and soft music was playing overhead. Jenny threw her arm around Molly's shoulder, drawing her in for a sideways hug. To their left, a group of people broke out into loud chatter, laughing suddenly at someone's joke. Jenny dropped her arm back to her side and laughed herself.

"Well, we're a pair tonight, aren't we? Come on, this is ridiculous. Let's go get some pad Thai and gossip like we're supposed to. I've had enough of this depressing grown-up talk."

Molly was voicing her agreement when she heard her phone beep. She fished it out of her green faux–alligator skin bag. "Oh, speak of the devil. There's a text from Scott."

She clicked open the message to read it, then reached out for Jenny's arm. "Um, Jenny. Scott says there's a voice mail from Bill on the home phone."

The noise of the restaurant seemed to have gotten louder, climbing to a pitch that seemed almost feverish in its intensity.

"I must have just missed his call," she said.

"What do you think that means?"

Molly started to sweat in the sudden heat of the room. "You know what I was just saying about Scott wanting me to quit my job?"

She looked at her friend.

"I think Shulzster & Grace may have beat him to it."

CHAPTER SIX

May

No

Molly sat with her back to the desk in her office, staring out at some seagulls circling above the bronze hat on the statue of William Penn outside. The sun was beginning to set on a brilliant, cloudless day, and she could see from the dense river of headlights on Broad Street that the traffic heading home had gotten thicker. She wiped a smudge of dirt off the window with a clean tissue and made a mental note to bring glass cleaner with her the next day.

A tumbling feeling was rolling against the inside of her torso wall like the pulsating motion of a massage chair. The baby had only recently started moving around in her belly, and Molly placed a hand over it now to feel the *thump-thump-thump* the baby made as he or she somersaulted around. Someone had told her once that early in pregnancy, the baby's movements would feel like a goldfish bumping against a fishbowl inside her, and Molly now knew the description was spot-on. It was odd to witness, to actually be able to *feel*, this person growing inside of her, feeding off of her, getting stronger.

If only her baby could pipe up with a little advice, she thought. She could use it.

Molly gave her belly a pat and looked back over the city. The crimson taillights of the cars looked like blood flowing through an artery. She couldn't imagine living anywhere but in this vibrant, busy place. Molly's phone buzzed on her desk, and she picked it up to hear Jenny's voice on the other end.

"Hey, Jenny. I was just wondering: will you still be friends with me if you have to come out to West Chester to visit me and the baby?"

"Nope." Jenny didn't miss a beat. "Not a chance. I'm not going out to the suburbs for you, woman, even if that baby's the cutest thing I've seen since the Philly Phanatic."

"Wait, what do you mean *if* the baby's cute?" Molly was smiling.

"Kidding. I'm kidding." Jenny's laughter sounded carefree. "Of course your baby's going to be adorable. You may have gotten knocked up, but at least the guy who did the knocking was hot." Her laughter quieted, and when Jenny spoke again, her voice was serious. "You still haven't decided what to do?"

Molly stared out the window. She saw the first hint of a moon peek out from behind the One Liberty Place tower. She loved when the moon was in the sky while it was still brilliant with sunlight. It felt like the universe was trying its damnedest to keep the world from slipping into darkness. Molly had sympathy for its stubbornness.

"Yeah, I'm thinking about it." She sighed. "It makes sense on a lot of levels. I'd have free, good child care. I'd be spending less money on groceries. Wouldn't have to worry about cooking most meals."

She toyed with a pen on her desk before sliding it into a drawer.

"And I'd have people around to talk me off the ledge when it all gets overwhelming—because you know it will. My parents are really nice to even offer."

There was a pause on the other end of the line. "But?"

"But it would mean actually moving back home. And I'd lose hours at work because I'd be spending so much time on a train. And Jenny, I can't sublet my house. Could you imagine me as a landlord?"

"Uh, no, I can't." Jenny whistled. "Not as nicely as you keep that place. You'd be stopping by every week just to make sure they're cleaning behind the toilet."

"They better, man. I just replaced that toilet." Molly smiled for a moment when she heard Jenny snort, but the familiar waves of confusion soon came crashing back. She told Jenny about her research into day care costs, and how placement in any of the centers downtown would cost more than her rent payment each month.

"So it looks like Molly Sullivan could be hanging up her Mary Tyler Moore hat."

"Yep." Molly had been patting and stacking the same pile of files on her desk for the length of the conversation. She stopped now and lined them up at the edge of her desk. "I could be."

"I understand," Jenny said. "You don't want to have to start turning tricks on Columbus Boulevard just to make rent."

"Yeah, I don't think the Children and Youth Division would be too happy with me carrying a diaper bag stuffed with G-strings."

Jenny chuckled. "Would your parents watch the baby full-time, then?"

"Yup. You know my mom is having a hard time slowing down after her retirement. And Pop's cut back on his hours so much at the hardware store that he basically just shows up once a week to make an appearance. They'd be thrilled, you know, if I did it. And you can't beat the price."

"It's just . . ." Jenny started to say.

". . . they're getting older, and it might be hard for them to manage once this baby's running around," Molly finished Jenny's sentence. "And I'd be living at home. In my old bedroom, in that twin bed with the lumpy mattress, surrounded by my Patti Smith and Alanis Morissette posters—only this time there'd be a bassinet in there, too. And you know how it is when you're with your parents for a while. It's like you go from a self-assured independent woman to that bratty teenage girl with braces within two minutes of entering the house."

Molly blew out a long breath. She could hear Jenny close a door, and the sound of a stereo got quieter.

"I know exactly what you mean," Jenny said. "Molly, how did we end up here? Last time I checked, we were complaining about boot-cut jeans and figuring out where to go on Friday night." She laughed, and the sound echoed like Jenny's old, deep laugh, not the forced chuckle Molly had been hearing from her lately. "And now I'm stuck in skinny jeans, systematically dismantling my own life, and you're about to pop out a kid and you don't even know where to put the crib."

"Pretty much," Molly said. "But wait a minute: you're laughing. This isn't about my homeless baby. You're talking things through with Dan, aren't you?!"

Molly heard the cheer in her own voice travel through the air. She didn't realize how much she needed something to start working out until she heard the lilt in Jenny's tone. And there was nothing like good news in a friend's life to make the sun shine a little bit brighter in your own. Especially if that friend was Jenny.

"Yes, Miss Marriage Counselor, Dan and I are talking."

"And?" Molly pressed.

"And that's it. Right now, anyway," Jenny said. "I'm trying very hard to separate our—my—issues from my parents', okay? But theirs was the most dysfunctional marriage to exist outside of Tom Cruise and Katie Holmes', and it got into my head. I still can't totally trust him. It's not all sunshine and rainbows yet, but I'm trying."

"Oh, Jenny." Molly tried to keep her voice level. She saw the moon go behind a cloud and grimaced.

"Hey, lady, I told you I'm a royal mess right now. You ever see a bag of salad mix that's been left in the fridge for too long? The leaves just melt into a jumbled mess of brown rot, right?"

Molly nodded, because she had seen it happen in someone else's house once.

"That's what my head feels like."

"But why?" Molly asked.

The phone was quiet for a moment. "Because I think you're not the only one who needs things to be just so."

Molly felt her eyes grow wide.

"Look," Jenny said. "Dan and I have been together since high school. Everything just fell into place for us: college, and our wedding, and getting our jobs. It was all so easy. I felt like we were just . . . *fated* to be together."

"Okay," Molly said. "And now you're not?" She felt confused. Jenny and Dan's relationship *had* been easy, which is why everyone they knew admitted jealousy of them at one time or another.

"When I couldn't get pregnant, I felt like one of the walls of our little world sort of crumbled. And then when I lost my job, another one came down. It feels like if one thing isn't right, none of it can be good," Jenny said. Her voice was bright. "Let's just say that instead of waiting for the other shoe to drop, I was proactive and dragged it down myself."

Molly patted her hand over her hair, thinking.

"It'll be fine," Jenny said. "Or not, I don't know. But at the very least it gave me the chance to watch so much of the Game Show Network I can now list every single French king that lived in the seventeen hundreds."

Molly smiled, and Jenny let loose with her old laugh again.

"But back to you. You're the one with the baby."

"Yeah, no getting around it, huh? Well, I still have a few more months of living the high life before I really have to decide—"

"Ha!" Jenny exclaimed. "That's you, Molly Sullivan. So laid-back, so casual. Easy, breezy . . ."

"Yeah, yeah, I get it. But I need some more time to figure out what I should do." Molly took a deep breath, looking over the traffic slowly making its way out of the city.

"All right, enough of this lighthearted chitchat," she said, and stood up from her chair. "I have about fifteen minutes to stuff a sandwich in my face and get pretty for this Stevens event tonight."

"Whoa, that's a big one, too," Jenny said. "Okay, then. I'll talk to you. And hey, it'll work out, you know. Your decision about moving home, I mean. And of course I'd visit you in West Chester, especially if the baby gets your personality."

There was a brief pause.

"Well, only if the baby has your personality," Jenny said. "Because seriously, if it ends up with Scott's, you're on your own out there."

"You're funny, Jenny."

"Hey, looks aren't everything. Honestly, though, Mol," Jenny said, "I'll keep you in my prayers."

"Prayers?" Molly leaned her head back to stare at the phone. "When did you start talking about praying? I don't think you've been to church since your wedding."

"I need all the help I can get, Mol," Jenny said. "I'm not doing such a good job of this on my own."

Molly bit her lip as she hung up the phone. The windows in most of the buildings across the alley from hers were dark now, and Molly heard the vacuums of the cleaning crew outside her office door. She watched the moon emerge from behind the cloud, bright and shining over the city below. The sky had turned into a painting of pastel brushstrokes, streaks of purple and pink flung across the horizon. The sun sank lower behind the skyline, and Molly wished it'd stay put just a moment longer. She didn't want dusk to fall, didn't want the moon to pass behind the clouds. She didn't like nighttime, or the darkness that came with it. At least in the light you can see what's coming next.

Thirty minutes later, Molly walked onto the deck of the Moshulu and surveyed the people milling around the hors d'oeuvres stations. The restaurant was a massive, four-mast sailing ship built in the eighteenth century. It had been converted into one of the most recognizable special occasion restaurants in the city, but Molly had been second-guessing her usually trusty instincts since she'd booked it. The Moshulu was anchored on the river next to Columbus Boulevard, a busy thoroughfare lined with strobe-lit clubs and open-air bars that pulsated at night with cover bands and loud drunks. Her taxi driver had had to dodge the partiers making their ways to bad decisions and sure hangovers on their way to Penn's Landing on this warm Thursday night, and Molly worried now that the venue she'd chosen might be too cliché, too expected for a PR event.

Thankfully though, one glance at the conservative crowd moving among linen-draped cocktail tables in their best tweed and Hermès scarves told her that her intuition had been spot-on once again. She felt the muscles in her neck loosen, drew her mouth into a serene smile, and stepped into the crowd.

Molly was wearing one of the maternity wrap dresses she kept in small rotation in her closet. This was one she'd found at an incredible discount online, and it was her favorite: black with a print of huge red poppies splashed all over it. It had a deep neckline, so she wore a camisole underneath to keep her embarrassing amount of new cleavage contained. Molly tugged at the inadequate piece of fabric. The long day had caught up with her, and as she moved through the crowd, greeting individuals she knew, Molly felt waterlogged—swollen and shifting, like someone had forced a swimming ring around her torso and refused to remove it. Molly got on line at the bar and chuckled to herself. If the floating Moshulu happened to sink into the Delaware River that night, at least the partygoers could use her as a life preserver.

Molly glanced around until she saw her client standing in the center of the room, talking to the president of the chamber of commerce. When the two men parted ways, she walked over to him, a glass of sparkling water in her left hand and a red leather clutch purse under her arm. Despite her physical discomfort, Molly felt confident. She'd managed every last detail of this event, down to the silverware in the guests' hands, and knew it had all come together to create a positive impact. By now, events like this were cake to Molly. And she definitely liked cake, she thought, eyeing a row of chocolate tarts lined up on a buffet table. It was no wonder she was about to burst out of her dress.

"Hi, Mark," Molly said now, and shook her client's hand. Mark Stevens, the company's vice president of marketing, smiled at her with his small, beady black eyes and gripped her swollen fingers in both of his hairy hands. Molly looked down at the brown tassels of Stevens' shining brown loafers and tried to pull in a deep breath of the ship's humid air, concentrating on getting through this evening. She told herself that in just a few hours she'd be alone, in the peace of her own home, in the quiet, dim light of her comfortable living room. There would be no small talk, nor aching feet, nor chattering, loud business owners making too much noise. Little did Molly know that this party would be the highlight of her night.

"So, what do you think of this crowd, Molly, huh?" Stevens gestured to the people filling the narrow space. Molly focused again on her client and looked around. Soft light bounced off the shine of the darkly paneled walls. The room reverberated with the mixture of low murmurs and sudden laughter of their guests' small talk. "Not too bad, right?"

Molly smiled and nodded once at her client. Of course it wasn't too bad, she thought. She'd scripted the entire evening. "No, not too bad at all, Mark. I think the homework we did before sending out the press releases really helped with the turnout."

"Ah. And that's why I hired you, Molly. Because you know exactly what I want." He winked at her, and she glanced away from his gaze as a middle-aged woman approached. She took her time walking toward them, swaying on her high heels, and flashed a dazed smile as she took Stevens' free arm. "Molly Sullivan, I'd like you to meet my wife, Susan," Stevens said. "Susan, meet Molly, the savviest PR specialist in town."

Susan Stevens looked like she was one gin and tonic away from falling asleep on her feet. Molly had to force herself to lower her gaze so she wouldn't giggle, and she noticed Susan's nylon-covered legs. Molly had been the one who helped Maidenform put stockings back in the dresser drawers of trend-conscious

women with her "Pantyhose, Like a Princess" campaign. It'd
been huge. She felt her confidence grow now that she knew Stevens was likely aware of the project.

Susan grinned at Molly now before lurching forward to shake
her hand. "It's *so* nice to meet you, Molly." Molly noticed that
Susan's consonants were slurring together. "I've heard *so* much
about, uh, you." Susan swallowed hard as a small burp extended
the skin around her closed lips. Molly tried very hard to keep a
straight face.

"Well, I'm in the mood to celebrate," Stevens proclaimed,
thumping his hands against his jacket lapels. "Susan, I can see
you're in need of another drink. Can I get you a little something
stronger than that water, Molly?"

Molly glanced at her glass and shook her head. "Oh, no,
thank you. Water's fine for me."

She saw Susan's eyes catch sight of her waistline and narrow.
Molly felt a flash of heat cross her face and stifled the groan itching to climb out of her throat. *Here we go,* she thought.

"Mark, I think *someone* might be expecting!" Susan cried,
winking at Molly. Molly could feel a sweat break out around her
hairline, the heat now rising up the back of her neck. Stevens was
one of her biggest contracts, and she needed to keep this conversation professional. Molly tried to smile, but couldn't help duck-
ing her head under the couple's intense gaze.

Stevens' eyes traveled over Molly's body, taking in her torso
under the tied belt of the dress. He clapped his hand on her back.

"Yeah, I thought you were looking a little in the family way,
Molly! Not like you to let yourself go." Stevens chuckled and
rubbed his own protruding belly. "You're starting to look like
me there, girl! Got a bun in the oven, do ya?"

Molly knew where this was headed, and she was weary of having to tell people that she was alone, that there was no father, that yes, she would be a single mother. It embarrassed her. She didn't want people to make assumptions about her based on her in-utero roommate, and each time Molly felt the weight of their judgment— even if she sometimes wondered if it wasn't just her own staring back at her. She looked at the jolly pair in front of her, their arms looped around each other, and even though she suspected Stevens was just trying to keep his wife upright, Molly felt a pang of jealousy twitch in her chest. Any other time she'd just file the whole experience away as a funny story to tell someone when she got home, but there was no one to tell. She thought of Liam, how he would've been waiting up for her with a glass of wine, how he would've laughed at her impersonation of Susan tipping forward in her heels. Molly stood in place, alone, and waited for the next round of questions.

"Well, that's just great, Molly!" Stevens was saying.

Susan parroted her husband's sentiment, nodding in rapid succession.

"But shouldn't you be sitting down?" Stevens used the ringed fingers of his left hand to smooth the few gray hairs that straggled across the top of his head. "Here, should we move to that table over there? A lady who's expecting should probably be home with her feet up on the sofa, getting waited on by her man, not out here with all these suits." He laughed, the broad sound rumbling from deep in his diaphragm. "I admire your dedication, though!"

Stevens looked at his wife for approval as Molly demurred. He rubbed his fingers down the corners of his mouth and appraised Molly again. Molly was ready to dive off the ship and just swim to a cab. She wondered what it was about being a pregnant woman that made people think it was okay to look her over like a show horse at auction. Molly tugged at the top of her dress again as Susan jumped in, her words so slurred it took Molly a moment to understand her.

"Oh, honey, you do look sort of *tired*. You should bow out early, rest a little bit. Doesn't your hubby feel better having you . . . you home?"

Molly felt the air close in around her at Susan's question. The oxygen raced out of her lungs like it was being sucked from a vacuum, and before thinking better of it, she reached out for Stevens' arm to steady herself. Blackness crossed over Molly's line of vision, and the party whirled around her in streaks of light and dark: people's voices calling out, the white shirts of the waiters moving steadily by, the up-and-down motion of the ship that was making her body sway on legs that threatened to buckle underneath her. She was overwhelmed by the odor of the brackish water lapping against the ship, by the exhaust fumes from the adjacent road, by the overpriced cologne of the wealthy men and women in the room. She felt her arms start to shake, sensed the sweat on her neck.

All of the elements of Molly's life—the baby, the house, this job, her parents, her friends—were circling above and around her like her own personal tornado, and she was standing in the vortex, alone, trying to keep the walls of the storm at bay.

She couldn't do this. She didn't want to do this alone.

She shouldn't have said no.

"Molly? Molly, are you okay? Molly, why don't you sit down?"

Molly heard the voices becoming clearer to her, as if she were being shaken awake from a bad dream. Her vision was blurry, obscured by the tears in her eyes. She was still shaking, and the pressure had not yet lifted from her chest. She saw Stevens pick up her bag from where it had dropped onto the floor, and she accepted it from him without making eye contact. Someone had taken the water glass from her hand. When she did raise her eyes to meet those of the people around her, she saw fear in them, and worry. She also saw pity. These people felt sorry for her. Molly decided then and there that this would be the last time she let herself have a panic attack in the middle of a crowded restaurant-boat.

Knocked back into the present by a cold slap of shame, Molly stood up straight, wiped her eyes with a cocktail napkin she'd crushed into her palm, and smoothed her dress. She took a deep breath to answer her client's wife's question. She had some damage control to do.

"Actually, Susan, there is no husband. I'm not married. The baby's father and I are not together anymore, so no, no one's waiting at home for me." She managed a laugh. "Just a comfortable couch, and some ice cream and pickles."

Susan frowned and grew quiet. Stevens glanced at Molly's left ring finger, as if verifying what she'd just said.

"You're not married?" he asked. His face was still jovial, but his voice seemed louder than necessary. "Whaddya mean you're not married? You're having a baby! I didn't think that actually happened to decent women like you." He stared at her, waiting. Molly felt the sweat cooling on her face and planted her swollen feet on the swaying floor.

"Mark, are you really implying that I'm not decent?" Molly had never anticipated that her professionalism would be called into question, but Stevens' company was a famously traditional one. There was a good chance they could drop her, not wanting an unwed pregnant woman to be at the helm of their public relations. Stevens sputtered, looking from Molly to his somber wife and back again.

Molly spoke again, her voice calmer.

"Look, I can assure you that my personal situation will have absolutely no impact on my professional work. I'm sorry I got dizzy for a moment there, but it *is* rather hot in here," she continued. Her voice was shaking, and she cleared her throat. Maybe if she could just pretend the last two minutes hadn't happened, no one would remember them by the time they got to their computers tomorrow.

"Anyway, my focus is on introducing you to some of the most powerful people in Philadelphia business development. There's nowhere else I'd rather be tonight than here, celebrating the success we've had." She turned to Stevens' wife. "Susan, don't you agree that this is wonderful?"

Molly smiled wide until she saw Stevens relax and begin to grin, too. He nodded, as if coming to an agreement with himself, and stuck out his thick hand.

"Well, congratulations, Molly. A new baby is always exciting, even with your, uh, predicament there." Molly bit the inside of her cheek.

"Hell, the old lady and I made four of them ourselves." He nudged Susan with his elbow. *Yeah,* Molly thought. *But you didn't have to rely on people like you to make sure you could afford them.*

"Thanks, Mark. I appreciate that." Tucking her bag under one arm, Molly looked around the room again, surveying the business leaders in attendance. She drew in a breath of air and took Stevens by the elbow.

"Look, I see Mary Keefer, the president of Stolton Materials, over there. I worked with her a while back, and she could probably help you with that grocery chain project. Shall I introduce you?"

She gestured toward the other woman and directed the couple across the room.

Thunder was rumbling across the dark sky when Molly emerged from a taxi much later, even though the spring evening had been mild. The city air felt heavy in its humidity, laden with damp and strangely quiet. The lone sound of the taxi's tires faded away, and Molly stood on the sidewalk with her keys in one hand, listening. She heard no televisions, no car radios. The usual traffic seemed to have disappeared from her street. There was no one else roaming the neighborhood this late at night. A sudden rustling sound from her left made Molly turn and jump just as a rat skittered out from under a car. It brushed the tips of Molly's toes as it ran by. She shuddered in revulsion, smoothing down the hair that now stood on end on her arms.

She walked up the stairs to her house with care. Even though she knew it was because of the coming storm, the absence of bird calls, of pigeons warbling, unsettled her, and she realized her heart was beating more quickly than usual. Molly reached the top of the steps just as a single flash of lightning ripped through the sky. Molly placed her key in the door, pushing the knob as she turned it. The door swung open too easily, and Molly had crossed the threshold before she realized that it hadn't been locked at all. She could sense a presence in the house. A roar of thunder rolled over the city, shaking the air with its threat.

She was not alone.

In the dark of her living room, Molly slowly set her bag down on the floor, freeing her hand, her fingers quivering, to slide a letter opener off of the entranceway table. As her eyes adjusted to the dark, she discerned the silhouette of a man sitting on her couch. Molly's heart began thumping in her chest. Her knees started shaking, almost giving way beneath her. Her breath was coming fast and hard, and she ran her finger over the point of the opener, testing its sharpness as she reached for the lamp. She thought about her phone, deep in the recesses of her bag, and debated opening the door and running for help. But before she could move, the figure on the couch rose, the form tall and broad, its sheer size looming over the room like the storm now pounding at her windows.

"Relax, Nikita. Before you go all ninja on my ass."

"Scott?" Molly heard the letter opener clatter to the floor, and switched on the lamp. Her voice shook. "What are you doing in my house? And why are you in the dark?"

"I—I still have my key. I—well, you never asked for it back. And I was afraid that if you saw me, you'd leave." Scott moved around the coffee table, bracing the small piece of metal on his palm as if testing its weight. He had an unsteady smile on his face as he watched Molly shiver beside the door.

"Well, this doesn't really make me want you to hang around, you know." Molly tried to keep her voice calm. "And about that key—" She stuck out her chin and set her jaw to stop it from trembling. All she'd wanted was to change into pajamas and fall into bed. "I think I'd like that back now."

"No, please." Scott pushed the key deep into the front pocket of his jeans. He was wearing a hooded sweater, so painstaking in its casualness it had to have been expensive. It hung from his muscled shoulders like a superhero cape worn by a child at play. His hair was carefully swept away from his face, and for once he didn't brush an absentminded hand through it. But an uncharacteristic stubble marred Scott's jawline, extending down his throat, and he scratched

at it, as if unused to its presence on his face. The scrape of his finger-
nails against his skin was the only sound in the house, the muffled
noise of the squall beating at the door outside.

"I need to talk to you, baby. We have to"—he looked around the
room, as if waiting for the walls to complete his thought—"talk."

He paused, silent, watching her. He was waiting for her reaction.

"What do you want, Scott?" Molly's voice caught, her mouth
suddenly parched. "It's one o'clock in the morning. I'm sure
whatever it is could've waited until there's daylight." *And wit-
nesses,* she thought. It felt too weird to have him there. Scott
cocked his head and walked over to where Molly stood. His green
eyes took in her entire face, stopping to rest on her hair and lips
before looking directly at her again. She was still shivering.

"I couldn't wait until then. I need you to let me back in,
Molly. Let me be with you. I want you to let me be a, a"—he
took his time with the word—"dad."

"Well, glad to see you've come around, Scott," Molly said,
and the words came spitting out of her mouth. "You've got a few
months' worth of ultrasounds and doctors' appointments to help
pay for, then."

"I know," he said, and his voice was soft. He reached up with
his free hand to smooth her hair over her shoulders. "I screwed
up by avoiding you."

Molly looked up at him, her face wrinkled in confusion.

"But I was hurt, Molly. First you dump me in front of fifty
people, then you come out of nowhere with news that you're
carrying my baby? What guy can handle that all at once?" Scott
looked at the floor, then took a deep lungful of air. "Listen, and
please just hear me out. Do you remember how I told you about
my mom taking on that new job at the firm she's at now?"

"Yeah." Molly said the word with distaste. Midnight visits from ex-boyfriends weren't exactly on her bucket list. "That was back when you were little. What does that have to do with us?"

"I told you that life changed for my family after that," Scott said. "How we suddenly had more money than we knew what to do with. How there were all these new toys piling up in my room, and all of a sudden I was in that . . . that Friends school in Jenkintown."

Molly knew that Scott's parents had paid almost thirty thousand dollars a year for his education there. What's more, they'd cut a check for much more than that to Penn State right around the time Scott was applying to colleges. He'd shown her a picture once of a wing in the business building that bore their names. He'd never known what it was like to take on a second job just to pay his student loans.

"But I never told you that I never made real friends once I transferred into that school, Molly, because I didn't know how. I never told you that for years I walked to class alone, ate by myself at lunch, then came home to sit in front of the TV while the cook got dinner ready."

"Okay . . ." Molly shifted her weight from one swollen foot to the other.

"Molly, my parents were so busy working to make a great life for me that they forgot to actually live a life *with* me. I had a tutor help me with my homework. Our housekeeper took me to karate. I was lonely and probably depressed, and nobody ever said a word."

Molly couldn't read any expression in Scott's face other than an uncharacteristic pleading in his eyes. He looked at her without blinking, the pupils shifting back and forth, his green eyes wet and imploring. Molly was aware that the baby had grown still inside her belly.

"I'm ready to be responsible for my own child, Molly. I want to try to be a father. I want a family—a good family." Scott shook his head. "Molly, I can't lose you."

Molly didn't answer right away. Panic gripped her chest, squeezing, forcing the air to move too quickly out of her lungs. She spoke her next words with care.

"Scott, this baby is the reason why I decided to *not* be with you. You think fifty-dollar bills are something to be given away like Tic Tacs. You act like appointments and deadlines are just *suggestions*. God, Scott. You think scrambled eggs come that way." The sound of Molly swallowing echoed in the room. "And you get mean. You get snappy when you get angry, and speak before you think, and lash out before you even know what you're hitting at. I just . . ." Molly shook her head. "I just can't."

Scott took a step closer. Molly moved backward. The front wall of her house pressed against her back.

"But you're wrong, Molly." She felt her breath coming in slow, shallow gasps. "That's why I'm here. That's what couldn't wait. I need you to realize that you were wrong."

"But you showing up at one a.m. doesn't change my mind, Scott," Molly said. "Something in my gut tells me it's just not right. That you and me together isn't good for any of us."

Molly saw Scott watch her as she placed her hand on her belly. She summoned up the rest of the courage that was still balled up inside her. "I don't want to be with you anymore." She hoped she was telling him the truth.

Scott dropped his hand from the wall. "So what are you going to do, Mol? Huh?"

Molly shook her head. She didn't have an answer for him. She didn't even have an answer for herself.

"I don't get it," Scott said, and the tone of his voice climbed higher. "You act like such a hipster, with your weird music and reusable grocery bags. You're in this empty house, all high and mighty because you're living by yourself, but sometimes it makes me think that maybe *you* think you're too good for me. That you think you're too good for any man."

Molly sputtered in surprise. She looked at the tall man standing in front of her, so at ease in his expensive clothes, the angles of his square face even more defined in the shadows dancing through the room.

"Me? Too good for *you?*"

Scott backed away from Molly. She stood straight from where she'd been leaning against the wall and squinted at Scott. He was pacing across the living room rug.

"Maybe that's what our problem was, Molly. You think you're better than me. That you don't need me or my money or my family, right?" He held his arms out wide. "Is that your MO, to prove that? That you're better off alone?"

Molly could feel tears prick at the backs of her aching eyes. She stared at Scott, a numb kind of shock now joining the adrenaline in her bloodstream.

Scott stopped to face her, and his next words felt like the cold gusts hitting the windowpanes behind her. "Do you really want to end up as alone as you're trying to be?"

Molly had to fight an immediate urge to throw open the door and race back out into the rain, into the squall, to get away from Scott, from the doubt. But this was her home. This was her life, and the happiness of her baby, and she had to defend it. So she remained standing where she was, shaking. Breathing.

"Is that all, Scott?" Molly willed the tears to stay where they were. "You just wanted to drop by with some kind words and a casserole?"

Scott sighed. "I'm sorry, Molly. I didn't mean to make you upset."

He planted his feet a little wider on the living room floor, nearly blocking Molly's view of anything else but him.

"But, Molly, you can't do this." Scott looked at her, waiting for a reaction she refused to give him. "You're my second chance." He let his words sink in. "I can't be left behind again."

Molly's legs felt as if they were liquefying beneath her. She put one hand on the door to open it, then stopped.

"Does Monica have anything to do with this?" Molly's voice sounded too high, too shaky behind the tears.

"What?" Scott stepped back, the surprise on his face genuine. "What does my mom have to do with this? She doesn't even know you're pregnant. *I* can't tell her."

Molly inhaled in one sharp breath. When she spoke, she said the words slowly, evenly.

"Scott, I think you need to go." She opened the door and stepped clear out of Scott's path. "And please don't show up here like this again."

Any swagger he had left fell away from Scott's tall frame, and his shoulders slumped, making him seem like the hurt little boy he must have been decades earlier.

"Molly, please don't do this."

"Scott," Molly said, "I have to."

Scott moved past her. Molly couldn't bring herself to look him in the eyes. He stopped, just inches in front of her.

"Please don't do this to me, Molly." His eyes sought out hers until she met them. "You can't leave me alone sitting in an empty house again. Not when we could be together. Not when we could have a family." He picked up Molly's left hand and touched her bare ring finger before looking back up at her. "Not when I haven't had enough of a chance to prove that I can be worth it."

Molly pressed her lips together to keep from speaking.

Scott tried to laugh, but the sound fell flat in the quiet room. His mouth hardened into a straight line above the angular set of his jaw, and he looked over her body, his gaze stopping at her swollen belly. "I miss my old Molly."

He brushed past her into the rain, bumping her shoulder into the door frame as he walked out of her house, and took each stair to the walk with such measured strength she could hear the reverberation of his footsteps.

Molly shut the door and checked the dead bolt twice to make sure it was in place. She rested there for a moment, waiting for her heartbeat to slow down, for the quaking in her muscles to quiet. Scott had told her everything tonight she wished he'd said months ago, but Molly didn't know if it was possible for a grown man to achieve in weeks the maturity he'd avoided for years. She moved toward the couch like she was walking through muddy water and sank into the cushions, avoiding the space where Scott had been just moments ago. Only then, alone on the sofa, did Molly allow herself to cry.

CHAPTER SEVEN

June

Yes

Molly used the heavy box in her arms to help push open the thick door to her townhome, then dropped the carton with a thud onto the mopped wood floors. She opened the closet door, carefully kicked her flip-flops off so that they landed squarely on a mat inside, then placed her bag in its designated cubbyhole underneath the entranceway table. A tidy pile of mail sat on top of the table, but Molly ignored it, choosing instead to look around at the casual grace of her little home: the dark beams of the ceiling, the light paint over the original crown molding and baseboards, the tall windows that illuminated her simple furnishings. In the quiet of the day, the air of her home was so still the sound of the door shutting didn't even make its usual echo around her empty dining room. The calm of the space around Molly was at complete odds with the turmoil roiling inside her swollen belly.

It was a miserable time to get the month's bills. She tucked the stack of envelopes inside the box on the floor. The container held

the last of her personal possessions from her former office at
Shulzster & Grace, and she'd refused any help carrying it as she
trudged through the heavy glass lobby doors for the last time.
These were her most precious items: her bachelor's degree from
Bryn Mawr and her master's—of which she was so proud—from
UPenn, a letter of praise from the very first client she'd ever repre-
sented, and a copy of the last letter Bill wrote in recommendation
of her promotion. The other two items she'd saved were a framed
photo from her first ultrasound appointment and a trophy given
to her by her goddaughter, Kailey: a gold-colored plastic woman
with pom-poms cheering atop a pedestal that read "Girls Rule!"
Kailey had given it to her for Christmas years ago and Molly had
kept it on her desk at every position she'd had since. Eight years
of PR success now lay in a cardboard carton at her feet.

Molly walked into the kitchen to pour a glass of water, groaning when she saw that, as usual, Scott had left the sink full of dirty
dishes. She'd worn a tank top and shorts for the day's mission, and
even with her thick hair pulled back into a high ponytail, she was
too aware that she was sweating like a pig on a spit. She was glad
she'd gotten permission to enter the office on a Saturday to empty
out her belongings. At least this was one humiliation she hadn't
had to suffer in front of everyone who used to respect her.

From her bag, Molly's phone whistled a tweeting sound. She
fished it out while taking a sip of water.

"Hi, Mom."

"How goes it, sweetheart?"

Molly blew air out through her nose, shaking her head at no
one in particular. "Well, I'm officially unemployed. I got all my
stuff out of the office today."

Emily made a *tsk*ing sound. "That fiancé of yours is going to love this."

"You're telling me." Molly felt a lump gather in her throat, making it difficult for her to talk. "This is like a dream come true for him.

"It could be worse, I guess." Her throat caught. "They did offer to extend me a short severance, so I'll still have my health insurance until the baby's born, and then Scott can add us on to his."

"Well, that's good," Emily said. "See? There's a silver lining after all."

Molly shook her head again. "But, Mom. I lost my job. And the thing is, I could've prevented it. I got lazy, and overwhelmed, and let stuff slide." The pitch of her voice climbed. "When has this ever happened to me?"

"Molly, honey, everybody makes mistakes."

"Not me, Mom," Molly said, more loudly than she'd intended. "*I* don't make mistakes. Or, at least, I never used to. Lately, it seems like all I do."

"Molly, what do you mean? What other mistakes have you made?"

The line was quiet for a moment.

"Nothing," Molly said. She was more subdued now. "I didn't mean anything by it. Getting pregnant probably wasn't the best move to make, though."

"But that's said and done," Emily said. Her tone was brusque. "So let's move on."

"Okay, okay." Molly laughed. "You don't have to get all tough love on me."

"A mother has to do what's necessary, sweetheart." Emily

chuckled now, her tone brighter. "You'll find that out in a few short months."

There was another pause. Molly was having a difficult time sorting through her thoughts.

"What does Dad think of all this?"

"Oh," Emily said, "you know your father. He's got himself starting another project to worry about instead. I think he's building a new mantel for the fireplace this time."

"Not a bad coping mechanism," Molly said, smiling. She glanced at the clock on the microwave. It was later than she'd thought. Scott had been due to get home from his charity golf outing an hour ago.

"Hey, Mom? I better go. It's almost lunchtime." She sighed. "I should get started on making my man a meal like a good housewife." The words tasted bitter in her mouth.

"It's not nineteen fifty-two, Molly," Emily said. "You can cook a damned meal without it being a statement against the women's movement."

"I guess so," Molly acquiesced. "But right now I feel like I've taken a couple steps back in life." She knew she was wallowing, and she could sense Emily losing her patience from the house in West Chester.

"It's not a race, Molly. You can take a couple of missteps and still come out ahead."

"I suppose. Just call me out if you find me cooking pot roast and potatoes on a Sunday, now, because it means I'm this close to playing backgammon in my spare time."

"Cut it out, child," Emily scolded, but she was chuckling. "That's exactly what your father and I have planned for tonight."

Molly laughed, glad her mother couldn't see her cringe. "Sorry, Mom."

"Molly, you'll figure it out." Emily's tone was warm. "Your dad and I raised you to chase after what you wanted, so don't you dare think you should stop now. Just keep in touch with your contacts and start over after the baby's born. Don't let this hiccup keep you from that."

For a moment silence hung in the air, then Emily continued. "No matter what Scott tells you, remember: it's not nineteen fifty-two. *You don't have to.*"

Molly bit her lip and looked toward the closed front door. The ornate stained glass window set above the entrance to her kitchen was dark. It caught her eye, and she made a mental note to scrub it clean so that it would reflect light again the way it was supposed to.

"Well, go enjoy your pot roast, okay?" Molly said. "Give Pop my love." She laughed. "And tell him not to hammer too hard."

Molly pulled the phone away from her ear before catching herself. "And, Mom?"

"Yes, Molly?" Emily never hung up before she did.

"Thank you."

Molly clicked off her phone and stood in her kitchen for a minute longer, turning to brace her hands on the counter and look out the window over the sink. The sky was as cloudy as the thoughts in her head. Other than two weeks over a Christmas break in college, Molly hadn't been unemployed since she first started busing tables at a Red Lobster while in high school. Even back then, when she had to soak her uniform every night in vinegar and water to get the smell of seafood and spoiled butter out of her clothes, she had loved making her own money. She still got a rush whenever she saw a paycheck made out in her name, and felt satisfied when she could check off bills paid each month. She'd worked to buy her first car, had kept up on the insurance, and had never had a credit card balance that she couldn't pay off right away. Molly still held the same attitude toward her finances. Unfortunately, she now lacked a job to pay those bills.

Molly looked around at the soft gray-blue walls and granite countertops. She made note of the cups lined up in straight rows in the glass-fronted cabinets, of the plates stacked with precision along the shelves. Her life had always been something she could keep organized, tidy. But she wasn't a PR specialist anymore. She had nowhere to go on Monday. It was one more piece of her life that had slipped out of her control, and Molly felt at a loss, like a huge abyss had opened up at her feet and she was about to step into it. It was as if she didn't have an identity to call her own anymore. She'd fallen off the grid.

Molly's feet ached, so she set her glass down on the counter and turned away from the window. She walked into the living room to put some music on the speakers and scrolled through the artist list on her phone in search of songs that were comforting and familiar before settling on some Fleetwood Mac. It reminded her of her father, and she needed that sense of security right now: green flannel shirts and carpentry dust, warmth and solidity. With a jolt of surprise, Molly realized that her father had all the characteristics of a tree. She couldn't help but laugh at the image. But Jack *was* stable, and rooted. A person knew that, even if he was quiet, he'd always be there when needed. She understood why her mother, who often reminded Molly of an anxious bird, flitting about, cackling at predators—always moving, always preparing—had settled into Jack's arms. He gave her shelter, and she provided him with purpose and entertainment, a reason to build trust. It was why they worked, and they loved each other for it.

Molly felt the baby shift in her belly and ran her hand over her stomach. She knew how important it was for her own child to have parents who could be that confident in their love for each other. Her thoughts shifted to her own current instability.

"*Fired*," Molly breathed. "I got *fired*." Because she'd dropped the ball and shirked her duties. Everything she'd worked so hard to get, trampled on like it was last week's gum wrapper. Molly had never been more ashamed of herself in her life. Stevie Nicks' nasal voice started singing "Landslide," and Molly sat back down on the kitchen barstool and put her head into her hands.

"Oh, mirror in the sky," she heard Stevie sing, her plaintive question ringing though Molly's thoughts, "what is love?"

She hadn't wanted to tell Jenny—poor Jenny, who was one of the most consistent workers at S&G and got laid off anyway, and who would give anything to have her old job back. Jenny could barely speak after Molly told her what happened. *But God bless the girl*, Molly thought. She certainly hadn't said one mean word to her. Her old friend had just taken it in stride, blinked hard once, and given her a hug. Jenny's resilience, Molly understood, was going to make her a very good mother one day.

"And what about me, little one?" Molly spoke to her belly, rubbing her hand over her protruding belly button. "I'm not so sure right now what kind of example I'm going to be to you if I can't even hold on to my dream job. What are you going to think of me?"

Molly heard footsteps and looked up to see Scott walk into the kitchen. She hadn't noticed him come in through the front door and knew by the bemused expression on his face he'd heard her talking to herself. He placed a pink bakery box on the island and reached for her.

"That baby's going to think he's the luckiest—or she, if it's a girl—kid in the world to have a mama who loves him enough to make raising him her sole job."

Scott wrapped his arms around Molly and pulled her against him. "I brought you those chocolate cupcakes you're always raving about. I knew you'd be hungry after packing up your stuff, *especially* since you insisted on refusing the help of a certain strong, able-bodied fiancé."

Molly gave the pink box a long look and loosened Scott's arm from her waist. "I wanted to do it by myself."

She knew he was trying to make her feel better, so she didn't understand why she couldn't bring herself to look him in the eye. "No need to bring a pity party with me."

"What pity party? This is perfect."

Molly rubbed her hands over her face, then back over her head, smoothing her ponytail. Now she knew why.

"Scott, we've been through this a thousand times. I lost my job. That doesn't mean I want to not have a job. It just means I need to find a new one."

Scott blew an exasperated sound between his teeth and dropped his arms from around Molly's swollen belly. His khaki shorts were smeared with dirt, and the hair that was normally swept back from his face now flopped into his eyes. Molly could smell the clubhouse rail whiskey on his breath, sickly sour and sweet, like cherries left to spoil on a countertop.

"Yeah, okay, Molly. And you explain to me how you're going to go on interviews and land a job with a belly out to there."

He reached into the fridge for a beer and cracked the top with the opener he kept on the refrigerator door. Molly's eyes fell on the dull spot the magnet had made on the fridge's finish and realized how much she hated that bottle opener.

"Molly, had you even thought about that? I think all that hear-me-roar mojo bouncing around in your head crowded out the common sense. No one's going to take on a woman who needs maternity leave two months after she's hired—I think even Ms. Steinem could've told you that. You're not going back to work right now."

Scott stood in place, distracted now by the peeling blue label on the bottle he held. Molly knew he was right. She hadn't considered how having the baby was going to play into her job search, and she found herself shaking her head in disbelief. The doorbell buzzed, and Scott walked out of the kitchen to answer it, patting her on the shoulder as he went.

Molly suddenly felt very, very tired. She rubbed her hand over the bump in her belly, feeling the baby move around, knocking against the space under her hand. Molly pursed her lips and gazed around the kitchen, the bare dining room, the inviting living area. She tried to imagine the rooms filled with a baby swing and play crib and activity mat and all the other myriad baby gear she kept seeing on parenting websites and in the magazines she'd been reading. This place was about to change mighty quickly, and she couldn't slow it down, or make it stop, even if she really wanted to.

It was such a very strange feeling to know that she was about to join her life—her entire *life*—with two people, and yet still feel like no one would come running if she needed help. There was so much happiness she was supposed to be feeling right now, but she couldn't quite touch it sometimes. It seemed like it was just past her fingertips, and she had to reach through a haze of uncertainty to get there, a fog so thick and unwieldy she was afraid it would never quite dissipate. And then she'd be stuck. Molly felt the baby kick again, as if in agreement—this baby who would soon enough need her to get her shit together already and focus on being its mom.

Molly thought about the parents she knew, parents she saw on the sidewalks, in the stores, and she realized something: nobody ever has her shit together. But some people do an excellent job of trying.

Molly could hear the deep rumble of Scott's voice as he talked with whomever was at the front door. The sound of his chuckle rolled back through the house to the kitchen, and she fought back the tears forming at the corners of her eyes. She felt like she was staring at her life from the outside, hands to the window-pane. She was just silent, watching the whirlwind of people—in utero and out—clamoring for attention, vying for the lead, tugging her along behind them. And for some reason, Molly had let herself get so out of control that she was listening to them instead of to herself.

"You okay there, Mol?" Scott was walking back into the kitchen with an armful of wrapped gifts, and Molly looked up to see his mother on his heels, floating on a cloud of Chanel No. 5 and hair spray, a camel-colored Birkin bag slung over her arm. Monica's grin was radiant, her white veneers flashing against the carefully lipsticked edges of her mouth. She dropped a large pastel-covered bag filled with tissue paper on the floor and reached for her future daughter-in-law.

"Molly! I just heard the news." Monica kissed the air beside both of Molly's cheeks and *tut-tut*ted Molly's gesture to stand up, motioning that she stay seated on the bar stool. She towered beside Molly in a pair of nude snakeskin stilettos.

"Your future father-in-law was driving me up the wall," she was saying, "hollering at that dreadful Phillies game on TV—"

"Oh, crap! I forgot that was on," Scott sputtered. He reached for his phone.

"Anyway," Monica continued, "he was hooting and hollering and driving me battier than usual—you'd think he was a physician for them and not the Eagles—so I decided it was a perfect time to run some errands. I was just coming through the neighborhood to do a little shopping for the baby and thought I would swing by to see if you two would like to join me for lunch, and then Scott tells me you're not working anymore, and I thought, 'Well! Now we have a reason to celebrate!'"

She looked back and forth between Scott and Molly, beaming. No one else seemed to notice that the air in the room had grown stifling. Molly felt queasy as the odor of Monica's perfume mixed with the smell of alcohol seeping from Scott's pores and wafted to her nostrils. They'd finally told Scott's parents about the baby one evening after Monica had made a comment on Molly's appetite at dinner. Monica had taken the news like a child being told she was going to Disney World. She came into the city now every few days with excuses of dropping off a gift or checking in to see how Molly was feeling.

Molly managed a small smile. "I'm not sure if your son told you the whole story, Monica." She glanced at Scott, who was picking at something in between his back teeth with a fingernail, clearly assuming no one would notice. Molly cringed. He wasn't going to be much help.

Monica smoothed her hair over one ear and winked at her. "Of course he did, darling. But I'm just so *happy* to hear it. Now, I know it isn't exactly what you want right now." Her words quickened once she saw the grimace cross Molly's face. "But you'll see, Molly, this will be a good thing."

Monica looked at Scott for affirmation. He nodded in obedience, tearing his eyes away from his phone to make brief eye contact with Molly. He offered her a shrug as an apology, and Molly felt herself take a shuddering breath. She might as well be alone in the room.

She no more wanted to be at home with a baby now than she did before she got pregnant. She wanted to be a Kelly Ripa, cute and perky with toned biceps, not a desperate housewife from some cable reality show. She wanted to emulate Ripa because she worked at a job she loved, made enough money to hire someone she trusted to care for her children while she was away, and then returned home to a tidy house to spend time with her little one. That's what Molly imagined as her future. Balance. Self-sufficiency. Control. It's what Monica herself had done for years, creating a legacy the likes of which Molly had kept in her sights for her own life. She closed her eyes for a moment.

Scott was speaking, having looked up from his phone long enough to join the conversation.

"You could always work part-time or at night, after I got home," he was saying to her. "Freelance or something."

"No, no, that won't do," Monica interrupted. "Look at all those years I wasted toiling away while you were growing up, Scott. It's a wonder you turned out as well as you did, considering that your father and I were never home and left you with that Bernadette woman to take care of you. Molly should be here, with you and the baby."

Molly shook her head in surprise. "Monica, I thought you loved your architecture work. Weren't you in school for years to do it?"

"I *did*, darling, and that was the problem." Monica rapped her manicured hands against the countertop. "I loved it *too* much. I was trying to help Scott's father create a nice life for ourselves, but look! You don't need to. You have us."

Scott moved to stand closer to Monica. Molly wondered why a mother's relationship with her son so often set up his partner to feel like the other woman, like a mistress tolerated as long as she didn't ruffle too many feathers. *Seriously, you two,* she thought. Monica was rubbing Scott's upper arm. *Get a room.*

"Monica," Molly said, "I'm still paying off my student loans from grad school. I kind of wanted to use my education while I'm still spending money on it." She paused to take a deep breath. She could feel her pulse racing, and she ran her hands over her hair again to push the stray strands away from her face.

"Well, then, don't worry about them." Monica laughed. "Scott, dear, you never told us Molly had loans."

Scott focused on his phone with a renewed, intense interest, and Monica turned her attention back to Molly. "Molly, consider them taken care of. We'll write you a check to cover the balance."

"I'm sorry, what?" Molly looked back and forth between Monica and Scott before remembering to close her mouth.

"Oh, stop it, Molly," Monica said. "You're going to have bigger fish to fry, darling. That baby's going to need his mommy. And now you've one less thing blocking your way to do just that."

Molly felt her body sag. Years of work, of budgeting to make more than the minimum payment each month, and in one fell swoop Monica could clear the lot. She'd wanted so badly to get to a place where she could be like Monica—hardworking, secure, with years of relationships invested in colleagues and business partners—and here Monica was, offering her an early exit off that same road. Molly sat where she was, breathing heavily, the muscles around her belly clenching with the effort. She should be happy, she told herself. Elated, to have less financial stress to worry over, to be joining a family capable of such generosity. But she felt the walls start rushing in on her again and struggled to fight off the feeling that an iron cage was clamping itself around her lungs, making her stay in place, struggling to breathe. She was supposed to feel grateful, Molly thought. She was supposed to be relieved. *Be relieved, Molly,* she told herself. *For God's sake, be RELIEVED.*

Monica seemed to sense the change in the air. "Well," she said, patting her bag with a flourish, "I want to talk wedding invitations. Who's coming to lunch with me? I was thinking either Tinto or the Fountain."

Molly's mouth watered. Tinto had some of the best Spanish food in the city.

"You're kind, Monica, but I'm actually not feeling very well," she demurred, avoiding the surprised look from Scott.

"Oh, you poor darling," Monica said, and took a step back from her. "Is it this heat?"

"I think so," Molly said. "I was going to lie down for a while."

"Oh, that's a shame. I was really looking forward to some mommy chitchat, too." Monica pouted.

Scott was still watching Molly, a frown creasing his forehead between his eyes. It disappeared as Monica turned to him in expectation.

"Scott, then? Shall we?"

"Um, yeah." Scott gave Molly a sidelong look. "Though I was starting to think you liked my fiancée more than you like me."

"Well, she is prettier," Monica replied, and patted the side of his face with her hand. "I'm kidding. Your fiancée just reminds me of me when I was her age." Monica smiled at Molly, then turned her attention to her son's attire. She took in the stains on his clothes.

"I'll pull the car around while you get changed." She kissed the air around Molly's cheeks again and stepped to the door.

Molly looked up at Scott. She felt the question on her face before she had to speak a word.

"I know what you're going to say, Molly. But you heard what my mother said." He leaned against the island where she sat. "Think about how much our baby is going to love seeing you every day, knowing you'll be there to take care of him. I can't imagine you'd be okay denying him that because you like your job."

"Well," Molly said, "at least I make my own money."

For a long moment, they stared each other down. Scott's face had taken on the hue of a raspberry, but when he spoke, his voice was soft.

"Molly. I can't have some stranger coming in here to raise *my* kid. We're not hiring a substitute mom," he said. "That's what I went though, and it can't be the same for him. I won't let *my* child grow up thinking he's not good enough." Scott's voice faltered. "I can't have him, or her—whatever—wondering what he did wrong to have to sit in an empty house, waiting for his family to remember he exists. It messes with a kid's brain, Mol. Do you really want that for our child?"

The gentle voice became a growl when Molly started to respond. Scott cut her off before she could say a word.

"You can't have it all, Molly," he said. It felt like he'd slapped her in the face. "You're smart enough to know that."

He strode out of the kitchen, looking straight ahead as he walked past her, and Molly could hear his heavy footsteps climbing the stairs to her bedroom. She struggled to allow her racing pulse to settle down so she could catch an even breath. Tears fell singularly from her eyes, taking their time carving salty paths down her cheeks.

Molly looked down at her hands. Her fingers were shaking. The light from the ceiling bounced around on her diamond ring, throwing splashes of white and yellow onto her pale skin. She saw how the huge ring overpowered her finger, making her hand look too small, too fragile. For a brief, quick moment, she allowed herself to imagine what a ring from Liam would've looked like. Its stone would've been small, the setting plain. It would've shone, though, and she could imagine the flashes of light throwing themselves out with abandon from the modest diamond. She would've been proud to wear it.

Molly felt a swift kick from the inside of her stomach and looked down at her belly. Tears rose up in her eyes with purpose now, before she could prepare herself for them. She hoped Scott wouldn't walk back into the kitchen to find her still sitting there, sobbing into her hands.

"Poor baby," she whispered. "I'm sorry Mommy and Daddy are fighting so much. We're just trying to figure out what's best for you. I swear to you, we'll be better by the time you come. We're really going to try, okay?" She took another shaky breath. "I'm going to try."

Molly stood up to refill her glass with water and glanced out the window at the darkening sky. There was a storm rolling in. She could smell the moist air coming in through the open window. She checked the clock on her phone and slid her keys from the counter. She heard heavy footfalls again as Scott came running down the stairs, and she blew a breath deep from her lungs as the front door slammed behind him. She waited a moment before going to the door herself. As she walked out of the house, Fleetwood Mac was still singing from the speakers, so determined in their harmonies on "The Chain," even though no one was there to listen. *Let Scott turn it off when he gets back,* Molly thought, closing the door. It was about time he realized that a world of music existed outside of Whitesnake anyway.

Thirty minutes later, Molly was wandering around the magazine racks of the massive Barnes & Noble on Walnut Street, looking for a pregnancy or parenting journal she hadn't already read cover to cover, when she saw Jenny's husband sitting at a table by himself in the in-store Starbucks with an oversized coffee cup in his hand. Without hesitating, she walked over to him. She hadn't seen him since that awful incident at her and Scott's engagement party.

Dan didn't notice Molly's approach, and she was able to get a good look at him before he registered her arrival. He was hunched over a stack of papers on the table, a pen held tightly in his left hand. His shoulders were tense, his feet planted wide on the floor. It looked like he was still in his work clothes. *Must be teaching summer school again,* Molly thought. Dan was always doing what he could to help his kids—and he said the extra money was nice, of course. He consistently looked the part of the standard-issue young, idealistic teacher, in his khakis, button-front shirt, and tie. His black Dr. Martens were shined to mirror-like quality, and his hair was cropped neatly close to his head. He looked tired, Molly noticed, but she wasn't sure if that meant he was up all night worrying about his struggling marriage or if the dark circles were just the result of another strenuous day spent manning the trenches in the classrooms of Philadelphia's public schools. She swallowed the lump in her throat when she saw the wedding ring in its usual place on his finger.

"Dan. Hi."

He looked up with surprise but seemed genuinely pleased to see her. He smiled wearily. "Hey, Mol, what are you doing here? Shouldn't you be off hobnobbing with the cream of the Philly crop? Here, sit down and take a load off. You look like you ate an inner tube."

Dan leaned over to take his school bag off the chair and placed it on the other side of the table.

"Oh, you hadn't heard?" Molly said as she sank down into the seat. "My hobnobbing days are over, buddy, at least for now. I got canned."

Dan choked on his coffee. "What? No shit. What for?"

"Oh, it doesn't matter. Let's just say I'm not as good a juggler as I used to be." Molly leaned back in her seat and placed her feet on the chair between them. It felt good to sit down.

"And what does Handsome Harry think about all this?"

Molly chuckled and shook her head, staring at the papers stacked under the pencil in Dan's hand. "Scott? He's why I'm here. We're having some, uh, *difficulties* agreeing on how to raise the baby."

Dan raised an eyebrow. "What did he say now?"

Molly laughed out loud this time, a genuine laugh, the whole situation suddenly just seeming absurd. "Oh, Dan. He's actually excited I got fired. His whole family's practically drawn up a schedule for me for when the baby comes—stay home all day to do laundry and breastfeed, cook gourmet meals, attend charity galas with his parents at night . . ."

". . . and bring him his midnight snack after you come home? Molly, that dude's messing with you." Dan looked at her now with an expression of real concern. His body was still, without the usual pitter-pattering of his pencil against a table or jitter of a leg. He waited.

"Nah." Molly shook her head. "He's not messing with me, Dan. He means it. It's like he wants me to be the exact opposite of the person he started dating."

Dan rubbed his hand through his spiky hair and sighed. "That's not good, Mol."

She sat up a little bit and squared her shoulders. "It'll be fine. We're just going through a rough patch. It'll be fine," she repeated. "He's just been in a weird mood or something."

"Molly, that's what the girls in my classes will tell their friends right before they walk into school with a black eye."

"Dan!" Molly stared at her friend, her eyes narrowed. "What are you talking about?"

"I'm just saying, be careful, Mol, okay? I gotta admit, I'm a little worried about you. Scott's been acting really shady ever since you got pregnant, you know?"

"Yeah." Molly sighed. "I guess you have a right to that opinion, huh?"

Dan was quiet.

"Look, I'm sorry he was such an ass that night. I'm starting to think we just need to keep him out of a twenty-mile radius of any alcohol, ever."

Dan still didn't speak. He started toying with the pencil, doodling circles around a corner of his grade book.

"How are you, anyway? That's why I stopped over." Molly leaned forward to catch Dan's eye. "So even though she's home now, evidently you're not talking with Jenny that much, if you didn't know I'd lost my job."

"No." Dan shook his head. "We've been talking, but not often, and not much. She's doing her standard shutdown thing she does when she's upset, and I've been trying to give her some space, but this has gone on too long. We just sort of circle each other at home. We don't talk, and she acts like she'll combust if I come too close. It's been, what, almost two months since she's been back? I can't take it. It's like she wants to believe I cheated on her."

Dan put his pencil down. He rubbed his eyes with the thumb and fingers of one hand, then looked at Molly. She was taken aback by the sadness she saw in his eyes.

"I hate it, Mol. I was so excited to have her back, but she might as well still be at her parents' house for all that's changed. I love Jenny more than I love tacos, but we've never not gotten along like this. I don't know if this job thing has her depressed, or if it's wanting a baby or what, but it's like she just took this as an excuse to block out me and anything that could hurt her anymore."

"Hmm. Jenny in shutdown mode. That's never good."

"No. It isn't."

Molly looked at him. "You know I'm dying to ask you about that night."

Dan gave her a withering look. "You're kidding me, right?" Molly shrugged her shoulders.

"Here. Look at this. Do you remember reading *Romeo and Juliet* in ninth-grade English?" He pushed an open book across the table to her.

"Shakespeare? Oh, I don't know, buddy. Sorry to say I hated English, and that guy William right there was a big reason. You may have to translate."

"Ah, you just didn't have the right teacher." Dan nodded at the page. "See, Mercutio starts making fun of Romeo for falling in love with Rosaline—you remember he loved her before seeing Juliet, right?"

Molly nodded, mainly to keep him talking.

"When Romeo tells Mercutio that he'd had a dream about her, Mercutio launches into this huge speech: 'I see Queen Mab hath been with you. / She is the fairies' midwife; and she comes / In shape no bigger than an agate-stone.'"

Dan looked at Molly, who shook her head in confusion. He continued.

"'On the fore-finger of an alderman / . . . she gallops night by night / Through lovers' brains, and then they dream of love; / O'er courtiers' knees, that dream on court'sies straight; / O'er lawyers' fingers, who straight dream on fees; / O'er ladies' lips, who straight on kisses dream . . . '"

Dan sat forcefully back in his seat and looked at Molly, triumphant.

Molly held up her hands, palms to the sky. "Sorry to disappoint you, bud, but that all sounded like Russian to me," she said.

Dan sighed in bemused exasperation. "Mercutio thought that love was fickle. Queen Mab was famous for being this tiny little enchanting fairy who could grant people's wishes through their dreams. She had the power to make them happy. Get what they want. She could do whatever she wanted simply by dancing into their heads"—Dan paused—"and working her magic."

"And this tells me nothing. Could you break it down in real-world terms for me?"

"Molly, c'mon," Dan said. He pushed aside the book. "What do you think? You think I really could cheat on Jenny? I've been in love with the girl since the first day of phys ed in the ninth grade. She spiked a volleyball straight into my head. She knocked me out." Dan shrugged his shoulders and blushed a little. "Literally and figuratively. She's my tiny little fairy who made my wishes

come true. I'm enchanted by her; always have been. There's just
no other way to put it.

"Of course there's never been anyone else. All I did was talk
to that girl because I found out we went through the same master's program. I don't know what Scott was thinking. Jenny's all
I've ever wanted."

He paused again. "I'm not her father."

Molly leaned back in her chair. "Yeah. That's what I figured."

"So now what?"

"I don't know, bud. I don't know. Wait for her to come
around? Stand outside your bedroom window with a boom box
Say Anything–style?"

"Don't think I haven't considered that, except that she hates
that movie," Dan said. "She never thought Diane was good
enough for Lloyd Dobler."

Molly smiled.

"Can I just tell you, Molly? Do you know how hard it is to
come home every night to a quiet house? Jenny'd always have the
radio on, and I'd walk in to see her dancing to 'Everyday Is Like
Sunday,' singing at the top of her lungs in what has to be the
worst impression of Morrissey I've ever heard. It was freakin'
adorable. She and I used to cook dinner together—"

Molly kept a straight face, but was secretly choking back a
sad smile. The only thing Scott ever wanted to do in the kitchen
with her was open a bottle of beer or fool around on top of the
island counter. Or both at the same time, if he could manage it.

Dan's voice had gotten quieter. "Now I can't stand to listen
to any band with an English singer anymore." He used the fingers of one hand to twist the napkin beside his coffee cup. "And
I used to really like The Smiths."

Molly raised her eyebrows.

"But it's awful," Dan said. "Climbing into bed without kissing her good night. Watching TV in separate rooms. Not talking over coffee in the morning. It's like she died, and I'm living with her ghost. There's just a hole."

Dan's voice had grown a little jagged, and he shook his head as if to snap out of it. "But she's not dead. She's sitting right there in our living room, watching *Wheel of Fortune* and pretending I'm not there right beside her, even though there's nowhere else I'd rather be . . . Have you talked to her?"

Molly shifted in her seat and uncrossed her legs. The doctor had warned her to not restrict the circulation to her ankles.

"Yes, but she doesn't give me much. She mainly focuses the conversations on me and the baby and avoids talking about you altogether. But I'm trying. I think you're right about the possibility of depression, though. Do you think this baby thing has really gotten to her?"

Dan nodded. "It's her own Queen Mab."

"And how are you with that? Can I ask?" Molly tilted her head to look at Dan's face.

"How do you think I am? Shitty. This hasn't worked out quite how I imagined."

Molly pressed her lips together, remembering the reason why she'd come out tonight in the first place.

"Listen," she said. "I'll try to get her out more—go to the gym, job-hunt together. Anything to get her out of the house and attempt to place her head squarely back on her shoulders. She's too smart to lose you. I know that, for sure. She does, too. She's just taking a little longer this time."

"Thanks, Mol. I appreciate it." Dan patted her knee in his

brusque, affectionate manner. "Hey, you should get home to your baby daddy and make up. Make him rub your feet or something. You look like you could use it."

"Hey, that's not nice!" Molly playfully swatted Dan against his shoulder. "You're my friend. You're supposed to tell me I look beautiful and have that certain glow. Not that I look tired with nasty feet." She grinned at him.

"Hey, you said it. I wasn't going to say anything about your feet, Captain Cankles. But pretty soon your fool fiancé's going to have to get a stroller just for you. Those things look painful."

Molly glanced down at her pathetic-looking ankles. She wished she'd changed into something longer so that Dan didn't really have to see the worst of the swelling on her legs. And the veins. Molly thought the varicose veins were the worst of the hidden curses of pregnancy so far. They hurt, and they were ugly. She hadn't been prepared for them.

"They are painful, but thanks, meanie. Men. You guys have no idea what we go through." As soon as she said it, Molly realized that Dan, of all people, was one of the more empathetic people she knew. She hadn't been talking about him.

"No, no, we don't, Molly. I'm not so sure about Scott, but trust me. Every day I thank God for making me a dude."

Molly spontaneously rose up and hugged Dan hard. Hugged him for being so caring, and for grading all of those papers and for wearing his wedding ring even though his marriage was on the rocks.

"What was that for?" he said, laughing. Molly didn't say anything. She just kissed him on top of his gelled, spiky hair. She and Jenny were going to have to have a chat. Dan grinned at her, then went back to his work.

CHAPTER EIGHT

July

No

❧

"You won't believe it when you see it. It's ridiculous."

"Ridiculous, as in gorgeous? Or ridiculous, as in so over the top even a Kardashian would think it's too much?"

Molly was standing in the middle of her living room with her phone pressed to her ear, staring at what she was pretty sure was meant to be a baby's cradle. Shaped like a capital D, it looked like a piece of furniture from a sci-fi movie, and it was here, in her home, resting on its back, taking up most of the space between her coffee table and the window. The smooth shape of the crib was built from white slats of wood that looked like someone had taken a stack of gigantic china plates and chopped them in half. Inside, quilted silk lined the mattress and sides.

"I'm not really sure, Jenny. He really outdid himself this time."

"Oh, no, Mol, that has the well-manicured fingerprints of Monica all over it," Jenny said with a laugh. "I think they've teamed up. Scott probably went to her for advice on what to get, and Monica was all, 'Molly's a modern girl! What's luxurious, yet edgy?'"

"'I know!'" Molly joined in, "'Let's get her something from *outer space*!'"

Jenny was full-on guffawing now.

"No, it's even better than that, Jenny," Molly said. "This has to be Scott's doing—Monica still doesn't know about the baby." She stepped to the other corner of the room to regard the cradle from a different angle. It was still enormous.

"She doesn't what?"

"I think Scott's terrified to tell her. This is all him. With her money, I'm sure."

Jenny's laughter quieted down until even the giggles faded. "It's really that bad?"

"It's really that bad."

Molly picked up her bag and shut the door of her home behind her, stealing one last glance at the white cradle hulking over its spot by the window. She shuddered and looked around her quiet street from her vantage point at the top of the steps. Even with Jenny on the phone with her, she found herself having to quiet her racing pulse. Molly couldn't remember a time when she wasn't tense anymore, when she wasn't conscious of the deep pit of anxiety that lay in her stomach like a rock. She felt like she was driving alone, steering through traffic on a busy round-about, trapped in an endless circle with no idea which exit to take. Molly listened to Jenny talk about nursery furniture and snorted. She didn't even know if she was in the right lane.

Scott had done this to her, Molly thought, but corrected herself. She had let Scott do this to her, opened the door for him to step into her head and try to take control. She thought she'd

made a decision and moved on, thought she was doing right by
the hefty baby now apparently doing knee bends in her abdomen. But if life was one long multiple-choice quiz, Molly was
just figuring out that the correct answer wasn't always the obvious one. And she'd never been comfortable with guessing.

Molly heard Jenny's voice fade until it sounded far away.

"Uh, Mol?"

Her voice got clearer again, and Molly realized Jenny had
been looking at her phone screen.

"That crazy cradle in your living room?" Jenny asked. "It
cost Scott—or his mom—six thousand dollars." Her voice was
quiet with shock. Molly peered back over her shoulder at the
cradle visible through her front window.

"Tell me you're joking."

"Um, no," Jenny said. "Scott's trying *hard*. That boy wants
to get back on your good side like I want a permanent blowout."

Molly moved down the stairs to where her car was parked.

"It sure seems that way," she said. "Though I kind of wonder
which would be easier to maintain, you know?"

Molly said good-bye before clicking off her phone and moved
across the sidewalk, taking one slow step at a time. Her body
was heavy and off balance from the weight of her belly, and she
trudged over to her car. Molly glanced over her shoulder once
more, almost expecting Scott to be standing next to the staircase
behind her, before unlocking the door and getting in. She maneuvered her silver Audi down Walnut Street and turned left onto
Broad, only beginning to relax once she entered the stop-and-go
test of patience that was the Schuylkill Expressway.

The sleek car had been her first purchase after she'd secured
her job at Shulzster & Grace. It was a year old when she'd looked

at it, with just a couple of thousand miles on it. She'd been searching for a car that was safe for driving roads like this one, and that would last her for years. Molly didn't need fancy headlights or leather seats or windshield wipers that sensed a drop of rain before she did, but she'd fallen in love with how this car felt when it moved. She was able to tap on the gas pedal and take off like a high diver off a platform, whipping through the air, feeling like she was testing the edges of safety, flirting with danger, but still in complete control. She loved the way she felt when she was racing down the Schuylkill, sunroof open, blasting Alabama Shakes, singing "Hang Loose" to the trees and open sky.

Molly stepped on the brakes again and checked the gas gauge. Friday afternoon traffic didn't make for a journey filled with wind in one's hair and the joys of the open road, and she was hoping to be able to stretch the tank until next week's payday. All Molly saw ahead of her, though, was a convoy of red taillights. To the right below her, runners meandered along the bike path beside Kelly Drive. Boathouse Row stood beyond them, acting as home base for the college students who were rowing crew, stroking in measured time against the slight current of the water. Green forests of trees, vibrant with the heat and humidity of mid-July, climbed the hills on her left, and Molly's car started and stopped with the traffic along the road cut into the steep hillside. She tapped the brakes again.

A six-thousand-dollar cradle was sitting in her house. *Six thousand* dollars, for a temporary crib the baby would outgrow in months. Molly saw the needle on the dashboard shift downward and gulped, nerves dancing around her stomach. She'd been so worried about the baby or her parents taking away her hard-won independence, but they weren't the threats. It was the worry that controlled her actions now. Worry, with all of its persistent digging and scraping, working in around the edges of her confidence until it started to fray. The worry had robbed her of the security she'd worked to take for granted.

If she had stayed with Scott, this child would never have had to worry, at least about money, Molly knew. And she understood that by walking away from Scott, she was asking her baby to grow up in a life similar to the one she'd had: one where he or she would work weekends at a restaurant, come home from soccer practice some nights to eggs and toast for dinner, and go to school wearing a cousin's hand-me-downs instead of trendy jeans. Molly wasn't sure of the point where, for a parent, simply taking care of your own basic needs ended and acting out of selfishness began.

Scott complained about the way he grew up, but worry wasn't in his daily vocabulary. He was a man who thought playing Ultimate Frisbee in the living room was a neat way to use lamps as goal posts. He used a bank card to take money out of an account, but rarely put funds in. His idea of a routine was making sure he got a shower before appointments and got to the clubs by midnight. And with that came an attitude that he was entitled to all the good in his life—and something was very wrong if he didn't get what he wanted. Scott was always in such need—of attention, of time, of validation—that Molly had stopped thinking about what he could give. And he could give a lot.

Molly thought of Valentine's Day last year, when she'd walked into the kitchen in the morning to find Scott standing at the stove with a spatula in his hand, looking at her with a sheepish grin as a pink pancake burned on the griddle in front of him. There was batter splattered on the stove hood, the counters were covered with flour and crusty egg whites, and there were more dishes piled into the sink than Molly used in a week, but he was trying. Scott, in his slouchy designer sweats with an apron tied around his waist, was trying.

Molly glanced at the light that glowed now on the gas gauge and eased her foot off the brake.

It was so much to process on a nine-month deadline. Molly swallowed hard as she merged onto the exit for I-476 South to her parents' home. She glanced up to see the city skyline in her rearview mirror. The smell of car exhaust still clung to the air wafting through the vents, and through the sunroof she saw a jetliner cut through the blue sky high above her toward the airport on the south side of the city. A billowing streak of white was left in the plane's wake, and Molly watched the mist dissipate for a moment before turning her attention again to the journey home.

Two hours later, Molly was wedged into a wicker chair on her parents' back porch, hands wrapped around a glass of lemonade. She ignored the possibility that she'd gotten so wide that she might require help to get out of the chair later. Emily was walking out from the kitchen with what Molly was thrilled to see was a plate of chocolate chip cookies. Her father was settled into his seat to Molly's right, paging through the day's edition of the *Philadelphia Inquirer*.

"Ah, Molly. What kind of world are we living in? Can you believe that Congress just moved to filibuster again? Damned politicians are so busy proving how right they are they forget what they're trying to accomplish in the first place."

Jack pushed the paper to the side in frustration, leaned forward to take a warm cookie from the china plate, and turned his attention to his daughter. Emily went back into the house, leaving the two of them alone. Jack nodded in the direction of Molly's protruding belly. "So, speaking of a filibuster, I hear Scott is trying to stonewall you on ending the relationship?"

Molly shrugged her shoulders. "It looks that way, if you go by the massive bouquet of flowers sitting on my coffee table at home right now." She didn't mention the spaceship cradle that rested beside it. "Pop, this is driving me crazy."

"Well, it does all seem a bit over the top, Molly." Jack's voice was grim. He wasn't a person who acted out when his emotions overwhelmed him. Molly always wished she could have inherited that trait. Instead of his voice becoming raised, for instance, the angrier or more worried Jack got, it simply became deeper. Right now it sounded almost guttural.

"It's like he's completely ignoring what you want out of this and forcing his way on you," her father said. "I don't like this at all."

Molly reached for a second cookie. The fresh air of the suburbs felt good in her lungs. She could hear her mother moving around in the kitchen behind them, placing dishes into the washer and cleaning the sink. She knew Emily was listening to every word they said through the open window.

"But Scott's always been big with his gestures, Pop. He tried to buy me a puppy on our third date, you remember? I just don't know if his heart is really behind all this, or if Monica's egging him on, or what. For all I know, he doesn't want this baby any more than he wants somebody scratching his stupid Porsche."

"But then he's just playing with you. It doesn't make sense."

"Scott's used to getting what he wants." Emily's voice came

sailing through the window screen in reply. "And he can't have Molly."

Molly snorted at Emily's need to be involved and steer the conversation. At least she knew which parent she *did* take after.

"You broke up with him for a reason, Molly. Remember that." Jack was looking at Molly with an expression so intent she found it hard to meet his eyes. "If it's the financial aspect you're worried about, your mother and I will do what we can to help you out, you know."

Molly sipped her lemonade and shook her head. "Thanks, Pop, but if I'm going to do this on my own, I have to learn how to manage. I'll figure it out."

Jack wiped his mouth with a paper napkin and took a long glance at the floor, where Molly's large hobo bag lay. She noticed her keys hanging out of the open side pocket, the weathered Audi key fob in plain sight, and sighed.

"I know what you're going to say, Pop," she said. "Don't rub it in."

"Hey, I didn't say anything," her father replied. He held up his hands in mock denial. "You're a smart girl. You'll figure out what you have to do."

Molly didn't reply. She'd once made the mistake of telling her frugal parents the cost of her monthly car payments, and she didn't think they'd ever gotten over the shock. But at the time she'd easily been able to afford them.

"But," Jack continued, "I do have a friend who works at that Subaru dealership in town if you want to trade it in and get a good deal on a used car."

Emily walked back out onto the porch and sank down into the brown wicker chair next to Molly.

"They have some really nice family wagons over there, dear," she said. "Your father and I drove by it the other day."

Molly inhaled and gave her father a sidelong stare, raising an eyebrow.

"Oh, eat your cookies, Molly," Jack chuckled. "We're only trying to help."

Again, Molly was silent. From the ornamental cherry tree to their right, a cardinal called out with an insistent, desperate voice, looking for his mate. Molly tried to imagine living at her parents' house again, sitting on this porch every day with them and the baby. She thought about withstanding the constant flow of Emily's advice, about stepping around her father's projects as she hurried to work and came home. She pictured what she knew of her parents' peaceful nights in the family room, quietly doing crosswords or watching the news, their routine interrupted by an infant's cries echoing through the house. She couldn't see how it could work. It wasn't going to be all fresh cookies and iced tea, not once she and the baby were actually here. From what she knew, babies were loud. Molly's parents were not used to loud.

Molly sensed the closed-in feeling swoop in on her again. Her parents started talking about the steep rise in gas prices along Route 30, and Molly looked around for something else to grab her attention. Her gaze landed on the old guitar her father had left propped in the corner, and she smiled a little to herself. Molly's most favorite mornings as a child were on days like this, sitting on that very porch on her father's lap while he cradled the guitar and taught her how to pick out the first notes to "Quinn the Eskimo." It had been her favorite song, and she still asked him to play it sometimes when she came home to visit. Molly's father caught her eye and gave her a knowing smile.

Emily had fallen silent, too, and the three of them quietly
looked out at the backyard. It was a pitch-perfect, gorgeous summer day. The tree leaves were reflecting sunlight in a way that
made them look shiny, and there was just enough breeze to make
sitting on the back porch under the ceiling fans comfortable.
Molly was always impressed that her parents kept the yard so
immaculate. It overflowed with trees that were covered with
blossoms in the spring, framing the small house with an illusion
of luxury, and they managed to keep gardens full of plants that
bloomed at different times throughout the summer. There was a
constant, vibrant flow of glorious blossoms in the yard from
May through September. It had taken years for her parents to
achieve what they were looking at now.

Molly glanced at her mother, who sat in her chair with her
head bent toward the sound of her wind chimes, smiling at Jack
across the table. Molly sighed, sank back against the cushions,
and looked out over the backyard again. Liam had been to her
parents' house a few times before they'd broken up. He'd loved
to sit on the porch, and used to joke with her parents that they
should turn the backyard into a spa retreat. Molly wondered if
she'd be sitting here now, having this conversation, if he had been
the father of the baby.

The breeze picked up and rustled the chimes, making them
clang furiously for a brief moment. As they shouted their tinny
song, a couple of puffy seedpods flew across the lawn. Another
gust of air rustled the cocktail napkins Emily had placed beneath
the cookie platter. Molly realized without a doubt that if she had
been expecting this baby with Liam, she would still be sitting
there, on the back porch of her parents' house, listening to the
breeze whistle by, just as she was now. But the difference was

that Liam would be in the seat beside her, chatting with Jack, offering Molly a plate with the last cookie. That didn't matter, though, Molly knew, because that image wasn't her reality. She turned the past few weeks over in her head, rubbing the spot where her baby's foot had just kicked, and watched the purple irises, brilliant and regal, stand tall among the other foliage in this peaceful setting. Molly wondered what a heavy rain would do to all of these majestic flowers, and for a strange, twisted moment, wished a thunderstorm would blow in and shred all of the happy damned blossoms to pieces.

An hour and a half later, Molly locked her car, carefully looking up and down the quiet sidewalk of her narrow street, her keys and phone gripped in her hand. Almost all of the parking spots were taken at that time of night in her residential neighborhood, and she'd had to park at the end of the block, farther away from home than she felt comfortable with. The sun had set, and the last soft rays of dappled light seemed to hover in the gaps of the densely leaved tree branches overhead. She walked quickly, briskly, planting the heel of each foot hard enough that she could break into a run if necessary.

Molly climbed the stairs to her brownstone and entered the living room, ensuring the door was still locked on her arrival as always. Instinctively, she checked the time on the clock above the mantel. It was almost eight thirty. From what she knew of children, most of the young ones had long been tucked into bed by this time. She had concocted a fantasy of a working single mom's evening at home. But the reality was, that mom probably wasn't doing something idyllic like putting a casserole into the oven this late in the evening. She was more likely frantically trying to feed and change her child and put her to bed without so much as a bath or a book, because she knew the crying baby was so over-tired by this point she'd take hours to settle down. Dinner for the mother would be a bowl of cereal at eleven o'clock while wearing pajamas she pulled out of the hamper because there weren't any clean clothes in the drawers. She would collapse into bed, exhausted, promising herself that she'd wake up early to prepare that last report for work, that she'd wash the bottles tomorrow, spend time with the baby the next night. Molly's fantasy was evaporating like the bubbles from the imaginary bath she wouldn't have the luxury to give.

Molly set her pocketbook on the entranceway table and looked around her tidy living room. She placed a hand on her belly and took one more glance at the clock, thinking of herself months from now, a woman with her arms full of all she was responsible for in the world. That woman was alone, and Molly would bet good money that having the support of people who loved her was a security she needed more than just being able to say she could do it on her own. Molly took a deep breath and leaned back against the closed door, defeated.

She'd just made a decision.

CHAPTER NINE

August

Yes

✦

"Jenny, I don't know about this. I swear, if Scott weren't working late, and if I hadn't spent the entire day scrubbing baseboards, I never would have let you talk me into this."

They were in Midtown Village, standing in the middle of Drury Street outside of McGillin's Olde Ale House, their old go-to for work happy hours. They had purchased tickets months earlier to see a concert later that evening, and Jenny had talked Molly into making a night of it. Jenny was now trying to psych her up to go into the pub and meet a large group of their old friends, but Molly remained planted in her spot on the pavement. Most of their former coworkers from Shulzster & Grace were already inside, and Molly dreaded having to face them for the first time since her mortifying exit. She felt uncomfortable and lumpy in black stretch capris and a silky pink tunic-style maternity tank top. Even with some cute flat flip-flops she'd picked up at Bloomingdale's and a couple of funky silver bangles on her arms and big hoops in her ears, she felt like a fraud. Only little, hip, cute people should be out at bars like this, she thought, looking over her friend. Jenny was wearing skinny jeans paired with an incredibly high pair of metallic gold sandals. Like Molly, she'd worn them with a tank top, but hers was shimmering and backless. She wore her hair down and had loaded up on the beaded jewelry. *She looks like a hippie goddess,* Molly thought. *And I look like Buddha.*

"Come *on*, preggers." Jenny did a sort of bounce in front of Molly and tugged on her hand. "It'll be fun. They're supposed to be our friends, remember? And when was the last time you actually went out and had a good time? I swear, that fiancé of yours is keeping you locked in your tower like Rapunzel."

"Well, my hair *has* gotten a little too long for my tastes . . ." Molly twirled the ends of her dark hair around her finger.

"You're ridiculous, and you're kind of driving me crazy a little bit. Your hair looks beautiful, as does the rest of you, lady. Have you taken a good look at yourself in a mirror?" Jenny waved both of her hands up and down at Molly's now-voluptuous form. "You're working this baby bump you've got going to the max, and you have that glow I always thought people were lying about. So, look. I didn't get all dressed up to stand outside in this heat. I'm trying to forget my sorrows, and we've got a fun night ahead of us. Let's go inside and get it started. What do you say?"

Jenny seized Molly's arm and pulled her to the doorway. Molly was no more looking forward to standing in that crowded bar than she was to childbirth, but she had to laugh at her friend's enthusiasm, and allowed herself to be pulled up to the bouncer before hesitating again.

"Wait a minute, Jenny," she said to her friend's back. "What sorrows are you talking about? You've got a perfectly good husband sitting at home, weeping into his spaghetti, wondering why you want to be anywhere but with him. *Especially* when he didn't do anything wrong."

"Don't you try bringing up my personal life as a stalling tactic, Molly," Jenny said. "I'm not falling for it."

Molly saw that Jenny had slowed down, though. "All I'm saying is that you guys are supposed to have patched this all up. I'm all about a girls' night, but you moved back home so you could make it better. I'm sensing some avoidance here."

Her friend was pointedly ignoring her. Molly tugged on Jenny's arm until she stopped walking.

"Jenny. It's like the only thing keeping you from being happy again with Dan is your own stubbornness. You can't be afraid of being content. It's not going to jinx you. It doesn't work that way."

Molly knew her best friend, and she also knew tonight was just another way for Jenny to run away from her issues. Jenny only knew how to walk a straight line, and any deviation from that paralyzed her. She'd always done so well in her life that she'd never had a chance to learn how to fix the bad when it happened. And now Molly was so exasperated she let the words tumble out of her mouth before she could run them through her usual filter.

"You know how you asked me if you were being a shit?" Molly finally asked. Jenny's eyes widened before she even finished her thought. "Well, you're kind of being a shit." She paused. "No offense."

Jenny gaped at Molly in shock. "When did Molly Sullivan get so blunt?"

Molly laughed. "When she saw her best friend making a dumb mistake, that's when. Isn't that what I'm supposed to do, save you from yourself?"

Jenny chuckled. "Yeah, I suppose so. I'll just have to remember that when it's your turn to get a talking-to."

Molly shook her head. "Nah. I've got my life locked down and under control. You know me."

She smirked, but the words didn't come out as blithely as she'd intended. Molly saw Jenny's look of concern and ignored it by digging around in her bag for her wallet. Ever since their last big disagreement, Scott had acted like an extraordinarily good-looking puppy that had been caught misbehaving. He spoke overly softly now, showering her with kisses and enthusiastic compliments, bringing her frequent bouquets of massive flowers. Molly was trying so hard to forget his gloating, his refusal to budge, but it was difficult with Scott's constant reminders that he'd hurt her in the first place, that he had something to make up for.

"I'm right, aren't I, though?" Molly asked. "About Dan? *I* feel guilty knowing he's got to be totally confused and heartbroken, and he's not even my husband."

"Yeah." Jenny tried to laugh. "But that's just because you like to fix everything."

"Still."

Jenny started to take a step, then stopped again. "I know, okay?" Her voice was tight. "You're right. Fine. I said it."

"So why don't you call him? Invite him out with us?"

"Because I don't really want to, Molly. I mean, I do, but . . . I don't know. I've been stubborn, and I admit I possibly made a dumbass move by moving out. And moving back in hasn't gone so well, either." Jenny used one hand to rub at her eyes. The air around them was heavy with humidity. They were just steps away from the air conditioning—and noise, and people, and sticky floors—of the bar. "But honestly, Mol, I was just looking

forward to a night out when I didn't have to *think* about any of
that stuff. Does that make sense?"

She was standing beside Molly on the sidewalk between the
street and bar, frozen. "Can I tell you something, Molly? Since
we're being blunt? It was almost a relief to think that maybe Dan
had cheated on me, that maybe he just wanted out, or was just
as selfish as my dad. Then I wouldn't have to feel like I was disappointing him anymore." Jenny looked down at the sidewalk.

"Disappointing Dan? The guy's been in love with you since
high school," Molly protested.

"Yeah, I know," Jenny said. "And I can't help feeling like I
should stop wasting his time. That maybe this marriage has run
its course."

Molly shook her head. "You're Catholic. Even if you don't go
to church, I know you. That's not a possibility."

"I'm serious, Molly. Maybe this was a sign he should get out
while he can. Find someone who can give him income and babies
and the perfect family life. A woman whose body works the way
it should." She took a breath. "Somebody who isn't broken."

"Shit, Jenny."

"Yeah, I know." Jenny looked to the side. "It finally hits the
fan, right?"

"Girl, what am I going to do with you?" Molly threw her arm
around her friend's shoulders and squeezed. "Dan didn't marry
you just to break up during an incredibly rough spot. It makes
total sense for you to need to take a breather. But for the last
time, you should let Dan be with you during that breather. Let
him help you. It's all he wants to do."

She was so exasperated. Of course Jenny was right about Molly's impulse to fix problems, but this issue had an easy solution.

Molly had always wondered why people needed to complicate perfectly good lives. Tonight, though, she could admit that it was often easier to see the answer to a question when you stood outside of the equation.

Jenny chuckled, then shook her head. "Okay, but you're still not getting out of this tonight. I'll sit down with him tomorrow and have a proper talk, get it all out on the table, I promise. But right now I just need something to shake me up. Get me out of this funk."

"Well," Molly said, showing the bouncer outside the front entrance her ID, "a margarita should get you started."

As soon as they entered the dark confines of the historic pub, Molly and Jenny spotted their old friends from S&G crowded around groups of two-tops shoved together, forming large islands of tables filled with bottles and half-full glasses. Laughter rang out at frequent intervals, bouncing back down from the dark wooden beams on the ceiling. Large mirrors that reflected the weak light to the packed room hung on walls that also featured framed photos of celebrities and antique photographs of the city. A gigantic American flag hung from the same dark rafters.

Someone in the group saw them enter and waved them over. The two women exchanged one uncomfortable glance before pasting brave smiles on their faces to approach their old colleagues. Molly maneuvered her belly around drunk men in loosened ties, their dark hair gelled and faces beginning to show the stubble of Friday night, and squealing women with South Philly accents, all freed for the weekend from the pressures of their work in the publishing and government and insurance offices of Center City. At the very least, she figured, she might run into somebody who had a lead or a contact for her—even if, as Scott kept reminding her, no one was going to want to hire a pregnant woman. Molly shook the thought out of her head. One of her favorite songs from the Pogues, "Fairytale of New York," began playing over the loudspeakers, and she bounced a little to the sound as she walked. Within minutes, she and Jenny were engulfed in laughter with their old friends. Molly allowed herself, finally, to relax, knowing it wouldn't be for very long.

An hour later, she stood between two stools at the long, straight bar on the first floor. She'd been surrounded by a throng of people three deep, but Pat, the middle-aged Friday night bartender, had recognized her and motioned for people to give her space to get through. Jenny was still back at the tables in the center of the room, surrounded by people and laughing her way through her third margarita.

"Molly Sullivan, old girl!" Pat reached out for one of her hands in a jolly, familiar gesture as his other pulled a pint from the tap. Liquor bottles stood like sentinels on the glass shelves behind him, stacked against the mirrored wall like guards of her past.

"Hey, Pat! It's good to see you!" Molly exclaimed, and leaned forward, using her forearms to prop herself on the bar. "It's been a long time, buddy."

"I'll say," Pat replied. "It's not often I get to see a beautiful face like yours around these parts." He didn't seem to notice the glare of the woman standing next to Molly. "What'll you have, Molly? Your usual?"

He dropped a handful of ice in a short glass with practiced speed and had his hand around a bottle of Johnnie Walker before she could stop him.

"Not for me, Pat, not today," she laughed, and backed away from the bar. "Or for the next couple of months or so." The bartender's eyes widened when he saw the reason for her restraint.

He quietly opened a bottle of sparkling water and poured it, instead of the whiskey, into the glass. He was nodding, but to Molly's relief, not asking questions. He tucked a slice of lime onto the rim and slid it across the bar to her without a sound.

"Well, you certainly made somebody speechless." Molly heard the laughing voice from beside her, and a forgotten shiver ran through her body. "I see you haven't lost your touch."

The shock from hearing a memory speak aloud rooted her into place for a moment. Then Molly turned to face the man who was now grinning at her, his nose scrunching up between the blue of his deep-set eyes in exactly the way she remembered. Her heart lurched in her chest, and Molly felt her face break open into a wide smile before she could catch herself.

"Liam."

His dusty brown hair was the same as it had been, his eyelashes dark and thick, and his eyes a shining cobalt. Molly felt her cheeks flush hot. The din of the bar seemed to fall away, and for a moment, neither of them said a word.

Liam was facing her, leaning against the bar with a casual lack of self-consciousness. His expression was open, and his genuine, elated grin made Molly feel for a moment like she did when she drove her car down an open highway: exhilarated, free, but still with the assurance that she was buckled up safely. Liam watched her, taking in her face with an appreciation that was honest, yet tentative. He held a full pint of Guinness in one hand.

"Molly." His voice still held the same earnest warmth. "Hey. It's good to see you again."

"You, too." Molly smiled and, for all her effort, could not make the muscles in her face go slack. "It's good to see you, too."

She couldn't think of anything more to add. For a brief

moment, with Liam standing so close to her, with the clamor of
pub-goers calling out for drinks muted by the sound of the blood
pounding through her veins, the weight of her troubles fell away.
For that second, Molly forgot that she was pregnant, that she
had a fiancé at home, that she was unemployed. She had no worries or fears about the weeks and months to come. They suddenly
became the minor details of her life, the extraneous, the silly
little minutiae that didn't really matter, especially when she was
surrounded by the noise of the bar and the dim light and the
knowledge that Liam was right in front of her. How Molly
wished she could live inside a bubble of that feeling.

Liam smiled at her and placed his beer on the bar. As he
leaned forward and lightly touched her elbow with his hand, all
Molly could focus on was the feeling of her nerve endings spark-
ing and the ocean-blue eyes of the man in front of her.

"How've you been? It's so funny to see you here. My brother
and I are going to that concert at the Electric Factory later and
stopped in on a whim to get a drink."

"You guys are going tonight?" Molly touched his arm before
she could stop herself. "My friend and I are going to that show,
too. I heard tickets sold out in twenty minutes." The band playing that night had recently exploded onto the popular scene,
bringing with it a mix of bluegrass and folk music that quickly
became trendy among other indie groups. Neither of them mentioned that it had been Molly who introduced Liam to the band's
music, years earlier, on an impromptu weekend road trip to
Maine because one of them wanted a lobster roll. Liam cleared
his throat.

"So, I just ran into a couple of the guys from the office." He
cocked his head, curious. He hadn't seemed to notice the swell

of her belly under her shirt. "Word on the street is that life has gotten a little, um, busy for you?"

Molly laughed at his polite phrasing. "What have you heard?"

"Well, let's see. Apparently, you're what they call a 'freelancer' now—" Liam grinned when Molly groaned.

"Well, that's the kindest way to say it, yes."

"—and that you, for all intents and purposes, have settled down."

So he'd known about the pregnancy, but was being discreet. Molly could have hugged him.

"I'm glad you're happy, Molly, really." Liam paused for a moment and watched her face. Molly was very aware of the distance between them, the inches between his body and hers, and the impulse to lay her hand over his and keep it there.

Molly's smile faltered. "Well, you know. Thank you." She swallowed hard. She noticed new laugh lines around Liam's eyes, and was startled by an urge to reach out and run her fingertips along them. She shook her head and chuckled. "I can't pretend I'm not itching to get another job, though."

"Well, yeah, I don't blame you!" Liam replied. "You were the best PR whiz kid S&G had in their arsenal. You were amazing. That's why I was surprised to hear that you'd left. I can't imagine you doing anything else."

Liam took a sip of his stout, and when Molly saw his bicep flex under his T-shirt she faltered in her response. She felt her cheeks heat up, picturing the tattoo that was etched into his right shoulder blade under the soft cotton. She'd discovered the circular Celtic cross, acquired after Liam returned home from a hiking tour of Ireland, one rainy Saturday afternoon when the Phillies game they were supposed to see got washed out and they found themselves otherwise occupied. This was months after Liam started with Shulzster & Grace. It was also right before Liam's on-and-off-again girlfriend from college moved back home from Colorado and asked him for another chance.

Molly had a necklace she kept at home that bore the same symbol as Liam's cross. She'd tucked it away, far in the back of one her dresser drawers, soon after she'd wandered into Barnes & Noble that fateful Friday night. The pendant was still there, safely cushioned in its protective box.

"How about you?" Molly asked. "Do you miss it at all?" She meant the job, she thought.

Liam shook his head and laughed. "No way, Molly. Becoming a teacher was the best decision I could have made. That job is the hardest, most fun thing I've ever done. It's a weird combo."

"That's funny. That's exactly what my friend Dan says."

Liam stood up straighter. "Wait, I think I know your friend Dan. He's Jenny Kim's husband, right?"

Molly nodded. Over Liam's shoulder she spotted Jenny at the other end of the room. She was sitting by herself, and as Molly watched, Jenny looked around before pulling her phone from her bag in a discreet motion. Molly knew she was scrolling through the notifications, having seen her do it thousands of times to check for a text from Dan. Molly saw her friend's shoulders sag for the briefest of moments, an uncharacteristic move for Jenny. A former coworker sat down in the seat beside her, ready to chat, and Jenny shoved the phone back into her bag in time to answer the friend's question, all without missing a beat. Molly bit the inside of her cheek and turned her attention back to Liam's eyes. Her blood began flowing a little more quickly once again. She could feel the baby moving inside her belly, reminding her of her place in reality.

"Speaking of married people, how are things with Stephanie? I saw the engagement announcement in the paper a while back," Molly said. "I'm glad it worked out for you."

Molly spoke the truth. Liam was one of the few men she'd met who deserved all the good that came his way. To her surprise, Liam shrugged and rolled his eyes to the side.

"Yeah, actually, it didn't so much. She decided to move back to Denver."

"What? I'm so sorry."

"Nah, it's okay. It wasn't meant to be. Her job was more important to her, she said."

Molly shook her head. "How so? What was she doing out there?" To Molly's further astonishment, Liam chuckled. He placed his beer on the bar.

"Ah, she decided to go into full-time missionary work."

"Okay . . ."

Liam laughed outright. "She became a nun."

Molly laughed, too, before she could stop herself. "Oh, no, really? Oh, Liam, I'm so sorry. I guess you can't really compete with God, right?"

Liam shook his head. "No, I suppose you can't. So, she's back there, and I'm back here, right where it all started." He fell quiet, his eyes sweeping her face before meeting her gaze again. Molly didn't speak.

"I gotta admit, Mol," he said. "I'm a little jealous of you."

Molly felt her eyes widen in surprise.

"I'm serious, Molly. It looks like you've got it all. Okay, so maybe not the job, so much"—Liam winced in apology as Molly grimaced—"but you have the important stuff. You're getting married. You're having a baby."

He took another sip of his beer and shrugged, looking away from Molly for the first time since they'd begun talking. "I can't wait to have children of my own one day. I think that's why I like teaching so much—I have a hundred and ten kids to take care of right now while I wait for my one. And here you are, already there."

He didn't miss the look of dismay Molly felt flash across her face.

"Did I just embarrass myself? I did, didn't I?" Liam laughed and looked around at the throngs of people in the bar. "I should go find my brother before I make it worse."

"It was good to see you, Liam." Molly's voice was soft.

He and Molly looked at each other for a silent moment. Neither of them moved. Pat swept Liam's empty pint glass from the bar—the bartender didn't ask if he'd like to stay for another—and broke the spell.

"It was good to see you, too, Molly. Good luck with everything." Liam reached his hand out and laid it on her belly, then withdrew it in a sudden movement. "Oh, I'm sorry. I didn't mean to do that. That was weird."

"It's fine," Molly assured him. "People do it all the time."

She could feel the warmth where his hand had been after he'd walked away. She took a breath and looked at the crush of people around her, the noises and smells of the bar flooding her senses again with a shock. She noticed that her engagement ring had gotten stuck on her swollen finger and, wincing with discomfort, twisted it until the diamond was centered again. She couldn't find Jenny among the groups of people around her, so she moved toward the bathroom. She was ready to leave for the show, and was determined to not look for Liam in the crowd once they got there.

Molly opened the door to the bathroom just as another

woman was walking out, shaking her head at Molly as if in warn-ing. Acting on instinct, Molly pushed her way into the room before she'd even heard the sound and rushed to Jenny when she saw her. Crumpled against the wall of an open stall, her best friend sat crouched on the filthy floor, arms wrapped around her knees. Her sobs were bouncing off of the dingy metal partitions beside the toilet. She was drunk, weeping, and mumbling about broken bellies. Molly patted Jenny's hair away from her face, where it hung like a curtain, wet from her tears, as if Jenny were a child who'd been bullied on the playground and left behind.

Molly watched her friend wipe the smudges of mascara away from her eyes with the back of her hand. Jenny had everything that was important in the world waiting for her in an apartment in Old City. No, Molly thought, she didn't have the baby yet, but when that baby did come, the child would be like a Sixers play-off game won in overtime: all the more exhilarating because the fight to get there was so much harder. Molly pictured Liam, single now, still out in the bar, talking with his brother. She had let him walk away because she'd thought he didn't want her. She'd moved on, but he had come back, because sometimes life's timing doesn't move by our own personal clocks. Molly bent down, moving awkwardly around the weight of her swollen belly. She slung Jenny's arm around her neck for support and helped her friend walk through the door.

Molly woke the next day with a brain like a mosh pit and a hor-rible need to use the bathroom, but she couldn't figure out how to get out of her bed. One leg was trapped under her C-shaped pregnancy pillow, the other tangled in the mess of sheets that snaked under and around her swollen body. She looked over her shoulder for help, but Scott's side of the mattress was empty save for a crumpled pile of T-shirts he'd left at the foot of the bed. Her back still throbbed from the pressure of being on her feet all night with a belly full of baby, and Molly pushed herself upright to extract herself from her self-induced trap. She rolled out of bed and stood, only to trip over another pile of clothes—Scott's shorts, this time, and for some reason they were on her side of the room. She threw out a hand to steady herself on the dresser and trudged out to the bathroom in the hallway.

Once there, she found a wet towel lying in a heap outside the bathtub. Molly stooped down to use it as a mop after her foot landed in the water pooling on the tile. She gulped when she saw that she was also clutching her fiancé's dirty underwear in her hand, and dropped the boxers into the hamper faster than she knew her swollen fingers could move. She used the toilet and brushed her teeth, worries of Jenny swirling through her head, battling for dominance with the exhaustion that lay thick over her brain like a storm.

Molly was still wearing the oversized T-shirt of Scott's she'd pulled on for bed the night before when she stumbled downstairs to the kitchen. She found her fiancé standing at the island in his pajama bottoms, barefoot and shirtless. He was scrolling through his email on his phone, intent, holding a coffee cup in his hand. Molly's heart began pounding in her chest, moving at a much faster pace than her muddled thoughts. She reached for a glass of water, but stopped at the sight of the coffeepot.

"Is that the same coffee from yesterday morning?"

Scott waited a beat before he looked up from his screen. "Huh?"

Molly sighed. "Did you wash out the pot this morning? You didn't do it yesterday."

"Oh, shit, no." Scott peered into his mug. "I was wondering why it tasted a little thicker than usual."

"See?" Molly said. "That's exactly what I mean."

"Were you talking about something?" Scott's forehead wrinkled into a question mark, and he lowered his phone to focus on Molly.

Molly's heart slammed itself against her rib cage now. Dismayed. She was so dismayed. About the coffee, yes. But it was also the towels, the clothes, the crumbs, the constant, constant mess, and she wanted to rip the mug out of Scott's hand and throw it against the wall, or smash his stupid phone to bits. She wanted to be destructive for once, to stop being so good all the time, to do something that would make Scott sit up and notice that this was all wrong. *Him,* she thought. Her entire life had been reshaped to wrap around Scott. Molly fought the urge to raise her voice and was completely unsuccessful.

"I'm *always* talking about something." Molly's voice was high-pitched, shaking. "I'm talking about how it's not right that our floors are your laundry hamper. Or how I'm tired of cabinets crammed with empty Pop-Tart boxes and overflowing trash cans I can't lift because you don't empty them."

Her chest was heaving, and she had to stop to catch her breath.

"Shit, Molly, calm down," Scott said. "I was just trying to drink my coffee."

But Molly had started, and after months of keeping silent, she wasn't finished. It was all so little, but it wasn't. It was huge and it was changing her life and he had to know. Scott was watching her with wide eyes, his mouth hanging open just a bit.

"Scott, this"—she gestured wildly at the mess surrounding them—"isn't me. This isn't how I want my house and my life to be. And I don't want our relationship to be like this. We don't have a housekeeper, Scott. And I don't want to do it all."

"Molly, where is all this coming from?"

"That's what I'm trying to tell you! This isn't new. I've talked to you about all of this before. I don't want to bring my baby into a world filled with candy wrappers in the couch cushions, or floors that are so dirty our socks stick to them when we walk. I don't want my child to think it's normal to have to take a bowl out of the sink and wash it before getting breakfast in the morning." Tears pricked up in Molly's eyes.

There was a moment of silence while Scott regarded her. Maybe she just wasn't meant to live with somebody else, Molly thought. Maybe she was the one with the problem. The olive color of Scott's eyes had deepened while she was talking. When he took his turn to speak, his voice was calm.

"So," he said, "why don't you go cry to Liam about it?"

"What?" Molly stared at him.

"I said, go find Liam. See if he cares. Hell, sleep with him if that's what you really want to do."

"Why are you bringing up Liam?"

"Oh, don't give me that, Molly." Scott turned to her. "I swung by McGillin's last night with my friends after work. I saw you getting all cozy at the bar with your old boy toy."

Scott watched Molly stutter as she tried to reply. "So are you cheating on me now, Molly? You get what's best of me, then run around behind my back with that tool?" He was glaring at her, the pupils of his eyes dancing to look at hers, but his tone wasn't angry. It was hurt.

Molly stood in place. She couldn't move. "You didn't speak to me. I didn't see you. Why didn't you say something?"

"Because I didn't want to have to punch the guy's face in, that's why."

"So you just hung around the bar and watched me talk with him?"

"Nah, I didn't hang around watching you," Scott said. "We went to a strip club instead."

He set his coffee cup on the butcher block island with a clatter, splattering the dark liquid all over its surface. Molly watched the stain spread across the wood.

"God, I can't even see you without picturing the way you were looking at him. You don't appreciate any of what I've given you, Molly. The attention. The love. And yeah, I'll say it, the life you lead because of me," Scott said. "You don't *respect* it. And I've had it, Molly. You need to back off."

Scott straightened and took a step toward her. "You're a control freak, Molly. Do you know that? Everything has to be perfect according to your crazy standards. You have these, these *rules*. It's suffocating."

"*My* rules?" Molly sputtered.

Scott's words felt like the stab of a knife into her lungs. She knew she should walk away, stop this from getting worse, but some stubbornness in her made her keep pushing. So Molly forged on, even though she knew they were spiraling out of control. Because she loathed the way he felt her up every time she walked past him, how he licked his lips instead of using a napkin after eating if he thought no one was watching, the insults he said were jokes, how he messed up her home and her confidence and didn't seem to ever, ever want to make any of it better. As much as she cared for him, it all felt like she was acting a role in a movie Scott was directing. So now that there was so much fear in her heart she couldn't find her way around it, Molly did the only thing she knew how to do. She focused on what she thought she could change.

"You leave dishes in the sink, all the time. We're attached to other houses, Scott. You can't leave food in the sink like that, or we'll get bugs. Same goes with the spills on the floor, and the counters. It shouldn't take this much effort to follow city health code."

"It's a few dishes, not a freaking landfill, Molly," Scott said. "I'm not going to do everything you want me to."

"Everything? Scott, I'm the *only* one who does anything around here. The groceries are in the fridge because of me. We have electricity because I write the bills. I clean the floors and do the laundry and make the meals. If I had any idea this was how you were going to be . . ."

Molly was so worked up she was sweating through her pajamas now. She could feel the cotton of Scott's T-shirt sticking to her back.

"What, Molly? What would you do?"

Molly was silent.

"This isn't just about a couple of dirty dishes, Mol, and you know it," Scott said.

"Then what else could it be?"

He just looked at her. "Tell me, what choices do you have?" Scott asked.

Again, she couldn't answer him.

"Go ahead, Molly," Scott said. "Leave me. If you hate me so much, think I'm such an *awful* guy, then break it off. In fact, run to Liam and see how well he can take care of you. How long do you think you'll be able to stay in this house once the landlord figures out you'll never be able to buy it?"

A strange kind of desperation filled Molly, making her feel like she had to cling to the moment, hold on, make the argument last. Because she didn't know what was going to happen after this. She didn't know what to do. This was the father of her baby. This was the choice she had made. And she couldn't let it all fall apart in front of her. She needed time.

There was a vein pulsing on the side of Scott's neck. Molly couldn't stop staring at it.

"You can't just—" Molly couldn't get any more words out. Scott's voice dominated hers.

"What? What can't I do, Molly?" Scott took a step toward her, towering over her with all the lean strength in his tall frame. Without thinking, Molly backed up and knocked her head into the refrigerator. A wine bottle that had been on top of the fridge fell to the floor, shattering into thousands of splintered shards. The wine splattered onto every visible surface in the kitchen. Scott was planted in front of Molly, facing her. She couldn't move. She watched wine drip off of her cabinet onto the countertop, leaving burgundy streaks in its wake, like blood seeping from a broken nose.

"Molly, don't you think I'm scared, too?" Scott pulled back. He ignored the mess and looked at Molly. "You're not the only one whose life is changing."

"But . . ." Molly tried to argue with him, but came up with nothing.

"But what? You act like I knocked you up on purpose. You've been with me for years, but suddenly want me to be somebody I'm not. And now I see you trolling the bars for better options? You paint me as the bad guy, Molly, but I think you've got it wrong."

"That's not how it was, Scott," Molly protested. "You know me better than that."

Molly didn't try to stop the tears from coming. They were deadlocked, she and Scott, just pushing back and forth in the tight space of their relationship, and neither one of them was going to get anywhere unless somebody stepped out of the way. Forgetting that she was Jack's daughter, Molly yelled louder than she'd ever heard herself.

"Scott, this isn't what I signed up for!" She was searching his eyes, looking for some softness. She wanted him to tell her he would make it all right. "Is this really what you want?"

"It ain't all sunshine and rainbows, Molly," Scott said, "so you can spare me the drama. But I'm not listening to your orders anymore."

Molly's head was bowed into her chest. She hadn't meant to get to this place. She hadn't planned this out. Her sobs broke over her huddled upper body like waves beating a beach's sandy floor. She couldn't fight to the surface, couldn't catch a breath. The waves kept pushing her down, and she had forgotten how to swim.

Scott backed away from her in a sudden movement and strode out of the kitchen. On his way out, he knocked his fist into the wall beside the doorway. Chunks of drywall crumbled from the dent he left behind and fell to the floor in a tinny waterfall of noise. Scott stopped for a moment, as if surprised by his own strength. Then he walked away without looking back.

Molly stayed, glued in her place against the refrigerator door, holding her breath. Her heart was still beating so hard that she began to feel faint, and she stared at the hole in the previously blank canvas of her kitchen wall. The stained glass above the doorway looked ridiculous above it, an intricate masterpiece, ornate and decorative, framing the glaring blemish. Molly took in deep breaths, trying to calm herself down, but every nerve in her body was on alert, waiting.

She noticed Scott's dirty mug lying on its side on the island, and at the sight of it, Molly shook her head hard, stood up straight, and began to clean. She was still shaking as she wiped away the spilled coffee and a few stray grounds from the rim of the cup. Her fingers trembled as she scrubbed the tan ring of an old stain clinging to the inside of the mug's white ceramic surface. She pulled the trash can over from the wall, shoved down the contents inside to flatten them, and began scooping in dustpans full of broken glass, willing her legs to work as she did. Pulling a plastic basket filled with cleaning supplies out from under the sink, Molly washed the cabinets, scrubbing them one at a time, the handles, the undersides. She mopped the floor and stood, wobbling slightly, on a stool to wipe wine stains from the tops of the doors. She did not slow down until each dish was in its place and every surface gleamed.

At one point, Molly caught sight of herself in the microwave door. Her hair was hanging around her face in knotted masses, and red blotches covered her face and neck. She had to use the bathroom again, but she could hear Rush blasting now from her speakers in the living room. She was allowing Scott to trap her where she was, barefoot and pregnant. Molly looked around her clean kitchen, searching for something, anything, that was out of place or needed an extra scrub. She was stuck in place, afraid to walk away.

CHAPTER TEN

September

No

They just didn't look right.

Molly blew out a hard breath of air in frustration and stepped back to stare at the nursery curtains again. One side was crooked, she knew it, and she wouldn't be able to leave the room until she straightened it out. Molly used a hand to knead a muscle in the small of her back, trying to work out a cramp while she scrutinized the window treatments. She'd been so excited to find brand-name curtains on eBay in exactly the same off-white, green-polka-dotted pattern she'd wanted, and, proud of her thriftiness, had purchased ribbon from a craft store to use as tie-backs. But she hadn't been able to get one of the ribbons to tie properly. Her patience was evaporating as quickly as the late-afternoon light, but with one final, stubborn yank, she managed to straighten the bow. Satisfied, she let herself walk out of the room. She was shivering with nervous excitement. This had to be like running your first marathon, and Molly was ready for somebody to fire the start gun already. There was only so much training a girl could do.

Molly heaved herself down the stairs with as much speed as the weight of her belly would allow. She had to brace her body against the banister as she did so, unsure of her balance this far into her pregnancy.

"Mom!" Molly called out toward the kitchen. "I'm going to run back to my house to grab another box of the baby's things. Should I just meet you at the restaurant?"

"Honey." Emily's voice moved back down the hall. "I don't like you traveling by yourself! Why don't you let your father go with you?"

"Mom, I'm perfectly capable of driving a half hour into the city." Molly rolled her eyes at the wall and dug her keys out of the diaper bag she'd started using as a pocketbook.

"But what if something happens?"

"Then I'll call you and drive myself to the hospital! It's not like I'm going to have the baby on the Blue Route," Molly replied.

"It's happened, Molly," her mother said, and sighed. "Fine. Have it your way."

There was a pause.

"But we're going to pick you up at your house before dinner."

The sound of the mixer started, making a familiar churning sound from its place on the laminate countertop in the back of the house. Emily was making a chocolate cake for Molly's birthday.

"Fine," Molly sighed under her breath, and shut the front door behind her.

There wasn't a sound in the house other than the echoes of Molly's movements. Her footsteps rang off the spare mopped floors as she padded up and down the stairs, gathering the last of the baby gear into a large plastic bin. Molly had left most of her dishes, cutlery, and pots and pans where they were, neatly arranged behind the pristine white doors of her kitchen cabinets. Her books remained sitting on the numerous shelves lining the tan-colored wall of her bedroom. She wouldn't be needing any of them once the baby was born, so she'd decided to leave them behind and list the house as-is on websites directed at students and staff of the local universities. She hoped for graduate or law school students as potential subletters, people too overwhelmed with their studies to even consider trashing the place, or a single professor with an eye for cleanliness and simple dinner parties. It was hard enough to leave this home behind. It'd been her first baby, and she wanted to leave it in the care of someone she could trust.

Molly closed the top of the bin and pushed it with her feet to the base of the stairs. Her lower back was throbbing with an awful kind of pain, and she knew she'd been overdoing it. Her parents had made plans with Jenny and her a month ago to go to dinner for her birthday, even though Molly had begged them not to make a big deal of it. But they'd insisted, because a birthday is a new beginning, Emily said. And one never, *ever*, she pronounced, ignores a chance to start fresh. So Molly would let them decide on Victor Café, of all places, the Italian restaurant famous for its opera-singing waitstaff. The last thing Molly felt like doing tonight was eating a massive meal of garlicky pasta and being serenaded by earnest young tenors, but her parents had been so excited to do something nice for her.

She grabbed her jug of water and walked over to the couch, collapsing into the deep cushions with a sigh. A small part of her wondered if she'd be able to lift herself back up when the time came, and she hoped her family would arrive sooner rather than later. Molly leaned her head back against the couch and closed her eyes for a moment, just a brief second, but it was long enough for her to fall off into the deep doze of the exhausted.

Another muscle spasm woke Molly just as a loud knocking started at the door, both of them jarring in their intensity. The cramp wrapped itself around Molly's abdomen, making her gasp with the pain of its intense grip.

"Oh, no," Molly said aloud. In an attempt to maneuver up and off the couch, she rolled to the side, making sure both feet had firm contact with the floor before pushing herself upright off the back of the sofa. The knocking came again, louder and more insistent this time. She knew that her parents, aware of the obnoxious sound the doorbell made, would avoid using the buzzer, but she wondered if she'd slept so long that they'd been out there a while and were impatient. It wasn't like them to knock like their fists were potential battering rams. Molly slowly made her way across the floor, grunting with each step. A deep sense of dread had spread through her body, as if her muscle aches were connected somehow to her intuition telling her not to open the door.

Molly swung open the door anyway, took one look at the person on the other side of the threshold, and fought the immediate urge to slam it shut.

"Scott."

He was leaning against the doorway, exasperation etched

into the tan skin of his face, as if he'd had to wait for hours. Scott looked like he was dressed for sailing, but that was a hobby not usually associated with someone terrified of water more than three feet deep. Molly looked at his slim-cut jeans and boat shoes. He was even wearing a lightweight blue sweater bedecked with jaunty nautical stripes. A vague sense of curiosity worked its way through her alarm. It looked, she thought, like Scott's mother had taken him for a doll and started dressing him.

"Jeez, Molly, you took forever." Scott ran his hand through his tousled hair. "Do you have a second? I need to talk to you."

"Scott, this might not be the best time," Molly replied. She placed a hand on her belly. "Also, I just don't want to see you. I told you I'd talk with you when I was ready. You need to give me some space."

"Molly, just let me in. I promise, I come in peace." He held up his hands, palms out to her in surrender, and took a step forward. "Honest."

"Fine." Molly ushered him through the doorway, looking around at the empty sidewalk outside before closing the door. She wondered when her parents were supposed to arrive. "But you're not sitting down."

She remained at the front door, one hand on the doorknob, at the ready to allow her ex-boyfriend's exit as soon as she could. Scott had been nonstop with the attention in the last few weeks. He called once a day and texted even more. His outlandish attempts to win her approval were beginning to make the space-age cradle look pedestrian. Molly's other hand rested on her lower back, willing away the pain that still throbbed against her kidneys.

Scott sighed and started to sit down on the living room couch before he registered her pointed glare and stood up straight again with uncharacteristic speed.

He rubbed his palms along his jeans.

"I know I've been a little pushy, Molly," Scott said.

Molly snorted.

"And that's why I wanted to come by. I need to apologize. I've been going about this the wrong way."

"Well, better late than never."

"I know, okay? And I'm sorry. I just started to get scared. I realized that if we weren't together, you know, as a couple, there was a very good chance I'd rarely get to see this baby, and I didn't know how to talk to you rationally about it." He winced. "During daylight."

Molly shook her head in surprise. "But that doesn't make any sense. What's with the sudden paternal instinct?" She regarded her ex with an odd feeling of sadness. "Are you confused? Did your parents put you up to this?"

Scott threw his arms wide.

"I'm not confused, Molly. And, um, I never exactly, uh, *told* my parents about the whole baby thing."

"Scott!"

"What?" Scott's hand was plowing through his hair, forming rows in his backswept mane like a tractor in a dusty wheat field. "Finding out about the pregnancy threw me off, and then you not wanting to be with me? I felt like a loser. You think I'm going to advertise that? My mom would've been crushed. You had all the cards in your hands, and I was reduced to just being the sperm donor."

Molly's jaw dropped.

"Cards? Sperm donor?" she asked. "I'm not playing a game,

here, Scott. We're not good for each other, which is why we broke up. I happened to have gotten pregnant. One had nothing to do with the other. The breakup would've happened eventually, whether I had a baby growing in me or not."

"Yeah, but—"

"Wait. Let me finish." Molly heard herself speaking the words she'd practiced saying, but found her confidence in them faltering with Scott standing in front of her, begging to make it all right. "There's no game here. I have to go about my life. And I have to start my family with the people who actually want to be in it."

"Molly. Come on. You can't mean that. All those years."

Scott's expression was downcast, and his eyes were so wide and imploring that Molly almost felt her resolve start to shift. Almost.

"I made this decision a long time ago, Scott." The next words slipped out of her mouth more easily than she could have anticipated. "And I'm sticking to it."

"We had fun times together, you and me!"

Molly choked out a laugh. "Scott, we fought half the time we were together! We want none of the same things. We couldn't even agree on what radio station to listen to in the car, let alone any of the big decisions. Did you know I'm planning to breast-feed the baby?"

Scott's face contorted in disgust before he could catch himself. He shook his head. "But can't I have changed my mind, Molly? I mean, look at you. You're awesome." He waved his arm in her direction in a sweeping arc. The gesture made her feel, once again, like she was on a stage, like this was all some sort of strange show. She just wanted to sit down.

"You're all independent, and you've got this good job. This whole house is baby-proofed already and you've got all this gear."

He paused and looked around the room. His gaze stopped to linger on the plastic bin by the stairs. "Wait. Why did you pack it all up?"

Molly set her lips in a line, her refusal to answer obvious.

"You're doing this on your own," he continued. "It's kind of a turn-on, you know. This Wonder Woman act? You not needing me anymore makes me realize how much I want you."

It was Molly's turn to shake her head. Another cramp had formed along her spine, exploding outward, and she leaned over a little as the ache got worse, wrapping from her back around her sides with a kind of fiery insistence she'd never felt before. She felt a pressure low in her torso, forceful and determined in its strength. She wanted Scott out of her house.

He had moved closer to Molly, and now he sidled in front of her, his arms outstretched in a gesture of apology. "Please, Molly, give me a chance," he said. "I'll still love you."

Molly took a step back. A hot wave of agony clamped itself around her abdomen, reaching for her belly button like the claws of a crab bringing in its prey. The heavy weight pushed against her bottom, and with a shock, she realized that this pain wasn't going to go away. Molly felt the pressure build, and she caught her breath.

"Oh, no," she said, for the second time in an hour.

She was in labor.

Molly forced herself to stand upright. The contraction had subsided enough for her to keep a straight face. Scott was staring at her, waiting for a response. He hadn't even noticed something was amiss.

"Scott. You don't love me." The panting in her voice was going to give her away. She tried to even her breathing. "You just like the *idea* of me. Just like your mother does. You know that."

Molly flipped open the lock on the door. "So I think we're through here. It's time for you to leave."

Scott groaned. He sounded like a little boy who'd been told he couldn't have more candy. "Molly, I don't want to leave. Not until you agree to give me another chance. Not until you agree to let me be a part of this baby's life. Of your life."

Molly shook her head in exasperation. She just wanted the man out of her house so she could figure out what to do next. She'd never wanted the company of her family more than she did then.

"We can talk about custody of the baby later on. Fine. There has to be a mediator present, though, and lawyers to put a plan in writing. That's the only way. I'm not having any more of these impromptu talks in my living room."

She tried not to gasp as she spoke. "And we're not getting back together, Scott, no way, no how. Now, please, just get out of my house."

"Molly, please."

Another contraction had started, moving more quickly this time. Molly moved to brace herself against the wall beside her entranceway closet and pointed at the door.

"Scott, go. We'll talk after the baby's born."

The contraction peaked now, stronger than the others, the pain vibrating from her center down her legs, up her chest, through her pelvis. She cried out against her will, and tried to fight the tears that were threatening to spill onto her face.

"Molly, what's going on? What are you doing? Talk to me, damn it!"

The next contraction started almost as soon as the pain from the other faded, its angry vise clamping down on her pelvis until it felt like there were knives fighting to leave Molly's body from below. She doubled over as Scott tried to hold her upright by the arms. He was still talking, still begging. She moaned again in spite of herself.

"Molly, I need to be here for you. You have to let me be a part of this. I'm the father of our baby." He was squeezing her.

Molly didn't answer him. Her knees bent suddenly with the weight of her contracting belly, but she refused to go down.

"Get out of here, Scott!" she cried. "Just go, damn it!"

No sooner had the words come out of her mouth than a furious knocking started from outside the house. The heavy door swung open, and Molly and Scott looked up in shock as in tumbled Jack, Emily, and, behind them, Jenny and Dan. Scott's hands were still clenched around Molly's upper arms, tight, holding her in place.

"What the hell is going on here?!" boomed Molly's father, his voice louder and more frightening than she'd ever heard it in her life. Emily rushed over to Molly's side as Scott let go of her and backed away. Her mother used her body as a shield to block Molly from Scott's view, while Jenny and Dan hung back in the living room, watching the scene unfold with anxious faces.

"Jack, I was just—" Scott's voice had become friendly.

"I don't care what you thought you were doing, Scott, you don't touch my daughter!" Jack took a step toward Scott, with Dan now right behind him.

Scott leaned around Emily to get Molly's attention. "Come on, Molly, don't you see? Don't let them do this. Don't let—"

A sudden contraction hit Molly with such force she couldn't breathe through it. With a scream, she collapsed onto the wood floor. She heard the gasps come from Jenny and her mother, and clutched her hard belly as if that could make this all stop.

"Get out!" she shrieked. Sweat was forming thick on her skin. "Get out!"

Scott stepped back, but didn't move beyond that.

"Make him *go*!" Molly begged. Before Scott had a chance to say another word, Jack and Dan each took him by an arm and towed him toward the door. Scott was struggling, trying to stay inside, not ready to give up whatever stake he still had there. Through a haze of tears, Molly saw Jenny's hands on Scott's back as the men forced him to the door, giving him one final shove as he went over the threshold.

When the door shut, every person in the room turned to look at Molly in apprehension. Her contraction had subsided, and for a wonderful, calm minute, she could relax against her mother's side, smiling at the sight of Dan with his arm around Jenny. But before she could take the next deep breath, she was doubled over again, panting in agony, as the four other people in her living room started scurrying around each other in confused panic.

"Oh my God, you're going to have the baby!" Jenny exclaimed. Molly watched her clap her hands in delight.

"Oh my God, you're going to have the baby?" Dan cried, looking around as if somebody forgot to tell him this was happening. "I thought we were going out for linguine!"

Molly groaned.

"Okay," Emily said. She hugged Molly tight and whispered in her ear. "You got this, Mol. You're going to be okay."

Molly's mother stood straight and took charge. "Jack, you go get the car." He nodded, and the next thing Molly heard was the slamming of the door. "Jenny, you go grab Molly's overnight bag from upstairs. Molly, you do have a spare bag packed here, of course?"

She nodded. Of course she did.

"Okay, and Dan?" Dan looked back and forth between Molly and Emily in a panicked stupor. His expression was one of sheer fear. "Dan, just go sit down and take a deep breath, will you?"

"Oh, God, I think I'm going to faint," he muttered, and collapsed onto the couch.

Jenny came running down the stairs moments later, the soles of her ballet flats slapping against the wood in their hurry. "I've got it!" she called out, jubilant, wielding the heavy bag like it was a Super Bowl trophy.

"I'm here, I'm here!" Jack threw open the front door to the house and then stood there, keys in hand, looking back and forth as if waiting for a stampede to rush his way. Dan leaped up from the couch, but stopped in his tracks.

"Holy crap, Molly," he yelped. "Holy crap. You've got stuff leaking out of you!"

Jenny threw the stuffed bag at him and ran to help Emily pull Molly up off the floor. Molly groaned, the pain so blinding that everything in front of her eyes had gone black. She barely registered the sensation of liquid streaming down her legs, too miserable to be embarrassed, and too preoccupied to care if someone cleaned it up.

With a grunting effort, her parents and friends formed a semicircle around her, shepherding her toward the door, all of them protecting her, moving in one heaving, tumbling, warm mass. Finally, they managed to ease Molly onto the doorstep.

"You can do this, Molly!" she heard Jenny say, and she felt her friend's thin hands around her shoulders, guiding her down the stairs. Another contraction burst its way around her torso, and Molly crumbled into the car, her mother carefully easing the back door closed behind her.

"See, Molly?" she heard Emily say, just as the lock clicked. As soon as they were all buckled up, Jack jammed his foot onto the accelerator. The tires of the car squealed and they jerked with a start out of the parking spot and onto the road. Molly pressed her head against the window, the glass cool against her moist forehead.

Emily couldn't help but get in one last word. "I *told* you it was a bad idea to come into the city alone!"

CHAPTER ELEVEN

October

Yes

The newborn's cry rose with swift crescendo, sailing through the room with the velocity and volume of a rocket. Molly stood at the foot of the bed holding her, her eyes half-closed, rocking back and forth in a stupor that felt close to sleep, but not nearly close enough. Scott lay still, holding a pillow over his face to shield his eyes from the slight sliver of hallway light that seeped in around the edge of the unlatched door.

The baby had been crying for twenty minutes, and nothing Molly had done would calm her down. She'd tried a diaper change, an attempt at feeding, another feeding, even dancing with her in the dark, and yet little Dylan Sullivan Berkus still lay draped over her shoulder, her perfect mouth open in an indignant wail. Molly's eyes were wet with exhaustion. She hadn't yet needed the deluxe video monitor Monica had gotten them, because Dylan was always with Molly at night, in her arms, wide awake.

Molly bounced their daughter, making *shush*ing noises. She wondered if she should try feeding her again.

A sigh, deep and rumbling, came floating under the current of the baby's noise. Scott, still huddled under the warm, wrinkled bedcovers, rubbed his hands over his face and his hair with a tense movement.

Dylan, her body rigid now with effort, continued to wail.

Molly knew the baby would cry even louder in Scott's arms. She wanted her mother, and only her mother would do, even when Molly's efforts didn't seem to be good enough. But Scott— Scott, who had to work tomorrow, who hated his inability to quiet the baby down, who couldn't handle not being able to *fix* the noise—Scott got to lie there, waving the white flag of a person begging for an excuse to surrender. In the quiet light from the door, Scott rolled over to face the wall. He positioned the pillow over his ear with an elbow and sighed again, the sound a frustrated groan of impatience.

"Just get her out of here, will you, Molly?"

Molly sat in the cold living room in her pajamas, having padded down the stairs in her bare feet with the fussing baby. Dylan was still crying, but the sound was softer now, with stretches of silence in between each rasping plea, as if she were waiting, listening for something that would break into the peace.

Molly and Scott were barely speaking anymore, other than to shout at each other in the middle of the night when Dylan started crying and Molly couldn't quiet her down. And it was always Molly to hold her, to comfort her, to go to her bassinet and change the diaper. She was breastfeeding every two hours.

Night was no different than day anymore, there was no beginning or end. It was just feedings and diapers, feedings and diapers, on a constant rotation of exhaustion and nipples that bled, and lumpy, hard knots in her engorged breasts that made her skin stretch until it shone. There was no sleep, because in between the feedings and diapers, the exhaustion and the pain, there were the tears. There were so many tears. Time held no meaning, because it was Molly, always Molly, to be the one to open her eyes and roll her body, still bruised and sore from childbirth, out of bed to reach for the baby. She'd ball up the diaper, change the soiled onesie, and pat the warm newborn on her tiny, frail back until, finally, she burped the extra air from her lungs, over and over again, while Scott snored.

He got so much sleep, Molly thought. He muttered through dreams, he rolled over to take up her side of the bed when she got out. While she hunched over their newborn, her breasts exposed and leaking, her skin clammy with postpartum night sweats, Scott stayed warm and asleep. Molly only knew it was a weekend when Scott emerged from the bedroom mid-morning in track pants instead of a business suit. How nice it must be, Molly thought, to know the difference between one day and the next.

She was sitting in the glider late the next afternoon, still wearing the same crumpled pajamas from the night before. They were damp and limp now, hanging against the new folds in her body with alarming conformity while the baby nursed. The past few weeks had brought her a new person to love—a person who looked like her and stared at her and draped herself against her mother's body like she was a blanket protecting her from the cold—but also physical pain, and the mind-numbing delirium of hours of wakefulness, and a partner who might as well have been just a craigslist roommate perpetually behind on his rent checks. She'd never felt so happy and miserable in her entire life.

Scott entered the room with a thud as the door knocked against the wall, startling the baby from her latch. He stood in the doorway, wearing a Penn State T-shirt and a pair of shiny basketball shorts slung low over his narrow hips. He rarely entered the nursery, and now hovered at the threshold, clearly uncomfortable.

"So, I had an absolute shit day. I was going to meet up with the guys for some pickup ball at the gym, blow off some steam. You don't mind, right?"

Molly noticed Scott was already wearing his new sneakers, tamping down the deep pile of the cream carpet. Her fiancé probably owned more pairs of shoes than she had clean underwear. She swallowed hard and readjusted their daughter against her chest.

"No, go ahead. It's not like you can feed her, anyway."

"Yeah, that's what I figured. I'll be home around ten thirty or so, unless the boys want to grab a beer."

"Is Dan meeting up with you?"

"Uh, no." Scott shifted his weight from one foot to the other. "He hasn't shown up to play since, you know." He cleared his throat. "So."

Scott moved across the carpet and planted a wet kiss on Molly's lips. He patted Dylan on her back with two hesitant movements, as if afraid she'd notice him.

"Do you need anything?"

Molly hesitated. They were surrounded by drawers stuffed

with baby clothes, a closet of designer crib sheets, expensive creams to help heal her stretch marks. "No, I'm good, thanks. I'm going to grab a shower and something to eat after I get her down."

Scott stayed silent for a moment, fidgeting. "Should I not play tonight, then?" His eyes shifted. "So I can stay here with you, and like, babysit?"

"Scott, go. I could use the quiet."

"Thanks, Mol. That's great." He spoke over his shoulder as he strode down the short hallway. "But I'll be up with you tomorrow morning. There'll be juice beside the bed and breakfast on the table when you wake up."

As Scott skipped down the stairs, his heavy shoes landing with a thud on each step, Molly took a sip of the water she kept in the nursery. She knew that Scott would go out that night after his games, drink from too many pitchers of watered-down Bud Light, and be so sick and stinking of buffalo wings the next day he would barely get up in time for work. There would be no waffles waiting for her, no newspaper at the ready on the kitchen island.

Molly stroked the soft auburn hair of the baby in her arms and felt some of the tension seep out of her body. It wasn't as if she expected Scott to wait on her. She was used to handling her responsibilities by herself. But his hurried promises—of breakfast tomorrow, or a weekend where he'd wash and fold all the laundry—just disappointed her when they didn't come to fruition. They were a reminder of what it could be like, to live in this house, to be a proper family, and that was something she couldn't dare to think about. She didn't need the acknowledgment of what was missing in her life. She just needed to live it as it was.

They still hadn't set a date for their wedding. In a surprising move, Scott had changed his mind and wanted to move up the date, but Molly was the one who held him off this time, saying they should wait. She was too tired to plan anything beyond what she was doing right at that moment. She was beginning to ask herself, though, how something that was supposed to be so exciting for both of them had turned into an inconvenience. Molly wondered at what point love had gotten pushed to the bottom of the to-do list.

Through the softly curtained panes of glass beside her she could see the brilliant oranges and reds of a fully leaved oak tree waving in a small rainstorm. The window was cracked open to the wet fall air, and Molly breathed in the smells of autumn in the city: a food truck on the corner selling hot coffee, the crisp leaves starting to break down under the feet of passing neighbors, and from somewhere, smoke curling from a fireplace. The setting sun broke through some dark clouds to shine across the city, peeking around the corners of buildings and bouncing off of the metal tags of the dogs that trotted happily through the puddles with their owners after work, reminding the world that the day was not over quite yet. Inside her house, inside this room, Molly felt the quiet settle her nerves. She leaned back in the chair, listening to the sounds of the street below, and felt the slight weight of her daughter, warm in her arms.

She gazed down at Dylan, who had fallen asleep at Molly's breast, her mouth still open, her hand resting against the swell of Molly's skin. She felt her heart rise in her throat. She ran her thumb across the baby's soft cheek and smiled in the stillness when she saw the tiny tongue move against it. She played with the thin nails that wrapped over the ends of her daughter's tiny fingers, nails so fragile and new Molly hadn't been able to cut them yet for fear of hurting her. She never wanted to hurt her. She wanted to protect this child forever from all the pain in the world, from the hurt that people could hurl at each other. Dylan had already heard yelling, and bad names, and frustration, and Molly wished she could take it all back, erase it, go into her precious growing brain and make it clean again. Her daughter was so new to the world. She needed to see the good in it before she had to experience the bad. Molly was already not living up to the standard she had set out to uphold.

Molly took in the sight of the miniature person she held in her arms. She wondered how her ears could have been so flawlessly formed, with their folds and dips, how her eyes knew to find hers as soon as they opened, seeking out her mother's face and voice and arms. From the moment Molly had placed her hands on her daughter's body that first evening, had picked her up to bring her to her chest, she'd wondered how she could ever have doubted how good life could be with her here. Because she was here, outside of her, moving and breathing and existing because of Molly, and in spite of Molly. Molly didn't understand why she'd thought she wasn't ready for this. For now, in the soft light of the evening, in the quiet of the house, with just the two of them, it felt like she'd loved this baby her entire life. She just hadn't known the strength of that love until she got the chance to meet her. And here she was.

Molly gently burped her sleepy daughter before laying her in the crib and padded out of her room, patting her waist to make sure the monitor was hooked to the band of her maternity sweatpants. She probably had about forty-five minutes before the little one woke up again. Molly moved through the house, picking up dirty burp cloths, stacking magazines on the coffee table, throwing out used breast pads. The pillows on the couch got fluffed. She swept the smallest speck of dust out of a corner. Molly wanted to keep busy so she wouldn't think. She needed to keep busy so the house, and everyone in it, wouldn't fall apart. She went into the kitchen to rinse out the suction cups of the breast pump and place Scott's dirty dishes in the dishwasher. She ran through the checklist in her head, tallying an ever-growing number of tasks. There was so much to do.

She put the last of the dishes away and checked the clock to see if she should just give up on the day and get ready for bed now. Molly's body ached, and she leaned against the countertop for a minute. She couldn't fathom going through the motions of taking a shower. She thought about being a kid in the springtime, years ago, when she'd play outside and a sudden rainstorm would pop up, soaking her to the skin. She remembered the awful chill, how it felt like she could feel the shivers of cold right down to her very bones. That's what this kind of tired felt like: like her insides were just rubber, her eyes fogged over with mist. Her head felt heavier than her belly had at the end of the pregnancy. But she had to keep going. Moving. She wiped down the countertops and poured water into the coffee machine, setting it up for the next morning. She had to keep nursing and diapering, folding the laundry and sorting the bills. Sleep would have to be something she fit in when she could.

And Scott? Well, Scott could play basketball.

Molly peered into the freezer and decided that her best option for dinner at this point was to pop a frozen Lean Cuisine into the microwave. It was only eight o'clock, but she knew she was going to go to bed after the baby's next feeding. She sighed and rubbed the back of her neck, looking around the kitchen. The floors could use a good scrubbing. She added the task to her mental to-do list.

The microwave timer binged, and Molly took the plastic tray out with her fingertips, instantly singeing her skin with some spilled sauce. As fastidious as she was about everything in her life, Molly still could never remember to pull on some blasted oven mitts.

"Damn it," she muttered, and threw the container onto the butcher block island she still used as a casual table. She lowered herself down onto the bar stool with a heavy movement and placed her face in her hands.

It's not fair, she thought. She loved that baby so much her heart sometimes felt like it was too big for her chest. But it wasn't enough for Scott. *They* weren't enough for Scott, and Molly found herself wondering what was so wrong with her that disinterest had replaced any love he may have once felt. Molly had dared to ask him to help a few times, but nothing had changed. Not Dylan's diaper. Not the dirty sheets on the bed. Not the empty roll on the toilet paper holder. She wanted to go back to work. She wanted to take control of a conference call, and meet clients, and wash her hair on a regular basis. Molly's world as she knew it was falling apart around her, and she was too tired to put it back together.

Molly scooped the first bite of the low-cal fettuccine Alfredo onto her fork just as the initial murmurs rose from the baby monitor. She held her breath and waited when it grew quiet, and then felt her whole body sag into itself as Dylan's wails started up again in a fury, bouncing through the speaker and echoing down the stairs. Molly took a deep breath, tossed the fork into the dishwasher, and set the full tray of food in the refrigerator. Dylan's cries filled the house now, pushing past the worries and to-do lists and pangs of hunger to stand front and center. Molly headed up the stairs.

"Seriously?"

Jenny was standing on the corner of 9th and Wharton, holding a sandwich in both hands, staring at the flashing neon lights of the restaurant that stood directly across the street.

"We couldn't go to Geno's?" she asked. She looked down at her cheesesteak with resignation, as if it were some salesman who'd come to her door at dinnertime and kept knocking. She sighed and took a tentative bite of her hoagie. "Geno's meat is so much better than this stuff," she said.

"No way!" Dan mumbled. His lips were wide open around the steak and onions he'd shoved into his mouth. He hadn't noticed the Cheez Whiz dripping onto his Converse high-tops. "Thif iv awesome!"

Molly looked back and forth between her friends. She was sitting at a table under an overhang at Pat's King of Steaks, rocking the car seat on the concrete floor beside her, even though Dylan had already fallen asleep. She was so tired it felt like her eyes were burning holes into their sockets, but she'd jumped at the chance to meet up with her friends, pulling on clean yoga pants and sneaking out of the house while Scott took a nap in their bedroom. He didn't like her going out as much anymore, saying it wasn't healthy for the baby to be out in the chill and that Molly should stay close in case she needed to be fed. But it'd been almost two months now. The air inside her home had grown

stale. Molly unzipped the car seat cover to peek inside. Dylan
was quiet, dozing in the warmth of her fleece cocoon. Molly
turned her attention back to her friends, who were pretending to
squabble like squirrels in a park.

"Do you see this?" Jenny was holding the dripping remains
of her cheese steak in her husband's direction. "This is how
much I love you. THIS. This sorry hunk of meat in a roll? Proof,
okay?"

She winced at the sight of a line cook glaring at her through the
glass. Not one of them had noticed that a window was propped
open.

"Proof of your love?" Dan was laughing. "Jenny, this is payback. Delicious payback, of course." He winked at Molly over
the top of his sandwich, bringing her into the conversation. She'd
never cared either way who won the war between the two rival
cheesesteak establishments that anchored the busy South Philly
intersection, but smiled at Dan's enthusiasm. She was just happy
to be out of the house.

"You know this is the only way I would've gotten her here,
right, Mols?" he asked. "Jenny had to leave me for a month, put
me through the wringer a little while longer, then come crawling
back feeling awful enough to agree to eating on this side of the
street."

"Well," Jenny said, and gave him a quick kiss on the cheek,
"guilt is a powerful motivator." She, too, looked at Molly. "I've
pretty much signed myself up for a lifetime of Pat's steaks, I'm
afraid."

Molly watched Dan, bent over a basket of French fries with a
content smile on his face. There was a fleck of Cheez Whiz caught
on the corner of his mouth. An image of Liam appeared in Molly's

mind—how they used to sit beside each other here, too, joking around just like Jenny and Dan were doing now. She thought about how the skin around his eyes had formed those laugh lines when they focused on her in the middle of the noisy pub a few months ago, their easy conversation after years of separation. Molly looked at her daughter and shook the thought out of her head.

A vintage Camaro pulled up to stop at the light on the corner beside them, its radio blaring Joni Mitchell through the open sun-roof. After a childhood of listening to her father's vinyl albums, Molly recognized "Both Sides Now" almost before the first chord had finished playing. A breeze scattered some paper napkins across the table, and she gathered them into a tidy stack, concen-trating on getting the folded edges lined up in perfect order.

Dan nudged Molly's leg with his knee. "Hey. Earth to Mols. What's up with you? How's life with Mr. Darcy?"

He imitated Scott's come-hither smile, complete with a toss of his spiky hair. Jenny didn't laugh.

"Mol, you look exhausted," Jenny said, and placed the rest of the cheesesteak in its paper on the table. Dan pulled it over in front of him and began eating again.

"Are you getting any sleep?" she asked.

Molly swallowed. "Not so much."

"Is he helping you out at all?"

Molly shook her head, lips clamped shut. The traffic light had turned green, and the Camaro paused for a split second before accelerating. The driver of the truck behind it lay on the horn, the sound a sudden, angry burst through the cool fall air, drown-ing out the delicate harmonies of the song. Molly heard Dylan whimper and rocked the car seat again.

"Is that what you were expecting," Jenny pressed, "when all of this began?" Dan had stopped chewing to listen.

"No, not at all," Molly said, keeping her gaze on the sidewalk. "In the beginning, no. Scott was always trying to impress me. I guess I figured that all the flowers and Sixers tickets would translate into dishwashing and diaper-changing once we got serious."

She looked up, but didn't like the expressions of pity she saw reflected in both of her friends' eyes. "Pretty stupid of me, huh?"

"You're not stupid, Molly." Jenny's voice was sharp.

"Okay," Dan said. "Let's say that either he changed, or he's just not the guy you thought he was. Say he's not Mr. Darcy so much as Mr. Homer Simpson."

"Mmm," Molly conceded.

"Listen, Molly," Jenny said, taking control of the conversation. She spoke firmly, but her voice was soft. "When I was being an idiot about Dan, you set me straight."

Dan nodded.

"And?" Molly felt herself stick her chin a little higher in the air. The evening breeze had picked up and changed direction, blowing now at their backs. Molly's oversized sweatshirt, one of the few pieces of clothing that fit her still-wide middle, did a poor job of blocking the chill.

"And I think you need to look at your situation with Scott. I'm concerned about you and a little worried for that sweet baby of yours."

Jenny was quiet for a long moment. Dan placed his hand on her back and rubbed a small circle there, as if working courage into her lungs.

"Look, Molly." Jenny sighed. "You gave me the bottom line,

so I'm going to bounce one to you. I made a mistake by almost leaving a relationship that was good—"

"I'll say," Dan said.

"—so why aren't you getting out of one that's bad?" Jenny asked.

"It's not that bad, Jenny." Molly swallowed. "We're just going through a rough patch."

"You said that months ago, Molly," Dan replied. He'd finished both cheesesteaks and wiped his hands clean of their grease. The napkins lay in front of him in a crumpled, stained heap. "Don't you think it's a sign that you haven't set a date yet? At this rate Dylan's going to grow up and get married before you two do."

"Well, having a baby is hard on a relationship. We have some growing pains to work out." Molly cringed as soon as the sentence was uttered. She knew how she sounded, and she watched Jenny's lips pull into a straight, hard line that told her she wasn't the only one. "I mean, that's what they always tell you."

"So, that's a reason for him to walk all over you?"

"I don't have a job, Jenny."

"So get one."

"Paying as much as S&G did? Enough to cover child care?"

"Is this you saying this, Molly, or what Scott's told you?"

"What are you talking about?"

"Molly, think about it. So you'd have to make some sacrifices. Maybe ask your parents to help out. Lose that cool silver bullet of a car and get something a little cheaper." Jenny was leaning forward. "But you can do it, you know. If you wanted to."

Dan nodded in echo. "You could do it, Molly."

She shook her head. "She can't have just a single mom as her family. It's not how it's supposed to go." Molly felt tears press against the backs of her eyes, weeks of the same conversation she'd been having in her mind now playing out in real time. "She needs a father."

"But she doesn't need an inept one, Mol. C'mon, you know that. And you can't think that getting married is going to change that." Jenny moved to Molly's side of the table and placed her arm around Molly's narrow shoulders, still muscular beneath the softness the pregnancy had added. She squeezed her tightly, and was slow to let go.

"Dude," Dan interjected. "Your relationship is like bad insurance."

Molly shook her head and pulled away from Jenny's arms. "What are you talking about?"

Jenny sighed. "Insurance. You know how an insurance company will weigh each case? They analyze an entity's liability versus its assets."

"In this case, look at Scott," Dan said. "It's all very logical. What is he bringing to your life, to your family? What is he taking away? Sometimes you need to compare one list to the other and make a choice."

"Jeez, you guys. You're ganging up on me here." Molly laughed and wiped her eyes with a free hand. "And who've you been hanging out with, anyway? Accountants?"

"Nah," Jenny said. "It's just a little something we picked up dealing with the bills for our new fertility treatments."

Molly avoided her friends' eyes, looking down at the car seat, and was serious again. "I can't have failed, Jenny. Not again. Not at *this*."

"Molly Sullivan, you will drive me nuts. You have a beautiful baby. You have your master's degree, and years of quality PR experience, and, of course, us. What more do you possibly need?"

Molly laughed again, and this time the sound was lighter, more genuine. But she felt Jenny's words slowly move into a pocket of her mind and settle there, locked away until she needed them again. The breeze had turned brisk, sending a shower of decaying leaves dancing among the tables, and she shivered in the sudden cold.

"Hey," Dan said, as Molly started gathering their discarded wrappers and napkins for the trash can. "Jenny and I were going to go to Yards later. Do you want to come?" Yards Brewing Company was one of their favorite stops in Manayunk, a hill-filled neighborhood on the far outskirts of Philadelphia where the condos were former paper factories and the bars drew professionals like the three of them out from the city on Saturday nights. Molly shook her head. Going out wasn't even an option.

"Homer won't let you out?" Dan asked. His voice was flat.

"It's not that. I've never left the baby for that long before." What she didn't say was that she'd never left the baby alone with Scott before. "Maybe next time?"

The question hung in the air like a helium balloon forgotten after a birthday party. The three friends gathered up the rest of their belongings in silence. It was time to go back home.

Molly shut the door behind her, giving Jenny and Dan a final wave as she did. Dylan was in desperate need of a change and feeding, so Molly carefully unclipped the harness of her car seat and lifted the tiny infant out. Her daughter, draped over her shoulder, helpless and reliant on her mother, felt small and fragile in her arms. Molly inhaled the scent of the skin beneath the soft down of her hair and kissed her head right above the ear.

Never had she held anything more worthy of her love. It was terrifying.

Molly was surprised that Scott wasn't in front of the TV until she heard voices coming from her dining room. She hadn't seen one of Monica's cars out front, or she would've tidied herself up before walking in.

"Molly, hello!" Monica's voice rang out like the false trill of a mockingbird. Scott sauntered into the living room behind her, casual in bare feet and worn jeans. Both had smiles on their faces that seemed stale, as if they'd been wearing them for a while.

"Hi, guys," Molly said. She tried to sound excited to have an unexpected guest, especially one like her future mother-in-law, but she knew her voice betrayed her. She'd been hoping to lie down with the baby for a nap. The excursion to South Philly had worn her out.

"Hey, I was worried about you." Scott's voice was silky, and he wrapped his arms around her as he kissed her lightly on the lips. Molly noticed that he didn't move to touch his daughter.

"Where were you all afternoon?" His mouth was close to her ear. "My mother's been waiting." Molly pulled away.

"Excuse me, Monica," Molly said, and without thinking smoothed down the wrinkles of her yoga pants with her free hand. "I didn't know you were stopping by, or I would've come home sooner." She looked around the living room. It was spotless.

Monica laughed, her voice high and loud, and walked over to kiss Molly's cheeks. She scooped Dylan out of Molly's arms before she could react and rubbed her finger against the infant's tiny nose and mouth, trying to make her smile. Molly almost cried out when she thought of the germs crawling into her daughter's mouth. "No need to apologize, darling. I was actually hoping to surprise you, anyway."

"Oh?" Molly looked from Monica to Scott. She twitched with the urge to snatch her daughter out of Monica's arms.

Scott scratched at the back of his head.

"My parents decided they wanted to give us a set for the dining room," he said. "Mom picked it out special for us and everything."

Molly stood very still.

"Well, we couldn't have you starting out together with an empty dining room, now could we?" Monica laughed. "I mean, now that you got a little jump on expanding your family, darling, we couldn't very well wait to give it to you for your wedding. You'll need it now."

Molly cleared her throat.

"Besides," Monica continued, looking back and forth between Molly and Scott with the benevolent eyes of someone used to people showing her gratitude, "your future father-in-law and I now have an excuse to get you a better gift once you do get married. Something that's more of an . . . *investment*."

She looked around at the house they were standing in, making sure they caught the hint.

"Something, say, to go along with the dining set." Monica was grinning now, her glossed lips stretching so wide the rouge on her cheeks folded into the wrinkles of skin. She held the baby aloft, as if in triumph. Molly saw her daughter wriggle in protest.

For a moment no one said a word. The air in the living room was hot in Molly's lungs.

"Well, shall we?" Monica clicked her tongue against her teeth, bringing them all to attention. "Don't you want to see your new dining room, Molly?"

They stepped toward the room, Monica's platform stilettos

clicking against the polished wood of the floor. Molly cringed when she saw the small nicks the heels left in their wake.

"Voilá!" With a flourish of her free arm, Monica stopped at the entranceway and let Molly walk ahead of her. Molly was no more than a step into the dining room when she stopped with a lurch, her body coming to a halt moments after her brain registered her shock.

Her dining room had shrunk while Molly was gone that afternoon. It had to have gotten smaller, she thought, for there was no way the furniture inside of it could possibly be that big. What sat in front of Molly was one of the most ornate dining table sets she'd ever seen. The chairs, all eight of them, were crafted in the Queen Anne style, ornate backs and engraved legs that had been covered in layers of varnish until they could be used as mirrors. They were set with plush off-white cushions, fabric so elegant and expensive Molly couldn't imagine how she'd ever clean them once they became covered in tomato sauce and pureed prunes in another year. The table was large enough to feed a high school economics class, which, Molly realized, was the exact course Monica and Scott needed a refresher in right now. She and Scott lived in a townhouse filled with furniture from IKEA. Molly highly doubted that Queen Anne had ever had a hankering for a self-assembled bookcase and carry-out Swedish meatballs.

Monica and Scott stood in place on either side of the doorway, staring at Molly in expectation of a reaction. Monica was waiting for something positive: glee, or unabashed excitement, possibly a fainting spell. She wanted her usual feedback, and Molly knew the routine by now. She caught Scott's expression out of the corner of her eye. He looked nervous, and Molly knew he didn't want her to disappoint his mother.

"Monica." Molly set her shoulders square and took her squirming baby out of her future mother-in-law's arms. "This was so kind of you. All of it. Truly. I don't know how to thank you."

"Oh, sweetheart, you don't have to say a word," Monica replied. Her tone was warm. "Edward and I just wanted to give you something nice you wouldn't necessarily buy for yourself."

Molly heard Scott muffle a snort.

"Besides," Monica continued, "now that you're at home and will have time on your hands, you'll need a place for dinner parties, right? We couldn't have you entertaining around the kitchen island anymore." She looked around the room and inhaled, as if holding the smell of polish and upholstery in her lungs would give her the high she'd need to power through her next board meeting.

"But," Molly started. Both Monica and Scott jerked their heads toward her. "Do you think, maybe, it might be a just little too *grand*?"

She meant the table, and the gift of the house. She meant the lifestyle. Monica sniffed.

"I don't feel right accepting such an elegant gift, Monica. I mean, I just fear the table getting banged up once the baby starts walking."

Monica's lip curled up. "Molly, you just keep the child out of the dining room. Do you think Scott was allowed to play as he liked around the house?"

Molly held her tongue. Scott's childhood home was about six thousand square feet bigger than hers. He wouldn't have been able to run though all of it in a day if he'd tried.

Scott laughed. "Yeah, right. I had a playroom, gated off from the rest of the rooms, and was constantly guarded by Bernadette. Mom, you wouldn't even let me *eat* in the dining room."

Monica shrugged her shoulders, as if saying, *Of course.*

Molly turned to Scott. "So where did you eat?"

"Why, in the kitchen, naturally," Monica answered for him.

"In the help's kitchen, Mom," Scott corrected her. "Right next to the sink, and in front of a TV Bernadette kept on the countertop." He glanced at Molly. "Ask me anything you want about *General Hospital* in the mid-eighties."

Molly thought back to the family dinners she'd had with her brothers and parents, all of them crowded around the round oak table in their kitchen. Sometimes they ate at five o'clock, sometimes at eight thirty after they'd all tumbled in from their various practices, soccer and field hockey bags piled up in the corner. They ate meatloaf or tacos or a jar of spaghetti sauce over pasta, quick meals one of their parents could throw together in twenty minutes, standing in their work clothes at the stove, Emily still in her pantyhose or Jack covered with the smell of sawdust. They used paper plates on occasion, drank water from the tap, and rarely complained about any of it because they were too busy talking about their days.

Molly watched Scott leaning against the doorjamb, his legs splayed in a practiced pose of relaxation, his hand running through his hair. Monica was chattering into the air. At the shrill sound of her voice, Dylan stirred in Molly's arms. She began to make pleading sounds and pecked her lips at Molly's chest, searching for nourishment. Molly saw Monica glance at her in horrified understanding, and Molly made her excuses, stepping with care up the stairs to the nursery while Scott and his mother discussed where to go for dinner that night. Molly wondered with vague seriousness if a restaurant as lovely as the luxurious Parc would allow her through the door in stretched-out maternity jeans.

Once in the baby's room, Molly closed the lid to the diaper pail, rubbed sanitizer into the cracked skin of her hands, and sat down with her fussy daughter in the glider to feed. Once Dylan quieted down, Molly could hear Monica and Scott laughing. They'd moved to the kitchen, and she could hear the faint clinking sound of wineglasses being set down on the countertop. Molly rolled her head around on her neck before pressing it into the cushion of the chair back. The ache that seemed to permanently occupy her chest had grown wider while she was downstairs, and she closed her eyes against the tired tears that, unrelenting, worked their way out.

Scott was in her kitchen, having cocktail hour with his mother before they met his father. Monica couldn't see the laundry piled on their bed, or the hospital bills that lay stacked next to the laptop in the bedroom, unpaid and ignored by her son. She didn't care that the dining room table she'd bought cost more than Molly could have made in three months, that it was heavier than anything Molly had ever owned, and that she'd given Scott one more bullet for the chamber when he wielded the weapon of money in Molly's face. Molly recognized the sharp pain in her breasts that occurred as her milk let down, and she felt Dylan relax into her meal. She was starting to accept the odd paradox that there was pain in everything, that it was as equally present in beauty as it was in hardship. She just wondered if she was still capable of telling the difference between the two.

CHAPTER TWELVE

November

No

"Sweetheart, you look wonderful!"

Before Molly could respond, her aunt Cookie pressed her warm lips to her cheek and wrapped an arm around her waist. With the other she playfully pretended to hide a plate filled with a half-eaten slice of cake behind her back before leaning toward Molly's ear.

"Tell me, you knockout, what's your secret?" She nudged Molly in her sharp ribs. "How'd you lose the baby weight already?"

A sudden burst of laughter rolled through Emily and Jack's home from the living room, bouncing off the white cabinets and sand-colored walls of the kitchen. Molly caught the sound from where she and Cookie stood beside the center table piled with tea sandwiches and deviled eggs.

"Cookie, you're sweet. I'm totally not going to admit to you that I'm wearing two pairs of Spanx under this dress." Molly winked at her aunt.

"Oh, thank God," Cookie said, and forked a crumbling pile of the vanilla cake into her carefully lipsticked mouth. "I was afraid you were going to give me one of those it-all-came-off-with-the-breastfeeding lines. Still, though, Spanx?" She eyed the sugar-dusted lemon bars resting on a cake pedestal. "I might have to invest in some."

The house was filled with a joyful cacophony of old stories being passed from one person to the other, the ripping of wrapping paper and popped balloons, the thrilled squeals of cousins chasing one another around a table. Molly's family members and close friends were crammed into every corner of the first floor, drinking iced tea and chilled wine from pastel-colored plastic cups.

In the very center of it all was her daughter, lying in her god-mother's arms, freshly changed out of her white baptismal gown and staring up into Jenny's face. Molly looked at Jenny, standing in the middle of an admiring throng of women, Dan hovering just enough outside of the circle to avoid being sucked into the chattering noise. Molly caught his eye, and he mouthed a plea for help. She hoped it was good practice for him, hanging around while a bunch of people admired his wife and a baby. Because it would be their baby in Jenny's arms one day. One day soon, if the pieces of the puzzle continued to click into place.

She was just about to walk over to the group and disentangle her daughter from Jenny's arms when she felt a weathered hand rest on her shoulder. Emily appeared on one side of her as Jack patted Molly's back.

"How's the baby doing, sweetheart?" Emily asked. "I haven't heard a peep out of her."

Molly held her palms up. "Yeah, I know. She must have inherited Pop's knack for lying low in a crowd."

"Ah, well, one of my grandchildren needed to." Emily nodded at Molly's brothers' children, who were using plastic forks as lances in a sugar-fueled jousting match while their parents hotly debated the spread in the Eagles game being played that evening. Molly felt Jack's chest move up and down with his silent chuckle. She noticed he'd changed out of his suit and into one of his plaid work shirts as soon as they'd gotten home from the ceremony. Even when he wasn't in his workshop, Jack had to be dressed as if he were. He acted as if he couldn't breathe in clothes that weren't made to handle sawdust and wood glue. He'd never been one to put on airs. Jack was who he was, quietly, and people accepted him for it.

Molly checked her watch. "Actually, I'm going to go feed her before she starts wailing. It's about time, anyway."

She felt her father plant a kiss on top of her head before joining the debate between her brothers. Johnny had worn a poorly hidden Eagles T-shirt under his sport coat to church and was now thumping his chest to prove a point. Emily shook her head, smiling, and returned to the kitchen to replenish the food platters.

Ten minutes later, after Molly had finally succeeded in wrestling her baby away from Jenny's protective arms, she settled under a throw blanket onto a wicker rocking chair on the back porch, which was blessedly absent of people but filled with the crisp, fresh air of early November. The partygoers were beginning to drift out of the house now, group by group, on their way to the bars and their homes to swap their high heels and ties for the comfortable jerseys and couches and flat screen TVs of afternoon football watching.

Molly pictured Scott at home, drinking a beer in front of his own television on his living room sofa, which she remembered was upholstered in brown leather, expensive and supple. She saw some of Scott in their daughter—in the narrow ridge of her nose, in her long fingers. Though Scott had been a presence in Molly's world for just a few years, the baby would be a constant reminder that he was once the central point of her life.

Molly played with Dylan's fingers and couldn't help thinking about the rest of Scott, the Scott she remembered from before. She could still picture the wink of his eye when he spotted her in a particular black wrap dress he liked to see her wear. She remembered the way he'd sweep a door open for her in a gesture as grand as the restaurant they were dining in that night. He had a way of looking at her, of making sure she was paying attention when he charmed friends and colleagues, that made her think her opinion of him mattered, that he was playing for her reaction. They'd gone skydiving together, about a year after they met, Molly absolutely terrified of heights but not able to turn down a challenge, and Scott laughing gently at her shaking fear, encouraging her in his own way. She'd jumped, just about fainting from an honest panic attack as she stood at the open door of the plane, the wind blowing so hard in her face she couldn't breathe. But when she'd finally landed on the ground on weak legs and saw Scott rushing toward her, exhilarated, to wrap his muscular arms around her and lift her off the ground once again, she'd been grateful. To him, for pushing her—because he did have to shove her out of the plane—and to herself, for letting herself trust that it would be okay.

Not that Molly had jumped out of an airplane since. She was stubborn, not insane.

Dylan moved her fingers out of Molly's grasp as she rooted for milk, startling her mother into the present. Molly hadn't talked to Scott much since the baby was born, except for a couple of stilted phone calls and one awkward meeting when he came out to West Chester. He was attentive, listening when she spoke, wiping the condensation off a table where his glass had been. He was trying to step back, court her again. There were no constant texts, no Porsche driving by the house. There was just the bouquet of pink and white dahlias that had been delivered yesterday. Scott had remembered his daughter's baptism.

Molly shivered in the rocking chair and pulled the blanket tighter around her and her daughter. A small gust of wind blew through the porch, rustling the leaves on the wide stairs leading down to the lawn. Molly listened to the wind chimes make a tinkling sound as their metal tubes collided together from their perch in the corner. They seemed, she thought, to make their prettiest music when their environment was the most unstable. It was no wonder she'd never liked them.

Molly placed her warm, dozing daughter up on her shoulder and patted her back. She looked out over the backyard, at the yellow and orange mums, the carefully weeded flower beds now cleaned and mulched for the winter. Coming back to her childhood home always seemed like a vacation to Molly after spending her days and nights in such a busy, noisy city. Staying here, though, on an open invitation, felt like moving around a set in some play she had never planned to see. Emily and Jack's home, in this rambling neighborhood in West Chester, with the old stone houses and whitewashed fences and spacious, landscaped backyards, wasn't real, even in comparison to Monica and Edward's. This wasn't authentic life, at least to Molly. Not right now, anyway. It was too perfect, and separate, and took a lot of work to maintain. Molly's life was grittier, her path still filled with gravel and potholes. She wasn't ready for an easy road yet, especially one already laid out for her. She was still content to keep walking and get to where she was supposed to go, eventually.

Later that afternoon, Molly was standing at the sink with a sponge in her hand, scrubbing the first of a staggering pile of dirty dishes.

"Molly, sit down. I can get these dishes," Emily said. "Jenny, will you take my daughter into the living room and make her relax? She's driving me crazy."

Jenny stood up from Emily's kitchen table and reached out a hand for her friend. "Molly, you heard the woman. Get your big ol' rear end in there and sit down."

"Hey!" Molly cried. "My butt is not that big anymore."

"Yeah, yeah, I realize that. And you've basically convinced me that no diet I ever go on will be as effective as the exhausted mama one. It's not fair."

Molly dried her hands on a dish towel, folding the white rectangle before placing it neatly on the counter. Her mother had been doing so much for her. She kissed Emily on the cheek, lingering beside her to give her shoulders a quick squeeze before she grabbed the last chocolate truffle from a tray still on the table.

Jenny followed her out of the room and sat down beside her. They could hear the vague rumblings of the Eagles game Jack and Dan had turned on downstairs.

"You okay?" Jenny had been quiet since the house emptied. She took a sip from her wineglass and smoothed her skirt under her legs, which were tucked beneath her on the couch. Her red heels lay piled in the corner by her purse, but Jenny still looked polished and chic in a pale blue shirtdress with a pleated skirt.

She'd worn pearls in honor of the sacred occasion, but even those managed to throw off a bohemian vibe on Molly's friend.

"Yeah," Molly replied right away, then paused. "No. How did you know?"

"Because you've been doing that super compulsive thing you do when you're upset and start straightening up everything in sight."

Molly stopped in the middle of organizing the magazines on her parents' coffee table and sat up straight, feeling embarrassed. She forced herself to relax backward into the overstuffed cushions of the couch. She'd taken off the shapewear she'd been wearing as soon as the last guest had left the house and now propped her feet up on the coffee table, careful not to snag her tights against the rough pages of the magazines. The music she'd turned on for the reception was still flowing from the old stereo in the corner, and she was glad to hear a ZZ Ward song playing. Jenny started singing along. "'Save my life, set me free,'" she sang, her clear alto softly rising over the music. Molly joined in with "'Yes or no is all I need,'" before both women let their voices trail away.

"I'm fine. I'm just annoyed that I finally convinced myself that I could do this single mom thing on my own—actually, finally, was okay with it all, and Scott had to swoop in and make me doubt myself all over again."

The baby called out in her sleep from the car seat in the corner, then settled back down into her nap before Molly could rise to check on her. Both Jenny and Molly watched her for a moment. Dylan was a sweet baby, easy to console when upset and content to stare at whoever held her when she wasn't. Little Dylan, with her dark reddish hair and Clara Bow lips and soft, smooth skin, whose tiny fists were curled up tight, wrapped up in whatever dreams infants who know nothing of the world can imagine. A sudden yelling rose up, muffled, from the basement.

"Wait, Molly." Jenny turned to face her on the sofa. "What are you saying?"

"I'm not saying anything." Molly sighed. "I'm just thinking, that's all."

"Well, stop thinking already," Jenny said. Her voice was higher than usual. "This is Scott we're talking about. One minute he's popping out of the dark to scare you half to death, and the other he's pushing you to get back together with him. It's twisted."

Molly didn't respond. She was staring at her daughter sleeping in the car seat with both hands resting on her small belly.

"Molly?" Jenny asked. "You have to know this, right?"

They were facing a large picture window, and the two of them sat for a moment watching a little girl ride her bike on the road below them, her father running along behind, one hand on the seat to keep her from falling. The girl giggled with laughter and pushed off even harder. The father lost his grip on the seat and slowed to a stop, watching the little girl pedal down the road without him. She squealed with glee.

Emily walked into the room before Molly could answer her friend. She carried a cup of tea and sank down with it into an armchair. She smiled at the two younger women, a tired smile that looked like it was stifling a yawn, and straightened the blanket over her sleeping granddaughter's socked feet. Molly watched her mother relax back into the seat and place her own feet, slightly swollen at the ankles in their pantyhose, on an ottoman.

"When will you be going to see Scott's parents, Molly?" Emily blew lightly over the tea in her mug and took a sip. "On New Year's Eve, if I'm correct? I do hope you're out of that party

before the celebrations really get underway. I don't want my
innocent grandchild being around that family when they've had
a few drinks."

Jenny sat forward, almost spilling the wine from her glass.

"I'm sorry, what?" She looked back and forth between Molly
and her mother, mouth open. "You're seeing Scott's *family* now?
What, in the name of hell—why?"

Jenny caught the wan look Emily gave her. "Sorry for my
language, Emily, but dear God, Molly, what's gotten into you?
You broke up with Scott so you wouldn't *have* to celebrate
another major holiday with his family."

"I know, I know," Molly said. "But they haven't met Dylan
yet. I kind of have to introduce her to them, and this is perfect,
because if we go early, we have your party to get to afterward,
so I don't have to be there long."

"But what are you going to do when you see Scott?" Jenny
asked. "He's probably going to take it as a sign that you want to
get back together." She shook her head in shock. "I'd rather you
give him a sign shaped like a good uppercut to his pretty face."

Emily chuckled into her tea.

"I was thinking I'd probably use the chance to finalize our
situation," Molly said. "Come to some sort of . . . resolution."

She shrugged. "Or maybe I'll just hide in the bathroom after
his parents look at the baby, and then I can sneak her out through
the back."

Jenny laughed. "No way in hell, lady. I've been to the Manor,
and it's too big for you to ever be able to find a back door without a tour guide, let alone get out of it. I think you're stuck."

Molly smiled at her friend, but neither one of them could hide
her apprehension about this meeting. Scott's parents had been

shocked to receive a phone call from the hospital telling them
they were about to become grandparents. Molly wasn't sure who
had made the call. Everyone had crowded into the labor and
delivery room when she was first admitted, groaning in pain, to
the hospital. Molly could only remember brief moments from the
scant hour before the baby arrived. She knew that at one point
she was screaming for the epidural that would never come
because she was already pushing. She remembered her mother
on one side of her, Jenny on the other, both holding a hand, and
then a leg, guiding her and cheering for her when she was saying
there was no way a baby could ever actually come out of her. She
distinctly recalled Dan throwing up all over his shoes and Jack
escorting him out of the room. And she remembered her baby,
the baby someone's gloved hands pulled from her and placed on
her chest, the infant girl who opened her eyes to look at Molly—
to give her one silent, personal look to acknowledge what she'd
known all along—before letting loose with a cry that announced
to them all that she had arrived.

But even as Molly's family had gathered around her bedside,
passing the bundled newborn around to each other like sandbag-
gers preparing for a storm, Molly was taking the blame in Scott's
family for the pregnancy, for deflowering their son, for giving him
a reputation in their community that he, by their accounts, did not
deserve and would never be able to live down. Not *their* son,
Monica had been heard to say. They were glad for the baby, but
Molly had taken a step down off the pedestal they'd built for her.
The relationship the two women had fostered over the years had
been rendered as unnecessary as the umbilical cord once connect-
ing Dylan to Molly. Molly was a mini-Monica no more. But still,
Molly felt she had an obligation to one day tell her daughter that

at least she'd tried to keep some semblance of the relationship intact, that she'd put forth the effort, even if it was small because she'd hoped to get away unscathed. She owed her that much.

Jack and Dan emerged from the basement, both flushed from what had been a tight win in overtime. Dan sat down on the floor beside his newly minted goddaughter, who was beginning to rustle against the stiff fabric of her seat.

Molly focused again on her best friend, who gathered the last of the discarded plates and cups still scattered around the living room and disappeared. She emerged now from the kitchen with a cloth to wipe any leftover crumbs from the coffee table. Before Emily could tell Jenny to relax, Molly started giggling.

"So, you do housekeeping now?"

Jenny broke into a little wiggle as she worked. She was so prim in her dress and pearls, bent over her cleaning, making them all laugh.

Dan spoke up. "Man, Jen, Molly should just hire you on as a nanny once her maternity leave ends. You seem to be getting a hang of this domestic thing."

Jenny's hands stopped in midair as she stared at her husband, the dishrag swinging from her fingers. She turned to look at Molly, who was regarding her friend with sudden interest. Jack and Emily watched them, listening.

"Huh." Jenny finished brushing the crumbs into her cupped hand, taking her time to form her question. "Are you still on the waiting list for that day care by Rittenhouse?"

"Nope. I took Dylan off of it when I decided to come back home."

"But you haven't been able to sublet your house yet?"

"Mm-mmm." Molly shook her head. "The last couple who

showed interest reeked of pot and patchouli. I could smell it even before they got to the door. I don't think I'll be able to rent it."

"That reminds me, Molly," Emily said. "I found a sweet little antique dining set on Etsy you might love. For the future, I mean." She coughed and took a sip of her tea.

"Well, either way, it's great that your parents are letting you stay here with them," Jenny said, nodding at them. "Though I'm sure it must be an adjustment for everybody." Jack cleared his throat and smiled at Emily.

"Which we're still happy to do, Molly," Emily said, "as long as you need us." Molly saw her mother slide her eyes to the side to meet Jack's. He shrugged and seemed to wait for his daughter's response.

"But it's a forty-five-minute trip to work each way," Molly admitted. "Without traffic, and only if the R5's on time."

"Huh. That's a shame."

"And I do feel bad to be such an imposition, though I know they love us a lot."

Jenny smiled at Molly's parents. Molly was quiet for a moment. She saw Dan biting back a grin. "You still hating that bank job?" she asked.

"You know it," Jenny replied. "The free lollipops don't make it any less mind-numbing.

"And it's a big commute now that you're back home?"

"Yeah."

"Huh."

"Yup."

Emily startled both of them. "Oh, for heaven's sake, you two! Look, Molly, your father and I don't mind in the least having our

most precious girls living with us, you know that. But we also
know that Jenny definitely has more energy than us old folks, so
by all means, girls, get to it already." She sat back in her chair
with a sigh, obviously satisfied.

"Okay then, Jenny." Molly could barely contain her grin.

"So, would you maybe consider—"

"Hells, yeah, I would!" Jenny grinned and threw her arms
around Molly's shoulders. Dan laughed out loud now, and Molly
saw Jack pat his wife on the shoulder and kiss the top of her gray
hair. "Girl, you got yourself a nanny!"

The women were still laughing at the sudden ease of their
new arrangement when Jack spoke up. "And, Molly, of course,
you know that your mother and I will be happy to help you as
much as we can on the, um, business side of your deal."

"You mean helping to pay Jenny?"

"Oh, that makes this even better," Jenny said. "I get paid to
hang out with Dylan!"

Molly looked at both of her parents, shaking her head. "You
guys, thank you, but I should be okay, especially once I trade in
my Audi and cut some expenses."

Molly thought of her weekly grocery bill. Now that she
wasn't binge-eating peanut butter–chocolate chip bagels and
Nutella each morning as a result of her pregnancy, she knew she
would save money there, at least. At the very least.

"I'll talk it over with Jenny." Molly nodded at her friend.
"And we'll go from there. But I'll keep you posted."

"We do know a good Subaru dealership," her dad reminded her.

Molly smiled at them, at Dan, at her baby, at Jenny.

"Thank you."

Dylan had started to fuss a little, and Dan picked her up out of the car seat, cradling her for a moment before handing her off to Molly. Emily and Jack excused themselves to the kitchen, empty tea mugs in hand.

"Okay then, boss," Jenny said, "that's probably our cue to go. We have an early appointment with the therapist tomorrow before Dan gets to school, anyway. I'll catch up with you soon so we can finalize the details."

"How's it going with the therapist?" Molly looked between her two friends. "If I can ask?"

"Of course you can ask," Jenny said. "Nothing's too personal once you know about the shots I have to take in the heinie."

Dan shrugged. "I think she lost her dignity right around the time we had a group of medical students observe her first uterine exam. At the rate she's going, if we ever actually do have a baby, Jenny'll be able to deliver in the middle of City Hall and not be embarrassed."

It was Jenny's turn to shrug.

She turned back to Molly. "It's going well, I guess. She's helping us sort out how many of our arguments were stemming from all this pressure, giving us ways to work through the stress together. And avoid the stress altogether, too, if we can. Our homework for next weekend is to go somewhere, out of the city, by ourselves, overnight."

"No kidding!"

"Yeah, I'm actually kind of excited." Dan wiggled his eyebrows, making Jenny elbow him in the stomach.

"So, what's the romantic destination?" Molly asked.

"New Hope," Jenny replied. She was referring to the sweet, tourist-filled town on the river north of the city. "Nice, right?

We're going to do a winery tour, and Dan agreed to let me take him to a play as long as he gets to choose a restaurant afterward."

"Ha," Molly said, watching Dan pretend to yawn. "So you're going to be eating at either a beer garden or a Sonic."

"Pretty much!" Dan said, and placed his hand at the small of Jenny's back to guide her toward the door.

"Well, I wish you a pleasant time anyway, Jenny, Sonic or no Sonic," Molly said, and followed them to the door, cradling Dylan in her left arm. "You guys deserve this."

Molly was truly happy for her friends. She would have expected to feel a pang of jealousy at the idea of a couple's get-away, but all she felt was peace, which surprised her. Molly leaned against the door, watching Jenny gather her belongings. "Let's iron out the details of this whole nanny thing after you come back, then. You know already—I don't have to be back to work until the start of the new year, so we've got plenty of time."

"Sounds good." Jenny picked her red pumps up off the floor and slipped them on. "Now, we are off to rest up before making our therapist a hundred and fifty bucks richer!"

Molly shut the door after her friends and leaned against it for a moment. She looked down at her daughter, who had fallen back to sleep in her arms. She had six more weeks. Six more weeks before she returned to her office. Six more until she had to leave her daughter in the care of another person. It was just a short time until New Year's Eve arrived: before the annual party, before the start of a fresh year, before she had to face her baby's father. Molly placed her lips against Dylan's smooth forehead. She had six more weeks before the rest of her life could begin.

CHAPTER THIRTEEN

December

Yes

Molly tightened the wool scarf around her neck and dug her hands deep into the pockets of her old peacoat. The sharp wind gripped small pieces of ice in its bitter bite now, and when she let herself gasp in the face of it, breathing it in, Molly could smell snow in the air. She kept walking, her head held down to stave off the brunt of the gusts that whipped through the alleyways she passed.

She'd had to get out of the house. Monica and Edward had insisted on coming by again to see the baby, pushing in through the doorway with the usual gifts—bags of toys and clothes and educational DVDs no four-month-old needed. Their breath smelled of the vodka martinis they drank each evening before dinner, whether they were dining out or staying in. But it was when Monica asked Molly to kindly leave the room, her own living room, because it made her uncomfortable to see her breastfeed her daughter, that Molly knew she needed to step out for a bit, even if it meant leaving Dylan behind with them all. Somehow she'd found her way to the Barnes & Noble where she'd first met Scott and had spent a solid hour sitting in a chair next to the literature section, just watching the space where he'd first walked up the aisle and into her life.

On her way home, Molly's steps slowed as she approached the building that housed Shulzster & Grace. It was a huge modern structure of steel and glass that sat like a roadblock at the halfway point on her walk to the subway. She adjusted the earbuds she was wearing and stared up at the glossy windows of the twentieth floor, thinking about who might occupy her old office now. She wondered if that person was as successful with client contracts as she had been in her heyday, or was as efficient with marketing and the schedules as she. The PR firm seemed to taunt her, laughing at her from behind the framework of its gleaming architecture. *Look at me,* it seemed to say. *You could have been here, but you screwed it up. Don't you wish you could still be here? Don't you wish?*

Molly bit back the taste of bile that rose in the back of her throat and pulled her coat closer around her, hugging her elbows to stay warm. When it got cold like this, Scott sometimes used to show up on her doorstep with a grin and two plane tickets to someplace warm. He'd convince her to call out of work, and they'd spend a long weekend in the Bahamas, or Costa Rica, or maybe Italy. Molly's passport had gotten more stamps in the first six months she was with Scott than it had in all her years before him.

She shivered again and looked at the huge glass entranceway that loomed over her, the doors through which she used to walk at least four times a day. Steam rose from the subway vents beneath her, its admittedly pungent warmth almost a respite from the cold. Molly stood in place, still, while the cars on Walnut Street honked at each other and the news helicopters *thup-thup-thup*ped overhead on their way to hunt the next big story of the night. Some passersby glanced at her with curiosity, but most ignored her presence, too wrapped up in their own problems to take notice of the small, sad woman standing alone on the busy sidewalk.

Molly turned away from the dark building and continued on her way home. She didn't like to leave Dylan alone with Scott. He quickly grew impatient when she cried, sometimes choosing to just sit on the couch and listen to her scream through the monitor rather than find a way to soothe her. He acted almost as if it was beneath his dignity to try to calm a baby down, Molly thought. But his parents were there, and she knew Scott would put on his best face for them. She just prayed they didn't leave before she got home.

Molly picked up her pace and hurried down the stairs to the subway station, cowering against the chill.

The snow was just beginning to fall the next day, a thin veil of white flakes cloaking the soot that covered the buildings outside her window. Molly sat cross-legged on the floor of the living room wearing her sweatpants and a Bryn Mawr T-shirt from her undergrad days, searching for Christmas gifts for her brothers. Dylan was dozing in her bouncy seat, and Molly was half-watching *Rocky Balboa* as she worked. Her cell phone rang, and Molly snatched it from the coffee table on the second ring. The movie had gone to commercial, and Molly turned down the volume of the television.

"Oh, sorry, Mol. Did I wake the baby?" Jenny's voice was bright and clear.

Molly glanced again at Dylan. She'd barely stirred.

"Nope, nope. You're good. What's up?" Molly clicked through pictures of camping gear online while she listened to her friend. She'd have to ask Scott for more money if she was going to be able to afford any of the items. He still hadn't added her to his checking account, no matter how many times she reminded him. She looked up to see that the commercials had ended and the movie was back on. Molly saw Sylvester Stallone move across the screen, rambling down the same Philadelphia streets she did every day. The volume was too low to hear what he was saying.

"Well, I just wanted to call and check to see if you guys were still planning on coming to our party this year." Jenny sounded tentative.

"What, for New Year's? We wouldn't miss it for the world. You know that. It's just . . ." Molly glanced at Dylan.

Jenny laughed as if she'd seen Molly's expression. "You have a little baby to care for now? Bring her with you."

"Jenny, we don't want to impose on you!" Molly said. "It's just that my parents have that party they go to every year, and Scott's parents are leaving for France that night, and we don't have a babysitter." Molly wondered how she'd convince Scott to pay for a sitter anyway. He'd gotten tight with his money since she'd had the baby. She tried to suppress the bubble of anger that flared in her belly like a fire, but it was there, as it always was lately, growing more persistent with each day that passed. Molly watched an image of City Hall pan across the television. It was the beginning of the scene where Rocky fights for his boxing license.

"Molly, I wouldn't offer if I weren't serious," Jenny insisted. Molly could hear Dan echo his agreement in the background. "We have so many friends who've started breeding we just decided that we'd better make the festivities start earlier this year so people can bring their kiddos."

"You guys are awesome," Molly said, relieved. She'd been worried she'd have to miss her first real social activity since giving birth. "The party's definitely going to have a different vibe this year, isn't it? With all of these little ones running around?" She laughed.

Jenny was starting to answer when Scott walked into the room.

"What's awesome? Did we win something?" He was dressed to go out, wearing his best jeans and a cashmere sweater his parents had brought him back from Milan last winter. He checked his hair in the mirror hanging by the front door. "Tell me. What'd we get?"

Molly put her hand over the phone's mouthpiece.

"Jenny and Dan are making their New Year's party kid-friendly this year. So we can take Dylan."

Scott groaned. "You mean you're making me go to that thing again? My buddy from work has tickets to the Sixers that night."

"On New Year's?" Molly said, surprised. She could hear Jenny whispering to Dan through the earpiece. "When were you going to tell me?"

"I don't know." Scott shrugged. "Does it matter?" He glanced at Dylan, whose eyes had opened while they were talking, and strode over to the staircase before taking the steps to the second floor two at a time. Molly was quiet for a long while. Hurt tumbled down her throat and into her belly like a waterfall, splashing there before spreading out, until it filled every cell in her body with the knowledge that she'd been trying to keep from rising like floodwaters for the past few months, or even years.

It was never going to get better. They were never going to be okay.

"Molly." Jenny's voice was clearer now. Molly'd forgotten she still had the phone up to her ear. "Is this worth it?"

Molly closed the lid to her laptop. She didn't feel like shopping after all.

"We have a baby, Jenny." She sighed, her tone even, willing the activity in her mind to abate. She stretched her legs out on the floor and noticed that her yoga pants were starting to get threadbare in the knees.

"Well, I'd like to know you'll be okay until I see you again."

"I'll be fine, Jenny. I have it under control. Don't spend your vacation worrying about me." Molly took a shaky breath, surprised by the sudden stab of fear she felt. "Are you guys going to be away for long?"

Jenny made an *mm-hmm* sound into the phone. "We'll be visiting Dan's dad and his stepmom for the rest of the month."

The fear turned to panic when Molly realized she wouldn't have her best friend around for two weeks. She stood to pick Dylan up from the seat and held her close. Her thoughts were competing with one another, coming fast and hard. She didn't realize that she was rocking back and forth in place.

"You'll be in Connecticut, right?" Molly tried to make her voice even. "They just got a ton of snow up there, I heard. And bonus for getting to hang out with Dan's folks."

"I know—they're just the coolest parents in the world, aren't they? I'm fantasizing about winter wonderlands and sleigh bells, and Dan's been talking nonstop about finally teaching me to ski." Jenny paused. "And it'll be nice to get away from Operation Procreation for a little bit."

"I totally agree." Molly was pacing on the living room rug. "And I'm not even the least bit jealous."

Jenny had been rustling some papers. The noise suddenly stopped. "Oh, no. Don't tell me. What are you guys up to?"

"He's insisting that we spend Christmas with his family."

Jenny was silent for a moment, then she said, "Wait a minute. He's never around and does nothing for you, but now you have to ditch your family to hang out with his? Do his parents even care about seeing Dylan?"

"Yeah, they do," Molly said. "A bit too much, actually. They love her. She's the second coming of Scott."

"So you're going to let him bully you into that, even with what happened the last time? I don't get it." Jenny's voice rose higher. "Are you trying to get pregnant again?"

Molly had stopped walking. She stood in the middle of her living room, staring at the television. Rocky was watching his son get browbeaten by his boss. Molly's body faced the door, her muscles tensed.

"God, no! I'm just trying to keep the relationship alive, friend. Gotta give the dying horse one more good kick in the ribs, you know?"

"Molly, his parents are dreadful. You're torturing yourself."

"Ah, they're not that bad. Monica's worked to make a good life for her family. You have to respect that." Molly was still standing in place, her mind not fully focused on the conversation.

Jenny snorted. "Yeah, because Scott turned out really well.

Is this the same Monica who once assumed Dan was part of the string quartet at a party? She's sort of—"

"—not too graceful, I know. I'll give you that. It took me a while to realize that about her," Molly said. "Too busy being dazzled by all the shiny jewelry and fancy cars."

Jenny was silent. "Well, I'll be thinking of you."

"As you sip your hot toddy with Dan beside the fireplace at some chic ski lodge?" Molly forced out a laugh. "You better not be."

Jenny chuckled, but it was a quiet sound, more reserved than her usual throaty laugh.

"Well, have a good Christmas, Mol. Let's sit down after the holidays and hash out the next step in our job-searching, okay? Because I know you won't let Scott keep you penned up in there too much longer."

Molly shifted on her feet and looked at Dylan, who had dozed off again in her arms. One day. One day soon. "You're still looking for another job?"

"Of course." Jenny laughed. "If I have to itemize one more receipt at that damn bank I'm going to end up stapling myself in the head."

After they said their good-byes, Molly placed her phone in her bag and laid a calm Dylan in her portable crib, spinning the mobile overhead as a distraction. She turned up the volume on the television just in time to catch her favorite scene in all the *Rocky* movies, a speech she remembered her brothers quoting from memory after she'd gone with them to see it over her winter break senior year. Rocky had just launched into his son with a lecture of epic proportions, and Molly sat down to watch it. There was always one line in particular she loved to hear her brothers recite: "If you know what you're worth," they'd shout, punching the air with glee, "then go out and get what you're worth." Molly had heard the same speech over and over again for a month that winter. She'd always rolled her eyes at their enthusiasm, but not today.

Today, Molly thought about her conversation with Jenny and Dan over cheesesteaks in October. She thought about the exhaustion of caring for Dylan by herself while picking up after Scott. She remembered broken promises, and impatient yelling, and getting to know a man who was as shiny and fast as the Porsche he drove but with the same unyielding shell. Molly'd been depending on a lifetime with a man she wasn't even sure she wanted to marry. She had to realize that a man wasn't like a house—no one should sign the papers when all she's considering is his *potential*. A fixer-upper is still going to have pipes that leak, and a roof that's collapsing, and a foundation crumbling beneath her feet, all of them problems she must learn to live with because she'd already committed to the loan. Molly jumped out of an airplane once without being able to see where she was going. She wasn't going to do it again.

Molly thought about this, thought about going out and getting what she was worth, all while she was sitting on a couch that smelled like the greasy potato chips Scott always dropped behind the cushions, picking at a hole in her sweatpants because, like a blind woman, she'd been counting on Scott to walk with her down a road she was never meant to be on to begin with.

Molly turned off the television and laid a protective hand on Dylan's belly, feeling the soft rise and fall of her stomach with each of her breaths. Once she was sure the baby would remain content, occupied with the shadows dancing in the corner of the

Pack 'n Play, Molly picked her way up the stairs, her feet landing on each step with a firm purpose.

Scott was sitting in front of the laptop, as he did most days at home now when he wasn't watching TV. He was surrounded by piles of hospital paperwork and unpaid invoices, playing a game, swearing as he frantically jabbed at the keyboard.

Molly stood at the edge of the desk, waiting for him to glance in her direction. She tried to keep the tremor out of her voice when she spoke. She thought of Rocky dressing down his son in the middle of a Philadelphia sidewalk and braced herself.

"Scott, I thought of something."

Scott cursed under his breath as a figure on the computer screen blew up in a mess of blood and machine guns.

"Huh?" he said, eyes still focused on the screen. "Can we talk about it later? I'm kind of in the middle of something here."

"It's pretty important."

He kept clicking away at the touch pad of the laptop, muttering under his breath.

"Scott. We're supposed to be getting married, right?"

"Yeah. What, are you still worried about the flowers for the church? I told you my mom was insisting on roses." He was dressed as if he could pop out to dinner at a moment's notice in his dry-cleaned sweater and perfectly slouched jeans. "Take it up with her."

"That's not it," Molly said. "You moved in here because we got engaged and had a baby, right?"

"Of course."

"And it's important to you that I be a stay-at-home mom, right?"

"Well, one of us has to do it, and I'm the one who has a job."

Molly reeled back like she'd been punched. She'd been with Scott for three years. Three years with him, and still, she stood there, shocked into a momentary silence: *How did I miss this?*

Molly moved over to the dresser that stood against the far wall and pulled out a pair of jeans and an oversized sweater. She could feel her body shaking as she changed clothes. She brushed her hair and pulled it back into a neat ponytail, refusing to pay attention to how dry her mouth felt. When she turned around again, her hands automatically clenched at her sides. She found it difficult to look directly at Scott's face, but forced herself to do so. She kept looking at him, kept the pressure of her gaze trained at his head, and started talking again, because she knew that at some point he would have to listen.

"Scott." Molly's voice was firm. "I can't do this anymore."

"Mmm," he replied. His eyes were locked on to his game. "Can't do what anymore?"

"This, Scott." Molly's exasperation weighted every word. "Us. I can't live like this anymore."

"Wait, what? What's the problem?"

Molly was breathing hard. "There are a few of them. For one thing, I've decided that I'm tired of you mooching off of me."

She had his attention now. Scott pushed his chair away from the computer and turned to look at Molly. His eyebrows were pulled together, dark over his green irises.

"What did you just say?"

She repeated herself, louder this time, her voice firmer. "I'm tired of you mooching off of me. It stops now."

Scott laughed. "Me, mooching off of you?" He shook his head. "You're kidding me, right, Molly? Aren't you the poor one?"

"Yeah, I am," Molly said, "because of you. And I don't know

how it's taken me this long to realize it. You insist that I stay home, yet I'm still the one paying the rent on this house. I'm the one watching her savings disappear, even though I'm engaged to a man who can afford to lie around the house in a seven-hundred-dollar sweater. You live here full-time, but haven't paid a dime toward the place." She paused to catch her breath. "You were never going to add me to your bank account, were you?"

Scott didn't say a word.

"I want you to start paying rent."

Scott was staring at her now, his eyebrows raised. Molly saw the surprise in his eyes and felt emboldened.

"Actually, back-rent, for the last eleven months you've been here, and money to help pay for Dylan's clothes," she continued. "And I need to have access to the bank account if I'm going to be the one taking care of the bills and groceries."

She took a moment to look at him, making sure not to break eye contact. "I don't think that's too much to ask, do you? I mean, considering that we're a family now and all."

Scott stood up. She used to love how tall he was, and strong, before the day it started to scare her. Now she just saw him, his chest at her eye level, and envisioned a wall. He was a wall, not big enough to block her way, and definitely not so big it couldn't be scaled. The computer game was on pause behind him, the voices of the gun-wielding soldiers yelling over and over again.

"We're getting married, Molly. I'm not paying rent to my wife." Scott's legs were planted wide as he stood between the computer and the bed, next to the door. "As it is, do you really think your name's going to be on the mortgage? My parents already have their lawyers working up papers for the landlord. I'm going to control the money."

Molly bent over to slip her feet into her boots, careful not to take her eyes off Scott for too long. She felt sick to her stomach.

"This is ridiculous." Scott's face was red. "You're home all day anyway. You shouldn't need money, unless you're renting some hotel room somewhere when I'm not looking. I'm sure you've got old Liam on speed dial."

Molly just shook her head in response. She'd heard it before.

She nodded toward the desk. "That's my computer. The cable you watch all the time on TV? I pay for it. The food you keep pulling out of the fridge while you leave the door hanging wide open? I buy that, too. And I'm finished buying it. You don't get a free pass anymore. Not from me, anyway."

"This is bullshit, Molly."

"I don't think so." Molly was fully dressed now and standing tall. "We have a daughter you need to pay attention to. We have a house to keep clean for her, and a college fund to discuss, and preschools to look into before she gets wait-listed. It's time to be a grown-up, Scott."

"I'm not buying into any of this," Scott said. "You liked me just fine a few months ago. I think something's going on with *you*.

"You cheating on me?" he said. "Got somebody else you think is better?"

"I really wish you'd stop accusing me of that." Molly sighed. "I can't believe you think I'd even have the *energy* to cheat, even if I wanted to."

"Well, something's making you feel pretty good about yourself to make you think you can start bossing me around."

"No, I'm on my own, here, saying that you can't walk all over me." Molly's anger continued to boil, but now she could barely contain a smile threatening to sneak onto her face. "Why do you automatically assume it's another guy? I'm getting a real job again, one in PR."

"Yeah. Good luck with that," Scott said.

"I've got two interviews lined up for next week." Molly watched Scott's face for a reaction. He said nothing.

"And as for us?" Molly continued. "I'm finished taking your crap."

He was shaking his head, muttering under his breath.

"Scott." He looked up at her, his eyebrows pulled together in angry confusion. "This part is over. I'm taking Dylan to my parents' for the weekend." Molly pulled the bag she kept packed for visits home out of the closet and hoisted it onto her shoulder.

Molly looked around the room, at the piles of his clothes dropped like used tissues in the corners of the room. "You can use the time alone to pack up your stuff and leave. I want you out of my house."

Scott stood in place, running his hand through his hair. Molly could see him thinking, reaching for some plan of attack, but she stepped to the door before he could make his move. Dylan had started crying for her from the living room, ready for a meal and some comfort from her mother. Molly slid around him and was about to step over the threshold to the hallway when she glanced sidelong at Scott. He'd started to sputter in indignation, and she knew he wouldn't block her way. The computer game was still making its machine-gun sounds, punctuating the tense air with the screams of some invisible character getting blown up, over and over again, as it repeated its loop. Molly leaned over, slammed the lid of the computer closed, and walked calmly down the stairs to her daughter.

New Year's Eve

Molly sat in her parked car on a densely tree-lined street in Merion Station, staring at the brick facade of a sprawling home. A half-moon driveway encircled an intricate English garden and brick wall. It lay between her and the front door. Dylan had fallen asleep on the drive, and Molly took a moment before disturbing her, trying to psych herself up to go ring Scott's parents' bell. She told herself that she only had to stay a couple of hours. She'd made sure that his parents had known ahead of time that she'd have to get home and let Dylan rest before Jenny and Dan's party tonight, so her early departure was already cleared. Now it was just a matter of going in.

Molly took one last deep breath and checked her makeup in the rearview mirror before getting out of the used Outback. She'd used a heavy hand to spackle concealer under her eyes, but there was no hiding the dark moons that seemed omnipresent on her skin. She took Dylan's carrier gently out of the backseat, hoisted the heavy red quilted diaper bag over her shoulder, and gingerly walked up the path. It was the first time she'd worn heels since she'd entered her third trimester, and as soon as she'd stepped into them Molly had understood why most young moms she saw wore flats. It was an occupational hazard to even attempt to navigate stone pavers on stilettos while balancing a car seat. Molly picked her way through the garden, focused on not toppling over into Scott's parents' lawn.

Molly rang the bell beside the front door of the narrow entranceway, marveling at how such a massive home could possess such an unwelcoming, cramped front porch. She knew that Scott had spent most of his life in this house, his parents having moved in right after Monica finished her architecture program and Scott's father landed his job with the Eagles. Every surface inside had something interesting to look at, a vase or a piece of modern art framed to impress. Molly had never seen so much as a speck of dust on any of the furniture in the house, and the outside of the home was maintained to Stepford-like quality as well. None of the work, of course, was done by the Berkuses themselves. The boxwoods were trimmed into even squares along the front porch, and Molly noticed that the new evergreens planted in orderly little planters along the walk were well-tended and perfectly spaced. While the rest of the homes on this affluent street were adorned in white lights and tasteful wreaths for the holidays, here the trees were topped with so much gold garland and glittering ornaments it seemed the Berkus family was determined that their holiday spirit be witnessed from space.

As Molly stood outside the entrance, catching her breath, she focused on trying to get her pulse to stop racing. She had just enough time to adjust the car seat on her arm and brace her shoulders back before the front door swung open with a clatter and Scott's mother appeared in the doorway. Her lean figure seemed to fill the length of the narrow space, and the diamonds in her ears flashed as she looked Molly over from head to high-heeled toe. Molly pasted an automatic smile on her face, set to endure the absolute awkwardness of this afternoon. A stranger would never have guessed that the two women used to bond over mani-pedis and afternoon leadership seminars. Molly's hand was clenched around the handle of Dylan's car seat, and she felt her heart thump with a little more forcefulness in her chest.

"Molly! What are you doing, standing out there in the cold? My granddaughter must be freezing. Come in, come in." She made kissy faces at Dylan, but didn't touch Molly.

Molly blew out the breath she'd been holding and followed Monica into the house.

Once in the foyer, Monica placed her hands on Molly's shoulders and maneuvered her into the expansive living room. As large as the space was, it was crowded with Scott's relatives, many of whom stopped mid-conversation to turn and stare at Molly. She hovered there in the center of room, like a decorative urn being presented for auction at Sotheby's, still clutching the car seat.

Monica cleared her throat and looked around with a wide smile. Her square white teeth, set in straight rows in her mouth, snapped together once before she introduced Molly to the general crowd, speaking to no one in particular but addressing the entire room.

"Well. Molly, meet Scott's aunt and uncle. You already know Trudy, of course, and the cousins. This is Molly, everyone!"

Monica bent over the car seat in a dramatic swoop. "And

this—this!—beautiful girl right here is my very own gorgeous little grandbaby. Oh, doesn't she look like Scott? Hello, sweet Dylan!" Molly couldn't help but feel like Scott's mother was acting out her own one-woman show.

Monica turned again to the rest of her family after hearing someone whisper. "Yes, it's Dylan. I know, her name is a little, well, *different*, but Molly is Irish, after all. You know how it goes."

Molly stood, staring at Monica in surprise, as the women rushed over to peer into the seat. The shiny demeanor, her smooth glamour, had all dropped away into a Northeast Philly accent now that Monica was inside, surrounded by her own family. Molly watched the women coo over the baby, mentally prepared to smack away any cocktail sauce–stained finger that made contact with her daughter's face. She still hadn't seen Scott, and she wondered if he'd declined to show up. She hoped he was there. She was ready to see him.

Monica finally acknowledged Molly again.

"Oh, let me take your coat, Molly. And let's get you off of those high heels. It's about time we saw you out of those sweatpants and UGGS, but my goodness, these certainly are high, aren't they?" she said. "Well, good for you for putting yourself together so well so soon after the baby was born!"

Monica turned to a woman standing next to her, a cousin, or aunt, possibly. "So many mothers today have to spend all their time with their little ones, but it's just lovely that she makes sure to take the time from this sweet baby for herself, isn't it?"

Molly attempted a smile. "Uh, thank—"

"Why, you only have a little bit of a stomach left, Molly! It's barely anything at all!"

"—you?" Molly lowered her voice a little, when all she

wanted to do was laugh. *Or scream,* she thought. *Really, either one would be fine.* "Um, Monica? Is there anywhere more private I could go to feed Dylan?"

Molly's daughter was stirring in her seat, with her face scrunched up in an expression that meant the hungry baby would be roaring for milk as soon as she opened those pretty blue eyes.

"Oh, honey, if you want to get settled in, Edward could feed her."

Scott's father came into the room just then, holding a can of beer in one hand. He was almost shouting into the ear of a middle-aged man next to him.

"They should just bench him, anyway! If his own QB doesn't trust him, why the hell is he still starting?" He clapped his great paw of a hand onto Molly's shoulder and bent over to get a look at Dylan.

"What do you think of dose Iggles, huh, little Dylan? Oh, my pretty little princess won't like football, will she? Just tutus and ballet class for you, sweetheart!"

"Dear," Monica addressed her husband, "I was just suggesting to Molly that maybe you'd like to feed the baby?"

"You were suggesting?" Edward's voice was jovial. "And here I thought I was in charge around this house!" He looked around at the small crowd for approval.

Molly watched Monica's head drop. She concentrated on her wedding rings, twisting the large, teardrop-shaped diamond around on her finger.

"Oh, I'm just joking," Edward continued. "Yeah, Molly, I'd love to feed her! Where's the bottle?" He looked around the floor for the diaper bag, and Molly felt her cheeks go red.

"Um, actually, Edward, I haven't started her on a bottle yet. But thanks for the offer."

Scott's father tilted his head and stared at her, his forehead wrinkled with bewilderment.

"How the hell does she eat, then? She's, what, four months old by now?" His voice was loud. Several people surrounding them turned to listen in. Monica's head snapped to attention.

Molly swallowed. "Edward, you know she's breastfed. I'm still nursing her." She stifled a smile at the look of horror that flashed across Edward's face.

"Oh." Edward sipped his beer and looked away.

"Still breastfeeding? Oh, my," Monica murmured. "My goodness, I thought only poor people and vegans did that anymore."

She gestured toward the staircase. "You can use the guest room upstairs, then, dear. Second door on your left. It has the pink wallpaper."

Molly excused herself and got upstairs as quickly as she could without making it obvious that she was nearly running in her stocking-clad feet. She shut the door to the guest room and settled herself onto the flowered bedspread with Dylan, a burp cloth, and her phone, placing her bag on the floor beside her. Molly's heart was running around in her chest like a rabbit trying to escape a predator. She was used to being around Scott's parents with him by her side, but now the dynamic had shifted. Interacting with both Monica and Edward on her own was a little like throwing herself into shark-infested waters with chum tied around her neck. Though in this case, the chum was her defenseless daughter.

Molly and Dylan settled into their feeding session. Molly leaned against the floral pillow sham with her eyes closed, the top of her dress pulled to the side so Dylan could nurse. She relaxed to hear the baby's soft grunting sounds and felt the small hand where it rested against her back, kneading the skin with a sort of absentminded concentration that didn't seem possible in someone so small. It was as if the small creature already knew her mind, already had it all together, and just needed to grow into a body big enough to make whatever she wanted happen. Molly wondered if she might not be a little jealous of her baby.

There was a brisk knock at the door. Before she could call out, it flew open, and the person she had been waiting to see broke into the room.

"Scott."

Molly tossed a burp cloth over her upper body in an attempt to cover up and tightened her hold on Dylan in a quick, instinctive move. She smoothed her hair around her shoulders with her free hand before taking notice of Scott's face. It held a strange expression, an unnerving combination of purpose and preoccupation. Molly reached under her hip to make sure her phone was still there where she'd placed it and adjusted the cloth over her bare chest again.

"Oh, relax, Molly. It's not like I've never seen them before."

Molly ignored his comment. "I didn't think you were here."

"My parents are throwing a family party." Scott stood at the foot of the bed, like he was unsure of where to go. "Why wouldn't I be here?"

He shifted from side to side in his shoes, which were scuffed on the top, most likely by the hand of an artisan cobbler in Europe.

"Anyway, I wanted to talk to you."

"Can it wait?" The house felt too quiet, and Molly felt her face flush hot. "I'd like to feed Dylan in peace, and then we can talk."

Scott snorted. "That name's not great, but I guess it was the best one out of all the crazy choices you were dreaming up," he said. "What was that one name on your list? Wait, it was Rhiannon, right? After that Fleetwood Mac song your dad likes so much?"

There was a moment of awkward silence while Molly watched him. Scott rocked on his feet, as if deciding what to do next. He was wearing a pair of tailored corduroy pants with a luxe button-front shirt he'd rolled at the sleeves. He looked as well-put-together as always, if one didn't notice the uncharacteristic way his eyes shifted, or how he kept running his hand through his hair.

"Seriously, can you go?" Molly said. "I'll talk to you downstairs, in a few minutes."

Scott acted like he hadn't heard her and moved toward the bed. Molly scooted farther back into the cushions, clutching the startled baby to her chest. She could feel her breath quicken.

"Molly, I just want to talk to you, and then I'll leave you alone. I promise."

Scott dropped down onto the foot of the mattress and looked at his daughter. Dylan had gone back to Molly's breast to nurse, her head and shoulders covered under the wide burp cloth, so that all he could see was a hand and her lower body in its brown tights and knit sage-colored dress.

"I gotta tell you something, Molly."

He inhaled.

"It's hard for me to feel close to Dylan." He glanced at the baby once again. "And it has nothing to do with her weird name."

Molly's arm tightened even more around the infant. "What are you talking about?"

"I mean, she's my kid. I made her, but big whoop, you know? I don't see me getting . . . used to her."

Molly swallowed. She stared at Scott's face, trying to discern some sort of emotion in his dull eyes. "And why are you telling me this?"

"Because it doesn't change the way I feel about you."

He glanced at her.

"I want you to know that you don't have to worry about me anymore. I know I've been going about this the wrong way. See, I've been thinking about you a lot. A whole lot, actually. You are constantly on my mind," Scott said. "You're in my head when I go to bed at night, and you're the first thing I think about when I wake up. It's like, I didn't need you when I had you, but now I can't live without you. I'm obsessed."

Scott had his arms braced on his knees, and was staring at his clasped hands. Molly's jaw had gone slack with shock. Before she could respond, Scott turned to look at her.

"Marry me, Molly."

She was still sitting on the bed, poorly covered from the waist up, with a child latched to her breast. Molly blinked, and wondered if she needed to get her hearing checked.

"I'm serious." Scott leaned toward her now, his face earnest and determined. "Marry me this week. We'll go to the courthouse, do something simple, just you and me. We can be like we were."

Silence filled the room after he said the words. Scott and Molly were both still for a moment, their eyes locked on each other.

When Scott glanced away, a strange sort of sensation shifted inside Molly's body, and she found her voice. A maternal center of balance had righted itself in her soul, turning her attention to the correct point on the compass. "Scott, I don't want to be like we were. Not before or after the baby. We're not good together."

She looked down at Dylan, at the closed eyes of her daughter, so content against the warmth of her mother's chest, before regarding Scott again.

"And you know that."

Scott moved closer to Molly. She couldn't shift away from

him, stuck where she was against the overstuffed pillows of the bed. He placed his hands on her arms, rubbing them up and down until her skin started to grow irritated from the friction. Molly wriggled her arms from his grasp.

Scott's eyes were pleading. "I don't want to lose you, Mol. I love you. You know that. You're the mother of my kid." To hear him beg this hard was unsettling.

"You just said you couldn't see yourself being close to her." Molly shook her head. "No."

"You know what I meant, Molly. I could figure out how to deal with her." He glanced at Dylan's form under the cloth. "I just need you."

Scott reached for Molly again and tried to pull her into his chest, pressing his lips against the top of her head. Molly cringed and tried to squirm out his grasp, holding the baby steady.

"Marry me."

"Scott, I—" Molly tried once more to pull away from him and, with a sudden burst of strength, pushed at Scott's chest until his hands fell off of her. She sat up straight, breathing hard.

"NO. This is not happening. *We* are not happening. This is it, we are done, and you may go." She pointed at the door and stared down Scott with a new fierceness she felt she had been waiting years to let loose. Molly watched as Scott's face changed. The muscles in his jaw tensed, and his eyes grew darker, more narrow. It was like he'd pulled on a mask while she was looking.

"Molly." His voice had developed an edge to it, sharp and hard. "What else are you going to do? You can't live without me."

Scott leaned back, and Molly watched him look her over. She knew now he was just trying to throw her off, make her insecure. She wasn't having it.

"You need me, Molly. We're supposed to be together," Scott said.

Molly let out a laugh that was low and sarcastic. "I'll be fine, Scott."

"Oh, yeah, you as a single mom, right?" He sneered at her. "Look how stretched thin you already were at S&G, Molly. You were a neurotic mess. And now you think you can handle it all?"

Molly didn't say anything. Dylan was finished nursing and had fallen asleep at her chest, but Molly didn't try to burp her, or move her, or even cover herself back up with her dress.

Scott stood up, gave one glance at the lump under the blanket that was Dylan, and walked away from the bed. Molly breathed in relief and slid her dress back into place on her shoulder. It was over. Scott stopped when he got to the closed door and, turning, took a step toward Molly before he opened it.

"I feel bad for you, Molly," Scott said. "You're making a huge mistake."

Molly looked down at her tiny daughter. Dylan was still sleeping at her chest, warm and small, folded around the contours of Molly's body. She hadn't fussed once the entire time Scott was talking. It was as if she hadn't even known he was there. Her mother had been enough for her, and that was all that mattered.

"No, Scott," Molly said. "I don't think I am at all."

Later that night, Molly stepped through the open doorway into her friends' home. Her hair was down now, curling around her shoulders in loose waves, and she'd pushed the sleeves of the cream V-necked sweater she'd changed into up her arms. She wore minimal jewelry—a watch, a pair of silver hoop earrings, and a necklace bearing a circular design that looked almost Celtic—but there was a hint of eye shadow glistening below her brows, and the shine of the room's lamps played against the gloss on her lips. Her skin was flushed a light rose color, giving her cheeks a pleasant hue. Her black pants made clean lines against her thighs, their fit smooth. Molly had pulled on the skinny jeans tonight, surprised and pleased that she could get them up over her hips. No one had to know that they didn't quite zip up all the way.

Dan was the first to greet Molly, and she walked into the room to hug him, smiling, aware of the murmurs here and there among the guests moving around the room. She saw the furtive glances passed between couples, friends, former coworkers, but then the chatter of the party fell back into its normal patterns, and she looked over her friend's shoulder to catch sight of Jenny, standing in the middle of the crowd, grinning at her.

Jenny walked over to Molly, her own face bright and cheerful. Glasses clinked around them, Florence and the Machine was playing from the stereo speakers, and Molly exhaled a breath she didn't know she'd been holding. She turned around to close the door on the cold night behind her. The last of the afternoon's clouds had cleared out, leaving behind a sky tinged with the thin rays of the setting sun. A few stars twinkled above the buildings among the pink and orange streaks, and as Molly pushed the heavy door shut with one hand, she caught a last whiff of the crisp air that swirled between the buildings and into the warm home like a kite bouncing along a shore breeze. She turned around again, ready to enter the party.

"Hey, hey, here are my girls!" Jenny set her glass, which was filled with something clear with a wedge of lime, on the counter of the open kitchen bar and wrapped her arms around Molly's shoulders. She drew her in close and hard.

"Wowsa, lady." Molly's friend leaned back, holding her by the shoulders at arm's length. "You smell awesome! Don't tell me you finally broke down and tried a new perfume."

Molly laughed, adjusting her weight so she could scoot the car seat she was carrying farther up her arm.

"Yeah, I figured it was about time. I don't want to be that old lady wearing the same stuff she bought at the drugstore with her allowance money when she was thirteen."

Jenny chuckled, but her attention had already been snagged by the little bundle of blankets in the carrier on Molly's arm.

"Well, if it's not Miss Dylan Sullivan! Hello, my precious girl." Jenny's voice rose to the unnaturally high level adults often adopted when they addressed babies. Molly started to tease her friend, knowing that Jenny would most certainly mock that voice were it coming from anybody else, but decided against it. She looked at Dan instead, who was watching and shaking his head with mock dismay. Jenny was still cooing at Dylan, so Molly placed the baby carrier on the floor.

"Come here, you. Man, she's beautiful, Molly. I mean, I know most babies are cute, but this one, lady"—Jenny jabbed a finger in Dylan's direction—"*this* one is a gem. Now, let me see my favorite goddaughter!"

"She's your only goddaughter, if I remember correctly." Molly smiled, unbuckling her daughter's harness. She felt pretty tonight. She knew the dark circles remained under her eyes, and that she looked more tired, more subdued, than she ever had at one of these parties, but she felt all right. She felt good.

Jenny took Dylan from Molly and held her close to her chest, rocking the baby in her arms.

"Yes, but even if I had a hundwed wittle godchildren, you'd

still be my favorite, sweet pea! Yes, you would!" Molly's best friend regarded the small infant, warm and secure in her little terry-cloth onesie. Dylan didn't make a sound. She just watched her godmother, her eyes moving over Jenny's face, taking her in.

"Jenny," Molly said, "thank you so much for having this again. The early party was such a great idea. Are there a lot of kids here?"

"Are you kidding me? Uh, yeah." Jenny nodded her head toward the back of the condo. "A bunch of them are camped out in our bedroom upstairs, watching *Toy Story 3*." She looked around. "Actually, I think that's where Dan just went. I'm sure he just wanted the excuse to go watch the movie again.

"You know, though," Jenny continued, adjusting Dylan, who'd begun to doze in her arms, "a party with kids is the only way we'd be able to see everybody, now that our friends are popping out babies like PEZ dispensers. Otherwise we'd be sitting here all by our lonesomes, and that's not fun."

Dan skipped down the last few steps of the carpeted staircase and headed over to the pair, smiling broadly, his spiky hair freshly gelled and sticking straight up from the top of his head.

"Okay, it looks like they're just getting to the incinerator scene, so I stocked them up on tissues. I figure we have a solid half hour before we have to think of something else to keep them contained. In the meantime, Molly, we've got food out in the dining room. Can I get you something to drink? Johnnie Walker on the rocks, right?"

"Um, not tonight, Dan. Jenny, what are you drinking? You always inspire me." Before her friend could answer her, Molly turned to Dan. "You know what? Surprise me. I'll have what she's having."

Dan smiled at Molly with an expression she thought was weirdly mischievous. "Okay, then, Molly, since you're playing it fast and loose tonight. One Jenny special, coming right up!"

Molly watched him pat Jenny on the lower back and wink at her. Jenny blushed red like Dan said she used to do in high school when he'd kiss her in the hallway, and they both watched him stroll back to the kitchen.

Jenny turned away to greet the friends who'd just entered the party, and Molly took a moment to look around. There were some groups of people she recognized, both from S&G and outside of it, mingling here and there. A few children played with quiet focus at a coffee table in the corner with some coloring books and cars. There were low flames flickering in the fireplace, strong enough to add ambience to the night, but far from being a danger to the fingertips of any curious toddlers. There were so many candles situated around the bookshelf tops and mantle they almost negated the need for the white lights that wove among them. Once again, Jenny had pulled off a stellar decorating job. The big Christmas tree in the corner and evergreen garlands placed here and there added to the mix to create a New Year's Eve gathering that felt inviting and special, even if this particular party was taking on a familiar, comfortable mood that felt more mellow than party-hardy.

Jenny's loud conversation had caused Dylan to fuss a little, and Molly took her daughter so that Jenny could finish her chat in peace. She smiled to hear the music wafting through the air and rocked the baby a little to the song's persistent beat. Molly was very aware that she still hadn't greeted a single other person in the room, but it didn't bother her. It was still early. She had just arrived.

"Leave all your love and your longing behind," she softly sang. "You can't carry it with you if you want to survive . . ."

"Okay, here you are, ladies." Dan approached with two short glasses in his hands, and Jenny turned to join her husband and Molly. She suddenly didn't look so well. Her face was pale, and she kept swallowing like she was trying to keep down a bad bite of food. She took the glass from Dan and took a deep sip.

"Hey, Jenny, you okay?" Molly's eyebrows were furrowed together with worry, a habit she'd picked up over the last few months.

Jenny glanced at Dan, then took another gulp of her drink, cringing. "I'll be fine, Mol. Just a little stomach trouble. Once I get some food in me, I'll be okay."

She motioned toward Molly. "Come on, try Dan's concoction. I'm anxious to hear what you think."

Dan grinned as he handed Molly the glass. He kept looking at her, waiting for her to try the drink. Molly watched Jenny take another sip of the iced liquid. She hadn't seen her friend drink this much since before she and Dan had started trying again for a baby.

"Mmm," Jenny said theatrically. "Thanks, Dan. You always get it right, don't you?"

Molly took a taste of her drink and instantly felt her nose wrinkle.

"But, Dan, this is water. I thought—" Molly looked at Jenny, then at her glass, and felt her mouth drop open. She thought for a second that she was going to lose her hold on Dylan, and grasped her tighter to her chest.

"Are you serious? You're—?"

Jenny squealed, softly, and bounced up and down in a little

dance in front of Molly. Dan threw his arm around his wife's shoulders, drawing her in tight, and the both of them just stood in place together, watching Molly absorb the news, grinning like cartoon characters.

"It's early, though," Jenny was quick to say. "Super early. I just found out a couple of weeks ago."

"A couple of weeks ago?! And you just told me now?"

Jenny bit her lip.

"Well, we wanted to wait for the right time. You know . . ." Molly could feel her face tighten up, and she swallowed, hard. "I mean, we wanted to surprise you. Don't be angry."

Molly exhaled through her nose and felt the muscles in her face soften. *It is a new year,* she told herself. *It's a new year.*

"How could I possibly be angry?" she finally exclaimed, then dropped her voice to a whisper. "This is the most incredible news I could have gotten! You're having a baby!" She wrapped Dan and Jenny in an awkward hug around Dylan.

"But I thought you weren't supposed to be finished with the injections until this month? What happened?"

Dan shrugged. "Looks like one of Operation Procreation's early exploratory missions met with some surprising success. We couldn't believe it."

"But it's real," Jenny said. "We found out right before we went to Connecticut. And I have the incredible morning sickness to prove it," she added, screwing up her face and sticking out her tongue. "Whoever named it morning sickness was a sadistic jokester. I do most of my barfing right around bedtime."

"Oh, no," Molly said. "Then, how are you handling all of this tonight? Will you be okay?"

"Eh, she's a trouper if I've ever seen one," said Dan. "You know how Jenny is. When it's time for the baby to be born she'll probably just push the kid out standing up and go back to whatever it was she was doing."

"No, I won't," Jenny interjected. "Trust me. But you gotta love his optimism, right?"

"I think Dan's probably right," Molly said. "Anybody who can take twice-daily shots in the butt for weeks must have a pretty good hold on pain tolerance."

"No," Jenny laughed. "That's just because of my sheer will and resignation to the fact that in order for a baby to come out of my vagina, a needle's gotta go into my ass."

Dan planted a kiss on the top of his wife's head. "She certainly has a way with words, doesn't she?

"Seriously, though," he continued. "She told me she wanted to go through with the party as usual. Jenny's the one who insisted."

"I don't want to lose the tradition," Jenny explained. "If we miss this year, what happens next year? Once we have the baby, it'd be too easy to say we're too busy or tired and not do it again. We have to make the effort if we want to keep it going."

Molly took a sip of her water and looked around. "I do love this, everybody getting together—even if they're too afraid to talk to me yet. But it's nice to have an excuse to not think about all the crap that happened in the last year. I'm all about celebrating the good right now."

"And," Jenny added, raising her glass, "unless you're pregnant, it's a damned good excuse to get drunk off your rear end and make out with somebody."

Molly laughed, then motioned that she was going to settle a drowsy Dylan off to the side. Some friends of Dan's from work—an art teacher who constantly reeked of alcohol and her defense lawyer husband—came up to talk to Jenny, so Molly took that as her excuse to step away.

Dylan had drifted off to a light sleep in her arms, but Molly somehow managed to transfer her back into her car seat without waking her. She felt proud of herself, soaking up another one of those little victories that made her feel like she could, really, take care of this child. She'd have to feed the baby soon, she knew— her breasts were starting to tingle from all the fluid packing them, waiting to be used, but for now the baby looked content.

The condo had gotten more crowded, and Molly maneuvered around the dining room table, piling a small plate with food, all the while keeping an eye on her sleeping daughter. The firelight from the stone fireplace in the adjacent room bounced off the crystal candleholders on the table, making Molly's skin glow with a warmth that made her feel at home, content.

A pair of boys, maybe seven and nine years old, raced by the table, knocking into Molly. She tottered on the high heels of her boots and might've fallen if it hadn't been for a strong hand that caught her elbow and steadied her. Molly turned to thank the man who'd helped her, but when she saw his face she breathed in so sharply her head felt suddenly light.

The man's eyes were the exact shade of blue the sky turns just before the sun breaks the horizon at dawn. Molly noticed, too, the dusting of salt-and-pepper through his dark hair, and the way the long fingers of his large hand wrapped themselves gently around her arm, supporting her, but carefully. He was slightly taller than she was in her heels and wore a navy blue sweater over a plaid, untucked, button-front shirt. The threads of the sweater looked so soft Molly had to restrain herself from running her hand over the sleeve. She knew without hesitation that underneath his shirt the man's skin would bear a tattoo that matched the necklace she wore. He was the teacher Jenny had been telling her about in teasing, vague terms, new to Dan's department, just transferred in from another high school across the city. Jenny seemed to have also conveniently forgotten to mention that he'd be coming to the party. Molly looked up again at his eyes. They were smiling at her, and the skin at the corners of them wrinkled into familiar creases.

"Liam." Molly's smile broke into a grin so wide she knew he could see every one of her teeth.

"Molly." Liam grinned back at her, then nodded at the floor. "You okay there?"

"Yeah, I'm okay." She felt herself blush, but recovered her composure. She looked over his face again, remembering every angle she once had memorized. "Thanks. If it weren't for you I'd be spending my New Year's scrubbing shrimp cocktail off of Jenny and Dan's walls."

"Can't let that happen." Liam laughed. "Don't you remember, I grew up in Baltimore? Any waste of Old Bay is considered a grave sin where I'm from." He picked up a bottle of porter from where he'd placed it on the table.

Molly shrugged, laughing, and glanced at Dylan, who was starting to stir in her spot on the floor. Molly picked her up and held her to her chest, hoping to comfort her so that they could stay in that spot just a few minutes longer.

Liam took a long look at the baby before resting his gaze again on Molly, his eyes focused on hers. "She's beautiful, Molly. Really beautiful. Are you both doing well?"

Molly nodded.

"Well, I can see where she gets her good looks. I do hope she gets her grace from some other DNA, though." He smiled to let her know he was teasing. Liam took a small sip of his beer before looking around the room. "Her father, maybe? Is he here?"

Molly shook her head, waiting for the flush of embarrassment to come. This time, though, it didn't. "No, he's not here. He's not exactly in the picture, you might say." Molly cleared her throat. "Actually, we're not together anymore." She made sure to look Liam straight in the eye, and was surprised when she saw his shoulders relax, felt the breath exhaled from his lips.

Molly held his gaze, waiting for him to speak. Her pulse throbbed as the blood rushed through her veins. Jenny caught her eye from the other side of the condo and gave her a thumbs-up. Molly shook her head, smiling, and turned back to Liam, but not before noticing that he'd seen Jenny's gesture, too, and was laughing.

He nodded his head and handed her a napkin.

"Well, since you're on your own, can I suggest you carry a couple extra of these around?" He looked down at Dylan again, who was staring right at him now, her eyes wide open, her face attentive. "And if you ever want some company when you, say, take her to the park, or maybe around dinnertime, I'm around, you know." Liam gave Molly a tentative smile. "I can pick up a mean takeout."

Molly's heart was doing flips now inside her chest, jumping around like the winning ball in a lottery pool.

"Though I think you'll be okay, Molly," Liam said. "I always knew you would be."

He set the napkins down on the table in a neat pile, then took a step back, turning to go.

"Hey, Liam." Molly heard the words come out of her mouth before she knew what she'd say next. And then she remembered. Of course she remembered. She'd never forgotten. "Happy birthday."

Liam's face broke into a grin so broad and so genuine it seemed to knock out all the other light in the room. He reached out and touched her arm again, then disappeared into the crowd in the living room. Molly stood there, smiling, the plate of cold shrimp still in her hand, staring at the spot where he'd been. Out of the corner of her eye, she saw Liam look back at her, as if he knew she was replaying in her head what he'd said to her; as if he knew she understood that this was another beginning.

The song changed over, and all of a sudden Liz Phair was blasting out one of her and Jenny's favorite songs over the crowd in the room. A few of Jenny's old girlfriends from college started singing along to "Polyester Bride," and Molly saw Dan shaking his head at his wife, who was crooning the words from across the room. Molly, too, found herself singing as she rocked her sweet baby. Maybe it was the skyscraping boots she'd pulled on tonight, but she felt taller. Straighter. She held her shoulders back, clasping Dylan against her heart with one hand while taking a big sip of her water with the other. Jenny caught her eye again and motioned for her to use the guest bedroom to breastfeed Dylan. Molly flashed her a quick smile, nodding her head, before leaving the room.

Dan had told Molly once that the students in his English class always ended every year debating Robert Frost and talking about the road not taken. Most of them were headed to college in the fall, and many of the kids were uncomfortable being at a crossroads in their lives. They worried about the choices they were making, that their decisions could lead them down the wrong paths, or to roads they weren't "supposed" to take.

Molly had told Dan that she thought the kids were focusing on the wrong issue. People were fooled into thinking they got to choose their path—life was just a road, one road, from start to finish. A person couldn't take an exit off, or decide to fly instead. She was stuck on the route she was traveling, whether she liked it or not, until she reached her destination.

"But Molly," Dan had said. "I can't tell these kids that. That's like telling them they have no choice in their lives at all, which is the exact opposite of what they need to hear right now. You can't tell a bunch of hormonal teenagers that they're basically screwed no matter which way they go. Half of them would be throwing themselves into the Delaware by graduation."

But Molly had stuck to her argument. She'd told Dan, slowly, thoughtfully, that she still thought it was the way a person chose to walk that defined her journey. She could decide to stop at a rest area, or avoid potholes, detour through the scenic lookout. She could travel so quickly that all the sights flashed by her in a blur, or she could choose to slow down when the road was leading her to a new discovery. She might take a break to go hike that trail she almost passed. Bad stuff was going to happen along the way—that was a given, and Dan's students should know that. But Molly insisted that the whole point of life was to use the bad, when it happened, as a stepping stone to get to the good. No one should trip over a branch in the road twice during the same walk. You fell once, brushed yourself off, and learned to watch where you were going.

"And the music, of course," she'd said, laughing. "You can't forget the music when you travel. Make sure to tell your students that. A little Fleetwood Mac playing 'Go Your Own Way' never hurt anybody."

Molly settled down onto the guest room bed to nurse Dylan. She looked around at the soft blue walls, the bamboo blinds, and tried to picture the room as a nursery. Her friends were having a baby. They were going to have a child who was special, and loved, and a reminder of all that was good in the world, just like the baby in her arms. And in a couple of years, that small child was going to be playing with all of the other kids running around the bedroom, and probably chasing Dylan around the coffee table, and stealing candy from that dish Dan always kept filled by the front door.

Molly ran her fingers over her daughter's fine red-brown hair, soaking in the warmth of her little body against her chest, the quiet of the peaceful room, the laughter on the other side of the door. She hoped this wouldn't be the last New Year's Eve party Jenny and Dan hosted. Molly wanted to be back in this house, with these people, this time next year.

After all, a lot could happen between now and then.

ACKNOWLEDGMENTS

When people ask how I write with three small kids at home, my best, most honest, and not at all graceful answer is this: by the seat of my pants. But there've also been two groups of people who've woven a support system for me over these last few years. The first group, my safety net, is widespread: my extended family and friends, my dear writer pals and fellow mamas. They've kept me buoyed with their encouragement and questions, from back when I first started writing One Vignette to now. In addition, Orly Konig-Lopez and Kerry Lonsdale had the brilliant idea to found the Women's Fiction Writer's Association—what an amazing group of writers—and the tenacity to keep with it as it grew. I don't think they know yet that WFWA was integral to this book getting to print (well, now they do!). I am so thankful for them.

And then—then!—there is the smaller group, my core, the ones who jumped in and really got their hands (eyes?) dirty and stuck with this book—and with me—as it took shape:

Julie Mianecki, my editor at Berkley. She has an amazing eye for detail, a readiness to listen, and not least of all, treated Molly as gently as I'd hoped she would on the last steps of this journey. I have loved working with her, as well as with the rest of the team at Berkley/Penguin. What a group.

My agent, Katie Shea Boutillier of Donald Maass Literary Agency, has been my champion, my friend, and my ass-kicker in equal measures. She saw something shiny in that lump of optimistic coal I sent her way years ago, and pushed me to keep polishing until I got out of my own way and saw it, too. I'm grateful that she believed in me.

My brother, Paul Ferguson, was one of my first readers, and definitely my most gung ho. His honesty kept me focused, his encouragement kept me going, and his hatred of Scott's character kept me laughing. Thanks so much to him and his wife, Sarah, for cheering me on, and for proving that a lawyer can actually be a really good proofreader.

My mom, Suzanne Ferguson, and my late father, Donald Ferguson, who mean more to me than I've ever been able to show them. My mom, who's been waiting for me to do this for years, has been both my security blanket and confidant. And my dad, who was in my head the whole time I wrote this (he would've hated Scott, too), and whose love for his family was fiercer than life; he taught me to write, and it's because of him that I do it now. How I wish I could place this book in his hands.

Molly Lynch is my friend and my second-draft reader and the best photographer this side of, well, anywhere. She's one of the funniest people I know, definitely the most sarcastic, and I seriously don't know what I'd do if she ever decided to phase me out. She makes life a lot happier.

Mary and Tim McGettigan, my aunt and uncle, for reading, for feedback (excellent work, Uncle Tim!), and, with Mark McGettigan, for keeping at the ready the Tröegs on tap. I'm especially thankful for that last one.

Donna Woodruff is the proudest mother-in-law a woman

could have. She tore through one of my earlier drafts and refused to give me an ounce of criticism, even though I begged. And the genuine encouragement of Mark Woodruff, her husband, has meant the world.

I want to mention, too, Thomas Bilodeau, my late father-in-law, who pretty much just made me feel like I could do anything I wanted. His son is a lot like him that way.

Annie Livingstone, whom I think of as "my" Annie. Everyone should have an Annie in her life, and I am so, so fortunate to have her in mine.

My husband, and my first reader, David Bilodeau. He's the love of my life, the brewer of my coffee, the giver of time, and quite truly the best decision I have ever made. I would not be doing this—writing, chasing my dreams, staying up way too late—if it weren't for his (gentle, constant, nagging) belief that I should. He makes me brave.

And finally, but at the root of it all, are my children. They never asked to have a writer as a mother, but seem to love me all the same. Saoirse Kate, Quinlan, and Cian, you are more than I ever hoped for in the world. Thank you for being the most loving, dynamic, endearing people I could ever have the joy to know and raise. I love you so.

READERS GUIDE FOR

All the Difference

by Leah Ferguson

1. *All the Difference* is a novel that follows one woman along two very different paths, which diverge when she must make an important decision. At the beginning of the novel, did you believe that Molly was going to say yes or no? Do you think she made the right choice?

2. Hindsight is something that we are privy to only after our choices have been made. How often do you side with yourself even in hindsight? How has hindsight led you to make stronger choices in the future?

3. Throughout the novel, Molly and Scott's relationship shifts from emotional and carefree to focused on the baby and barely functional. Would it have made sense for them to stay together for the baby's sake?

4. Molly refers to the songs and lyrics of Fleetwood Mac throughout the novel. Are you familiar with their music? How did it shape your imagination while reading?

5. Scott's immaturity in both paths of Molly's life is prevalent. Did you feel that Molly had unrealistic expectations of him or that he wouldn't have been capable of change?

6. Under stress, Molly compulsively cleans to control her environment and calm her emotions. What tricks do you use to soothe yourself during stressful times? Are yours as helpful as Molly's?

7. Jenny's difficulty in getting pregnant made Molly feel guilty about her unplanned pregnancy. Have you ever been handed something another person was working hard to achieve? How did you deal with their feelings? Has the opposite ever occurred?

8. When Liam decides to give his relationship with an ex-girlfriend another chance, Molly lets him go. Were you proud of her for this? Do you believe in second chances when it comes to relationships?

9. Oftentimes people seek safety and comfort in the familiar. Describe some of the ways the characters in the novel fall into their comfort zones.

10. Toward the end of the novel, Scott pleads: "You're in my head when I go to bed at night, and you're the first thing I think about when I wake up. It's like, I didn't need you when I had you, but now I can't live without you. I'm obsessed." Did you believe him or do you think he was upset for not getting what he wanted? What does this statement suggest a relationship with Scott would be like for Molly?

11. In Chapter 12, Molly observes: "Emily and Jack's home, in this rambling neighborhood in West Chester, with the old stone houses and whitewashed fences and spacious, landscaped backyards, wasn't real, even in comparison to Monica and Edward's. This wasn't authentic life, at least to Molly. Not right now, anyway. It was too perfect, and separate, and took a lot of work to maintain. Molly's life was grittier, her path still filled with gravel and potholes. She wasn't ready for an easy road yet, especially one already laid out for her. She was still content to keep walking and get to where she was supposed to go, eventually." How is the comparison between her parents' home and Molly's life symbolic? How can seeking solace in chaos work to Molly's benefit?

12. In Chapter 12, Molly recalls her skydiving experience: "But when she'd finally landed on the ground on weak legs and saw Scott rushing toward her, exhilarated, to wrap his muscular arms around her and lift her off the ground once again, she'd been grateful. To him, for pushing her—because he did have to shove her out of the plane—and to herself, for letting herself trust that it would be okay." How has Molly grown throughout the novel? Do you think the Molly at the beginning of the book would have the same outlook?

13. When considering the two possible paths of Molly's life, did you think she could end up without Scott in either? Are our destinies predetermined? How much control do we have over them?